THE Walls OF Arad

CAROLE TOWRISS

Four Diamonds
PUBLISHING

The Walls of Arad

THE Walls OF Arad

To my God, my refuge and my fortress,
in whom I trust.

To my mother, who will always be
my foundation and my encouragement.
I love you.

Lord, you have been our dwelling place
throughout all generations.
~PSALM 90.1

GLOSSARY

sabba • grandfather
abba • father
imma • mother
savta • grandfather
habibi • sweetheart (Egyptian, to a male)
habibti • sweetheart (Egyptian, to a female)
neshika • kisses
khamsin • sandstorm, sirocco
wazir • vizier (ancient Semitic, reconstructed)
shiva • first seven days of mourning
shloshim • last 21 days of a month of mourning

HEBREW MONTHS OF THE YEAR

Shebat • January-February
Adar • February-March
Abib • March-April
Ziv • April May
Sivan • May-June
Tammuz • June-July
Av • July-August
Elul • August-September

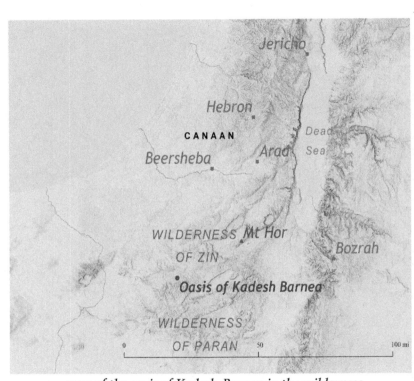

*map of the oasis of Kadesh-Barnea in the wilderness
and the city of Arad on the edge of Canaan*

Zadok's Family
(Egypt/Israel)

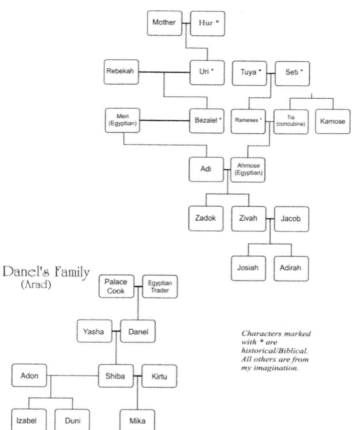

Danel's Family
(Arad)

Characters marked with * are historical/Biblical. All others are from my imagination.

CHAPTER 1

**Oasis of Kadesh Barnea, Sinai Peninsula
Late 13th Century B.C.,
Late winter, 22nd day of Shevat**

"YOU WANT ME TO WHAT?" Zadok stared at the white-haired woman sitting beside him, her face as serene as if she had just asked him to pass her a cup of water.

"Marry her. I want you to marry Arisha."

He'd seen the girl around Miriam's tent. Not often. She tended to stay inside, away from the gazes of others. "Why me?" He wiped his sweaty hands on his tunic. Marriage was not a topic he enjoyed discussing. "I'm sure there are any number of young men who would be more than happy to take her as a wife. She's very pretty." Her wavy, light brown hair and sad eyes floated through his mind.

"She doesn't need those others. She needs you." Miriam's wide grin plumped the apples of her cheeks, giving her an endearing child-like look despite her age.

"Needs me? What do you mean she needs me?"

Her eyes twinkled. "Are you going to repeat everything I say?"

Zadok jumped to his feet. "Are you going to tell me what you are talking about?"

"Sit down." Miriam spoke without looking up or raising her voice.

Clenching his jaw, he pulled his cloak tighter against the cool morning breeze drifting through the long, orderly rows of canvas tents. "You know what happened the last time I wanted to marry someone."

She flipped the manna cakes in the pan over the fire in front of her tent. Apparently satisfied they were nicely browned on both sides, she put two next to a handful of dates on a plate and handed it to Zadok. "Marah was a selfish, spoiled child, and her father was no better. They couldn't see past tomorrow and had no faith in Yahweh's provision." She grinned. "But you will be perfect for Arisha."

"And why is that?"

"Arisha is from Arad. In Canaan."

"In Canaan?" He pointed north. "That Canaan?"

Miriam raised a brow. "You know of another?"

He bristled. "And I am perfect because like her, I am not a true Israelite."

Miriam's eyes—the same piercing eyes she shared with her brother Moses—held his. "I watched your *sabba* lovingly build every piece of furniture in that Tabernacle." Her bony fingers pointed to the structure hidden behind the animal hide curtain on the other side of the sandy walkway in front of them. "Your grandfather crafted the Ark of the Covenant, over which the very presence of Yahweh rests. And I watched *his* sabba Hur, along with my own brother Aaron, hold Moses's arms up to heaven all day so we would not be slaughtered by the Amalekites. That man gave his life for Israel. You could not be more Israelite if you were Jacob himself."

"But still, my mother is half Egyptian. And my father—"

Her gaze softened as she placed her hand on his cheek. "I know your father. And I have known you since you were a tiny being in your mother's belly." She put one manna cake on a plate for herself. "I don't care about your blood. I chose you for your shepherd's heart. Arisha is ... she has been deeply wounded. I would like to give her more time, but I can't. She needs to marry. She needs the gentle nature Yahweh gave you, so her heart can fully mend."

He shook his head.

"I have talked to Yahweh about this."

He waited until a pair of priests passed by on the aisle between the first row of tents and the outer wall of the tabernacle. He didn't need anyone else hearing this bizarre conversation. "You've talked to Yahweh?" He finished his manna cake and picked up the second. "Have you talked to her? Wait—how do you talk to her? Does she speak Hebrew?"

"She doesn't need to. I can understand her quite well. Our languages are very similar. Not like Egyptian. And no, I haven't spoken to her because I wanted to speak to you first."

Zadok pondered her words as he savored the sweet manna. "I cannot marry someone I do not love."

"You will."

Zadok blinked. "I will what? Marry someone I don't love?" Could she possibly be ordering him to do that?

Miriam laughed. "No, no. You will love her."

"How can you say that?"

Miriam waved her hand. "I know these things. This isn't the first time I've done this. It's just the first time I've been so open about it. I usually just ... nudge people toward one another. And I'm always right." She set her plate down.

"Why be different this time?" He ripped a date in two and removed the seed, then handed her the meat.

"I don't have much time left." She bit off a small piece of the fruit.

He studied her face, but he couldn't tell for certain what that meant. Was she ... ?

"I'm failing. I can feel it. I want to know Arisha is in good hands before I go."

"Does she know?" Why did he care? He barely knew her.

A smile slowly crept over Miriam's face. "Why do you ask?"

"I-I just know how close to you she is. This will be hard for her."

Her smiled widened. "See? You care for her already. Besides, you should be married by now, as well, shouldn't you? How old are you now?"

"I was born twenty-three summers ago. And most people seem to share the opinion of Marah's father." Zadok dropped the plate on the sand at his feet. "You may have been thinking about this for some time, but this is the first I've heard about it, and I need to think." He slapped his hands against each other and stood. "I'll let you know."

As a Levite, Miriam lived on the inner row of tents around the Tabernacle. Preferring to avoid the busyness of the only entrance to the courtyard, she'd pitched her tent all the way at the north end of the row.

Zadok strolled south along the wide walkway, the Tabernacle on his right, and tents of the Levites on his left. Halfway down he reached Moses's tent. Moses lived exactly east of the tabernacle, across from the wide opening. Aaron, as high priest, lived next to him.

Zadok cut between the two tents and stepped into Judah's section. His tent was behind Aaron's. Sabba Hur had lived there many years ago, when he and Aaron were Moses's closest advisors. He'd shared that tent with Abba, and Kamose, the Egyptian captain of the guard who had escaped with the Israelites. Joshua's tent was behind Moses's so he could be close to the leader, though as an Ephraimite, his tent would normally have been exactly opposite Moses, on the west side of camp.

Zadok turned and strode south, continuing through the tents of Zebulon. As he walked, he tried to make sense of what he'd heard.

But he couldn't.

Why would Miriam pick him? She knew he wasn't suitable. She

knew his ... failings. It was an absurd request. He would just have to tell her *no*.

He walked beyond camp to the southern springs where the livestock were kept, and hopped over the rock wall. Now, where were his sheep?

There, near the smallest of the springs. His beautiful sheep. The only creatures he felt truly comfortable with. Sheep were so much simpler than people.

He scanned the group—all accounted for.

Well, actually, they weren't his. Most of them weren't, anyway. He was the shepherd for the priests. Three years ago, Aaron had come to him to ask him to take his small flock, the one he'd begun to build for his future, and turn it into a flock for the Tabernacle. Once they reached Canaan, the priests would need at least two lambs every day, more each Sabbath. Over one thousand lambs every year. Only the best lambs would do. Only the best shepherd.

"Zadok!" A young boy waved him over.

"Micah." Zadok ambled toward the boy and tousled his hair. "How are my sheep?"

"Everybody's here and happy. Reuben is finishing the milking, and Jonah says a couple of the ewes are looking very uncomfortable." Micah laughed.

"All right. I'll go check on them. Thank you." He clapped Micah on the shoulder and headed for the ewes he knew were nearing time to deliver. It was early in the season, but not unheard of.

Jonah knelt by one of the expectant sheep. Jonah was Zadok's most recent but his best hire yet. He was eighteen—the oldest— and big, strong, and willing to work at night with Reuben to guard the flock. Zadok paid the boys in milk, a commodity he had plenty of.

"How is she?"

"I think she might drop this lamb tonight." Jonah rubbed his hand down the ewe's back.

"All right. I'll stay with her. You watch the flock."

"Can I help?" Jonah's eyes pleaded.

"I need you to watch over the sheep, but there will be plenty more ewes waiting to deliver. If you can find someone else willing to work for me and to stand guard, you can help next time."

Jonah's shoulders drooped, but he nodded and loped off.

As the ewe wandered away from the flock to find a quiet place, Zadok followed from a distance. It was unlikely she'd need help, but he wanted to be close by, just in case.

At least she wouldn't be asking him any uncomfortable questions about his life.

～

"*N*o, I won't! Why can't I just stay here with you?" Arisha grasped Miriam's wrinkled hands and pulled them to her chest, fighting to control her voice. The tent she shared with the old woman closed in on her, shutting out everything but Miriam. Her blood pounded in her ears and her heart thumped against her chest. Her legs wobbled. How could Miriam do this to her? How could she throw her away like this?

"Arish—"

"Please, please let me stay here with you." She grasped Miriam's tunic.

Miriam withdrew her hands and placed them on Arisha's wet face. "You are a woman, and it is well past time for you to marry and create a life of your own. You cannot live in mine any longer."

"But I don't want to. I don't know how." Arisha buried her face in Miriam's shoulder and sobbed. "I'm afraid," she whispered.

Miriam embraced her and rubbed circles on her back. "No, no, my child, you mustn't be afraid. Yahweh has created marriage for us, and it is a good thing. It is not something to be feared."

Arisha pulled back and narrowed her eyes. "But you never married."

"I almost did."

"What happened?"

Miriam gestured to a cushion.

Arisha released her and sank to the floor, immediately missing the comfort of the woman. She swiped the tears from her cheeks and tried to slow her breathing.

Miriam stepped outside the tent. While she was gone, Arisha studied the tent that had been her only real home—at least, the only one she could remember. Soft cushions stuffed with wool, covered in sheepskin, were scattered over the floor. Their extra tunics were neatly folded in the corner. Skins of water occupied another corner. Sleeping mats lay rolled up along the back wall.

She was safe here. How could she leave?

Miriam returned with two cups full of hot water, then sat across from Arisha. She reached into a bag and withdrew mint and sage leaves and dropped a few into each cup. "It was long, long ago, back in Egypt. His name was Eliab. We were two months from marrying, and he was killed in the brickfields."

"Oh, Miriam!" Arisha's hand went to her mouth.

"Obviously I was devastated. I knew I would never love anyone else like I loved him. I thought ... I thought my life was over. I wouldn't come out of my house for a month."

Miriam stirred the leaves in the cups. "Then a friend had a baby. Her *imma* had died when she was very young, and I had always helped my imma with Aaron and Moses. She begged me to come help her, so I spent several weeks with her. And then another friend needed me, and another ... and I realized I found it very fulfilling."

Arisha shook her head. "But you never married."

"Yahweh gave me something else. I could have sought marriage again; I *chose* not to. But it wasn't because I was afraid. I chose another way instead." Miriam took her hand. "What would you be choosing?"

Arisha released a slow sigh. "Nothing, I suppose."

"Exactly." She fished the leaves from the tea, then offered a cup to Arisha. "I'm asking you to trust me, Arisha. I *know* this is the best life for you."

Arisha's eyes filled with tears once again, but she blinked them back. "When do I have to do this?"

"Not until you are comfortable with him."

Arisha's eyes widened. "Truly?"

Miriam laughed. "Of course. I am not trying to get rid of you."

Arisha frowned. It certainly felt that way.

"You may not believe me, but I am doing what is best for you." She took a long sip of tea. "I'm happy living alone, helping other people. I am quite demanding, I love to be in control, and I hate taking orders. It would take a very special sort of man to live with me. I never found another one like Eliab." She shrugged. "But you, my sweet, would not be happy. We were not created to live alone."

"But I am not alone! We have each other. Why can't it stay that way?"

Miriam set her cup aside, then took Arisha's hand in both of hers. She waited until Arisha's gaze met her own. "I know you're afraid. But I have known this man since he was a baby. I know his father, and knew his grandfather and his great-uncle. He is an honorable, gentle man, and he will never abandon or mistreat you. You have trusted me so far. Trust me now."

Arisha sniffled and managed a nod as Miriam exited the tent. After a few moments, Arisha left as well. She wandered north along the walkway. The sun hid behind the Tabernacle but hadn't quite set, leaving her in the shadows.

A pair of Laughing Doves flew over her head, their snickering call lightening her heart. They were the most beautiful of the desert birds. She picked up her pace and followed them.

North of camp, two enormous springs were joined to two on the east by a small river. Miriam said they supplied enough water for everyone even in the hottest summers, but she hadn't been here long enough to know. The river fed broom bushes and date palms stretching toward the sky, standing like watchful sentinels all along the east and north sides of camp. Low hills protected them on the south and west.

She reached the largest spring, the one directly north of camp.

A warm breeze blew in off the mountains far beyond the spring, tossing her hair over her shoulders. She gazed north, where the desert gave way to cliffs, then to the hills of Canaan. When she escaped months ago, she never would have imagined a place a lovely as this.

Women came and went, carrying skins full of clear water to their waiting families. Always the women, always alone. Miriam said marrying brought man and woman together, but from what she saw, women stayed with women and the men were still with the men.

Why should she marry anyone if she would still be alone?

~

ZADOK SWATTED AT THE WETNESS on his cheek and rolled his head away. Too early to wake up. Wet pressure jabbed him in his neck, and after a moment, his nose. He opened his eyes to a year-old lamb nuzzling his face.

He reached up to rub the animal's head. "What's the matter? Can't find your imma, *Neshika*?"

Zadok's gaze wandered skyward. Yahweh's protective cloud hovered, the fire of night giving way to the puffy white of day. The cloud was not only a reminder of His pronouncement that Israel wait here, outside Canaan for forty years, but protection from the sun and heat while living in the desert. Zadok breathed a quick prayer of thanks.

The yearling baaaed at him, then nuzzled him again.

"Fine, I'll get up."

He sat up and rubbed his eyes, squinted against the sun at his flock lying around him. He stretched and groaned. How much sleep had he gotten? Not much. The first lambs of the season had been born. After the first ewe delivered, he discovered another in distress. Nearly ended up pulling the lamb out of its mother that time. And then of course he had to sit and watch as the mother licked the baby clean, and the lamb in turn began to suckle. There wasn't a more satisfying experience in the world than seeing a newborn stand and begin to walk.

"Zadok?"

He twisted toward the voice. "Jonah? You're still here?" He stuck out a hand and Jonah pulled him up.

"You looked like you could use the sleep, so I stayed a while longer than usual. Reuben isn't here yet, but Micah is. Are you up now?"

Shivering in the cool morning air of early spring, Zadok brushed off his sheepskin cloak he'd used as a blanket and shrugged into it. "Yes. Thank you for staying. You can go now. Get some sleep yourself."

Jonah nodded, then picked up several skins of milk he had gathered and jogged toward camp.

Zadok picked up the lamb at his feet, checked its ears, eyes, looked in its mouth. "Doing well today, Shika. Now run off." He moved to another lamb and did the same.

A third cowered near its ewe trembling. He knelt beside the lamb, ran his hand along its back, down its flanks. What was the problem? Gently taking hold of the head, he pulled the nose toward him. There it was—a nasty scratch on her face. He reached for the horn in the bag tied to his belt. "Hold on, girl. Hold on." He removed the skin cover, then dipped two fingers into the ram's horn full of olive oil and rubbed the cool liquid into the wound. The lamb jerked her head at first, but calmed as the oil soothed the sting. "Better now?" He drew his fingers over the rest of her head, checking the rest of her skin just in case.

He strolled through his flock, inspecting the youngest and the oldest. All present and doing well. He glanced at the low wall they had built soon after Yahweh's decree. Huge rocks dragged and rolled from the rugged hills south of camp sectioned off an enormous area for the remaining sheep and goats they had then. Three semi-sweet springs fed by an underground river nurtured a pasture, full of grass and safe from predators.

The majority of the animals they had brought from Egypt had

been lost on the way to Mt Sinai. Expecting to be in Canaan in a matter of weeks, many had been slaughtered for food. Others had died for lack of water. The grassy area had been set up for those who wished to continue to keep their flocks, but most lost interest quickly. They kept a sheep or a goat or two, just for some milk, but no one wanted to start breeding animals here, thought it was too much trouble. They wanted to wait until they reached their new home.

Zadok wanted to have his flock ready when they got there. He loved the work, loved the animals. He had built up a small flock, and intended to have quite a good-sized one before they reached their permanent home in Canaan. Joshua had told him about the grassy hills in the south, perfect for raising sheep. Dotted with springs, there was enough water and food for any flock. It was all Zadok had dreamed of since the first time he held a newborn lamb.

And when Aaron asked him to give it up ...

But he could still work with the sheep, and he was doing what Yahweh wanted.

Now the lush pasture of Kadesh was basically his. The low hills that surrounded them on three sides and the noise of the people kept the sheep safe from most predators, but Zadok took no chances and kept at least two people with the flock at all times.

With the springs, the hills, and the date palms, the oasis had been a perfect place to wait out Yahweh's judgment of forty years.

But it wasn't Canaan. Not the land they had left Egypt for. No one over twenty who escaped that day had been allowed to live to see it because of their unbelief when the scouts returned with their report. Zadok's parents were still alive, but all four of his grandparents had died. There were few left now.

His eyes darting back and forth, he scanned the hills, as he did several times every day, searching for anything that might harm his animals. He turned to see Moses coming toward him.

"Your flock is well cared for, Zadok." Moses smiled as he took stock of the sheep around him.

"Thank you. That means a lot coming from another shepherd."

"There are times I miss caring for one of Yahweh's simplest creations." Neshika loped near and nudged Moses's leg. The old man bent to pick her up, his staff hooked on his arm.

Zadok marveled at his agility. Even at one hundred twenty years old, Moses moved with the ease of a man a fraction of his age.

As Moses held her and stroked her nose, she nuzzled his chest. He laughed. "She's quite affectionate, isn't she?"

Zadok smiled as he rubbed her ears. "That's why I named her *kiss*."

Moses gently set the lamb on the grass. He leaned on his staff and was quiet for several moments. "I hear Miriam asked you to do something."

Zadok huffed, then leveled his gaze at Moses. "Do something? She asked me to marry someone I've never even met."

"What did you tell her?"

"I told her I'd have to think about it."

Moses shrugged. "Could be quite an adventure."

A chill ran through Zadok. "I don't *like* adventures. That's why I'm a shepherd. I like peace, calm, predictability. It's the same year after year, season to season. The rains come when they are supposed to. Lambs are born when they are ready. The sun rises every morning."

"A life like that can be tedious, my son."

Zadok crossed his arms and gazed at the far-off mountains. "Maybe. But it's safe."

"Safe from what?"

"Danger ... risk ..."

"Heartache?"

"Maybe."

Moses studied Zadok and stroked his white beard. "Are you going to hide in the pasture your entire life?"

"Maybe." Years of keeping his voice low around the sheep kept Zadok from raising it, but his chest tightened.

"Just because they didn't understand you, doesn't mean everyone won't."

"I won't go through that again."

Moses's eyes were gentle. "Miriam wouldn't let you."

Zadok rubbed his thumbnail on his lower lip. "I just can't," he whispered.

Moses pursed his lips. "Have you considered that this is what Yahweh, and not just Miriam, wants from you?"

Zadok breathed a heavy sigh. "Why would you think that?"

"For one, Miriam rarely makes decisions involving others, especially to this extent, without hearing from Yahweh. Second, she has known you since you were born. Do you really think she would do something so serious, on her own, if she had any inkling it would hurt you? And third, in my experience Yahweh seems to take a particular delight in turning our world end over end when we are at our most content."

Moses turned and left without waiting for a response.

Most content. Was Zadok content? He'd limited his world to a narrow, carefully controlled existence, designed to keep out pain and loss. It worked, as far as that went. He had been free of pain and loss since ...

But content?

Probably not.

CHAPTER 2

23rd day of Shevat

*A*RISHA RELAXED ON THE BANK of the spring and slipped off her sandals. She rolled her neck and sighed as she dug her feet and hands deep into the warm sand, the heat drawing the tension out of her body.

Winter dragged on. There wasn't as much rain here as there was in Arad, but there was a little. At least there would be an abundance of flowers popping up all over the oasis—something to be thankful for. A few anemones already bloomed, their deep blood red blaring against the sand.

She wrapped her arms around herself in the cooling evening. Miriam hadn't said anything today, or yesterday, but her silence on the matter was loud enough. She was waiting for Arisha's answer. Arisha observed the families as she wandered through camp on her way to the spring; she saw women and children with more women and children. The men were always off drilling for the oncoming wars with the Canaanites, or even when back in camp, they huddled in groups by themselves, away from the women.

A trilling nearby drew her attention. The same pair of Laughing

Doves gathered twigs and sticks and piled them haphazardly in a bare spot in a broom bush. The small nest looked like a stiff breeze could blow it away. Arisha chuckled dryly. Did they not care if their eggs were safe? Not care about their children? Like her mother.

She dropped her chin on her knees. Surely all parents couldn't be like hers. Miriam wasn't. Moses and Aaron weren't—she'd seen them with their children and grandchildren. There must be others —many others. Or Israel wouldn't survive.

She raised her head. The birds were still busily collecting sticks. She looked closer ... only one of the birds picked up the twigs. Which one? The more brightly colored one. She searched her mind. Someone once told her the female was always duller—of course. So the male gathered the sticks and ... brought them to the female? She weaved them in and out and crafted a nest, hopping and jumping to test its strength.

Arisha tilted her head. They worked together. Male and female together. She had never seen that before. Birds were not people, but still ...

Pink and purple shot through the sky as the sun crept lower. A shiver ran through her. Better get back to the tent before dark. She pushed herself up.

She ambled through the tents of Issachar on her way to the tent. Giggles caught her ear. A father tossed his squealing little girl in the air while the mother laughed. Strange, she'd never noticed anything like that before. Up ahead, a woman swept out a tent. That was more familiar. But then the father walked up with a child in each hand, and kissed the woman on the cheek before they all ducked inside. To her left, a family sat around the fire together.

She stopped. Could it be that until now, she had seen only what she was used to seeing? Expected to see?

The next morning, Arisha quietly slipped out of their tent and gathered manna for Miriam as she had every day since she'd arrived. She returned and stirred life into the fire.

Miriam was usually up by now, but she'd been tired lately. Perhaps she was still sleeping.

Arisha picked up the pottery vessel Miriam said she'd carried from Egypt and turned it over in her hands. Not a single crack. The pot looked like it had been made last year, not almost forty years ago.

The fire flared and she poured a small amount of water in the pot and placed it on a pair of stable sticks over the fire. She opened the jar of manna and dumped two portions into a bowl, then sat back and waited for the water to boil. Down the row of tents, other women and girls did the same. Children ran in and out of tents, their laughter filling the air. Eagle owls screeched as they swooped overhead, returning to their nests after a night of hunting. Ominous Nubian Vultures circled low, searching for those unlucky enough to die before the sun climbed out of bed.

The bubbling water called her attention back from the azure sky above her. She poured the water into the bowl and stirred the manna into a hot cereal, then divided it into two bowls. She reached for a skin and two cups, and poured two goat's milk. Miriam still hadn't appeared.

Stuffing down growing apprehension, Arisha rose and peered into the tent. Miriam still slept, her unmoving form facing the back. Arisha bit her lip, waited to see if Miriam's chest rose and fell as she breathed. At last, shallow movement. Should she wake her, or let her sleep? She returned to the fire and took her bowl in hand. She scooped a handful in her mouth, barely noticing the burning sensation on her tongue. A few more bites. Worry took over again and she stepped back inside.

"Miriam?" She knelt and touched the woman's shoulder. No response. She gently shook her. "Miriam?" A groan, slow movement. Arisha released a breath.

Miriam rolled onto her back. She blinked several times, then fixed her gaze on Arisha. She smiled slowly. "Arisha, what's wrong?"

"You just slept so late. I was worried."

"I did?"

"I've made the morning meal. Most have already eaten."

Miriam's eyes grew wide. "Oh, my. I'm sorry, child. I'll rise right away."

"I'm not trying to hurry you. If you are not well, rest. I only wanted to be sure you are well." Arisha searched her face for any sign that Miriam was ill—or worse.

"I'll be out in a moment." She patted on Arisha's cheek. "Don't fret."

Arisha placed her hand over Miriam's. Miriam could tell her not to worry, but that wouldn't stop her. Arisha could see what was happening. Miriam was nearly one hundred thirty years old. She was becoming slower and slower every day. And it had all happened so quickly. Even last month she was quick, active and strong. But now, day by day she seemed to grow weaker.

Miriam's mind was as alert as ever. Was her failing health behind this sudden marriage plot? Was she afraid to leave Arisha alone if she ...?

No, Arisha refused to think about that as she sat by the fire, waiting. She set the full bowl and cup next to her.

Miriam appeared in the tent's doorway. She smiled broadly, the same smile she always had for Arisha, but her hand gripped the pole to hold her up.

Arisha's heart sank to her stomach, and the little manna in it threatened to come up. Apparently, she was going to have to think about it, whether she wanted to or not.

~

THE CRACKLING FIRE MIMICKED THE tension in Zadok's heart. Trapped between his sister and her husband, he wished he'd stayed and eaten with the other shepherds instead of coming home like Imma had begged him to. He took a deep breath and braced for another verbal onslaught.

"It wouldn't hurt you to at least talk to her." His sister's dark eyes narrowed.

"Zivah—"

"Just talk to her."

"I don't even know her."

"Maybe that's because you've been hiding from everyone."

"I am not hiding. I'm taking care of the sheep, as Aaron asked me to do." Twice now in three days someone had accused him of hiding.

She waved her hand in his face. "Excuses, excuses. You're just afraid it will happen again."

The words stung. He wouldn't let her see it. "Maybe I'm just happy with the way things are."

She jabbed her finger in his chest. "You want to be alone for the rest of your life? Surround yourself with your sheep?"

"Sheep aren't so bad."

"Well, you can't talk to sheep, and they don't keep you warm at night. And to whom will you leave them when you die?"

"Zivah, what a morbid thought!" Jacob threw a dark glance at her.

She ignored her husband. "He needs to think about these things instead of continually pretending nothing is wrong."

The tent flap opened and his mother exited the tent. "Zivah, leave your brother alone."

Thank Yahweh Imma came out when she did. No telling how much longer Zivah would have gone on. She meant well, but ...

"But Imma, I'm trying—"

"I know what you're trying. But stop."

Zivah huffed.

"Why don't you go back to your own tent for a while and let me talk to your brother alone, hmm? Come back later for the evening meal."

Zivah rolled her eyes, but rose and left. Jacob winked at Zadok before following her.

Imma sat next to Zadok. "So, *habibi*, what are you thinking?"

"Before my dear sister started attacking me, I was actually considering it."

"Considering what? The marriage?"

"No, just meeting her." He stared at the fire. "Have you met her? Zivah seems to think I haven't because I've been hiding."

"I've seen her with Miriam a few times. I've never talked to her. She doesn't come with Miriam when she comes to visit Moses, or Joshua." Her brow wrinkled. "Which she hasn't done in a while." She popped a date in her mouth. "What changed your mind?"

"Moses. He came out to visit me by the flock a couple days ago."

She laughed. "Ah, Moses. He's good at that. A question here, a comment there, and soon your entire way of thinking has been turned upside down. I heard many stories like that from Abba."

"Upside down is right." He kissed Imma on the cheek and rose. "I suppose I should go tell Miriam. I don't know if I'll be back soon or if she'll have me stay a while."

A few moments later, he strolled up to Miriam's fire.

Miriam stood to meet him. "Zadok. I've been expecting you."

Expecting him? A typical Miriam thing to say. He hadn't decided himself until a few moments ago. "I'll meet her. That's all I agree to for now."

"Excellent. Stay for dinner. I'll invite Moses and Aaron, and Joshua—"

"And I can talk to her?"

"No ... she'll be in the tent. But she can watch you, and get to know you a little."

"Watch me?"

Miriam winced. "She hasn't agreed to meet you yet."

Zadok threw his hands up. "What? You mean you went through all that with me and she hasn't even agreed yet? Maybe we should just forget it then."

Miriam grabbed his sleeve. "Zadok, wait."

He halted. Waited a moment.

"Her mother sold her to a family as a servant when she was about five or six years old."

Zadok felt like he'd been head butted by a ram. "*Sold* her?" How could any parent do that?

"Then they sold her to another family several years later. After that, she did something—she's still not sure what—and she was left at the door of the temple."

"Temple? What temple?"

"The temple of Asherah. She was raised along with the other daughters of the temple as a *qadesh*."

"Which is ...?"

"A woman consecrated to the temple."

He winced, closed his eyes. "Doing what?"

"For several years, she recorded offerings, cleaned the temple, served the priestesses ..."

"Then ...?"

"She learned that every woman of age is expected to attend the annual fertility rites each autumn."

Zadok thought a moment. Then it hit him. "You mean as ... as one of the *participants?*"

"Yes."

His stomach roiled. He almost didn't want to ask the next question. "And then what?"

"She escaped. And I found her."

He pinched his brows together. "Found her?"

Miriam looked over his shoulder. "In the broom bushes. She had learned to gather manna as soon as it appeared before anyone else came out, then she just hid out all day at the north spring. That lasted for a week or so. She's been with me since."

He sucked in a deep breath, then let it out slowly, trying to understand everything she had just said.

"There's more to the story, I'm sure. I don't know how she got here alone, or out of the city. But that's all she's told me so far, all she will say."

"But how can I marry someone who does not worship Yahweh? It is forbidden."

Miriam smiled. "Ah, but she does."

"How can that possibly be?"

"A man there taught her about Yahweh. He worked in the palace, which was next to the temple and somehow he found her. I don't know how he knew the things he knew, but he told her many of the stories of our people. She knows about Egypt, the escape, Joseph, Moses." She raised a brow. "Still, she has no sense of family, of marriage. Of real love. She knows little of our laws. She doesn't trust anyone but me, and that's only after many months with me."

"Then how do I get her to trust me? If she ever agrees to meet me?"

"You'll have to earn her trust. Be very gentle. Go slowly." Miriam laid her hand on his arm. "Show her that you are truly interested in her. Listen when she talks, never be in a hurry around her, look at her, ask questions, answer hers, never be dismissive. I think you can figure it out. For now, just sit and talk to everyone else. And smile."

~

*A*RISHA PEERED THROUGH THE NARROW slit between the tent flaps at the man Miriam spoke to. He was older than she expected. Or maybe he just looked older. Why wasn't he married? He was tall and his shoulders were broad. He slipped off his cloak and handed it to Miriam. The huge muscles on his upper arms showed under his short-sleeved tunic as he moved and sank to the ground. If he ever got angry ...

Miriam strategically placed him so Arisha could see his features, but so he wasn't on the far side of the fire. He had a kind face.

Aaron passed the plate of manna cakes to Zadok. "Still getting harassed by the others for not taking part in the training exercises?"

"Yes. Marah's father has a great deal of influence."

Moses touched Zadok's shoulder. "Don't worry about what Marah's father says. Those who love you know the truth. And soon enough, so will everyone else."

Zadok remained silent.

Joshua took the manna. "I've seen him fight. He'll be ready when we need him. And you mustn't forget it was his uncle Kamose who trained me in the first place."

"Great-uncle," corrected Zadok.

Moses nodded. "That's true, but the best of soldiers lose their edge without practice."

"He cannot be a warrior and shepherd at the same time. I need his full concentration if we are to have a flock ready by the time we enter Canaan." Aaron's glance shifted from Joshua to Moses and back.

Joshua raised his hands. "I'm not arguing. So, Zadok, how is the flock? Ready for lambing to begin?"

"I already had the first two. Both at night, of course."

"Can't have you getting too much rest."

Zadok laughed.

Arisha studied him as he sat before the fire in front of her tent. His low, soft voice soothed her, and his easy laugh delighted her. What would it be like if he were sitting at their fire, their tent?

She could only begin to wonder.

～

ZADOK RAN HIS FINGERS ALONG the tent ropes, checked the knots to make sure they were good and tight.

Jacob hovered. "You've eaten the evening meal with her and Miriam every night for a week."

"Yes, I have." He wasn't going to give him any more information than that.

"So are you going to ask for her?"

"It's not that simple, Jacob."

"Why not? You want her; Miriam wants you to have her."

Zadok swallowed and counted to five. "Who says I want her? Besides, I have to earn her trust first."

"Her trust? Why does she need to trust you? What's not to trust about you?"

And that is why Miriam came to me, and not to one of the hundreds of thousands of other young men in Israel.

Arisha needed someone who saw more than a pretty girl who would make a good wife, who would give him many strong sons, and be easy to live with.

Zadok rounded the corner of the tent. "Leave it alone, Jacob."

"Fine. Then why are you here instead of with her, anyway? Tired of her already?" Jacob laughed.

Zadok turned from the tent to face his brother-in-law. "She said I should spend the Sabbath with my family."

Zivah peeked her head around the tent. "She said what?"

Zadok folded his arms across his chest. "She wanted me to spend the Sabbath with you." Though the wisdom of that idea was now lost on him.

Zivah's face brightened. "I like her." She jerked her head toward the front. "Food's ready."

Zadok took his place next to his mother, who put her arm around him and dropped a kiss on his cheek. "Hello, Imma."

On his other side sat his niece and nephew, Josiah and Adira. With Jacob's dark curly hair and Zivah's olive skin, the children were beautiful. Adira would have men standing in line asking to marry her. Thank Yahweh that wouldn't be for many, many years.

Plates of manna and cups of milk made their way around the circle. Zivah helped her daughters balance their bowls on their laps.

"When do you bring her here, habibi?" Imma turned her pointed gaze on him.

"Sometime when Jacob is not around."

Jacob jerked his head up from his food. "What? That's not fair!"

Zivah touched Jacob's shoulder. "You can be somewhat ... abrasive, husband. A bit much to take for someone new."

He bumped her shoulder with his. "You don't seem to have any problem with me."

Zadok laughed. "Because she's just like you."

Zivah glared at him. "Very funny."

"In fact, maybe you shouldn't be here, either."

She tossed a manna cake at Zadok's head, but he stuck out his hand and caught it.

"Nice catch." Jacob nodded approval.

"Imma, I'm done. Can we go now?" Adira, the youngest, looked at her mother with wide, pleading eyes. "I want to go play in the water."

"Is Josiah finished?"

"Almost." The child spoke through a mouthful of manna.

Adira stood and wrapped her arms around Zivah, placing a slobbery kiss on her mouth. Zivah giggled and used her sleeve to dry her face.

Zadok concentrated on his food. He'd avoided marriage—and relationships in general—for so long. After spending a week with Arisha, was he ready to admit he missed it? Longed for it?

"I think I'll take the girls to the river, then." Zivah collected the plates and rose.

"Leave the plates, Zivah. I'll get them. Take Jacob with you."

Zivah glanced from Imma to Zadok to Jacob and back to Imma, who raised her brows. His imma wanted to talk to him. Again. How old was he?

Imma waited until they were out of sight, then handed him a bowl of dates. "So, habibi. Now you've met her, spent time with her. Tell me about Arisha."

Before he could answer her, his abba strode up to the fire pit. "I'm sorry I am so late. I was helping a young family expand their tent. A baby is coming soon." He reached for Zadok. "My son, welcome home. It's been a long while since you've eaten with us."

Zadok rose and embraced his father. "Good evening, Abba." He sat and waited as Imma served his father the remaining manna cakes.

"Thank you, Adi."

She turned her flashing brown eyes on him. "Now. Arisha?"

What to say first? His mind suddenly went mushy. Abba's laughter penetrated the haze.

"Ahmose! Hush!" His mother glared at Abba, who continued to chuckle.

"Well, she's beautiful. She's very quiet—doesn't talk much. She's been talking more lately, the more time I spend with her."

"Are you ready to try this again?"

The old pain threatened to overtake him. He shuddered and shoved it deep in his mind. "I don't know. Miriam says Yahweh told her to do this. Wants me to do this."

"But you are still wary?"

He nodded.

Abba set his plate aside and leaned near. "Arisha knows who and what you are already. There will be no sudden changes, no surprises."

Did she know? Everything? He needed to make sure Arisha knew right now what she'd be getting into if she married him.

Which was still a big "if."

Because he'd never let anyone do that to him again.

CHAPTER 3

9th Day of Adar

AANEL STOOD AT THE WINDOW in his workroom, high in the outside wall of the fortified city of Arad. The southernmost city in Canaan wasn't the biggest. In fact, it was quite small compared to some. Hazor was almost twenty times bigger. But Arad was well protected and prosperous. Sitting on the crossroads of two trade routes, Arad boasted the best of everything and wanted for nothing.

He scanned the fields below him. The wheat was ripening nicely and the second crop of barley had been sown. The scent of apricots, peaches, and plums wafted up. Ten years ago, he had commanded that the fruit trees be planted under these walls, not so close as to be helpful in breaching them, but near enough to allow the fragrance to fill the rooms. One of his best decisions as *wazir*.

How far he had come since his time as the cook's son! But growing up in this palace had taught him all of its secrets, and in many ways he was even more effective than those who were handed the job from the fathers and their fathers' fathers. Then suddenly the wazir at that time was left with no sons, no grandsons, no nephews or even cousins, and the principles of Yahweh Danel had sought so desperately to learn had shown the king he could trust Danel more than anyone else. That Yahweh could take the son of an Egyptian trader and make him the highest ranking man not in the royal family still amazed him every day.

He glanced at the retreating sun, then at the water clock in the corner of his spacious room. It was almost time for the evening meal. He descended the steps from the floor of sleeping rooms to the kitchen on the ground floor, his knees creaking.

A young girl called to him as he entered the room. Always warm due to constant fires, and bright because of the many windows, the kitchen held fond memories for him.

"Ishat! How goes it today?" He kissed the girl on the cheek, causing a pink glow to appear.

"How many times have I asked you not to distract my help, old man?" A gray-haired woman smacked him on the rear, laughing.

He laughed with her. "I'm sorry, Sisa. Is his food ready?"

"Of course. Poisoned as always."

"You do realize your husband eats it first."

"Why do you think I poison it?" She smirked, and Ishat giggled.

A portly man with a balding head and ruddy cheeks entered the kitchen from steps leading down to a room underground. While Mepec tasted the food and wine, Danel thought through what he had accomplished today, and what remained for tomorrow.

Food supplies had been obtained. That shipment of cedar should have arrived by now. Perhaps he should send messengers out along the road to meet up with them. A delegation from Hazor was due the day after tomorrow; he needed to make certain the rooms were readied. The troublemaker in the kitchen had been reassigned to the prison detail—that should be a deterrent to any other agitators.

The kitchen—a pang pierced his heart. Ever since his mother died, the king trusted no one to cook his meals, leading him to compel a servant—at the moment Sisa's husband—to taste every-thing before he ate it.

Mepec arranged the king's golden cup and plate on a tray, and followed Danel down the hall to the throne room. Stepping through an archway, they entered a large room with a single throne against the far wall. They passed hand-smoothed wooden beams that supported a high ceiling, and the stone of Baal in the center of the room. The orange light of day's end poured into the room through the windows set high in a western wall.

The ruler slumped in his gilded chair, tapping his fingers on the adorned arm. He held his staff even though no visitors were present, nor were any expected.

Danel silently took his place next to the king, at his right elbow.

Mepec set the tray on a pedestal next to the throne. "Your meal, my king." He stepped back and waited by the door.

"I assume it's safe, since he's still here." He shoved his staff at Danel, who took it. "So far, anyway."

Danel took the staff, bowed and backed away from the throne, remaining at hand should the monarch need him.

The aging King Keret of Arad ate in silence for a while. He looked older than his sixty-two years. He wore his gray hair cut just below his ears, as was the custom in Canaan, but it was quite thin. Probably from worry—he'd spent most of his adult life loudly wondering when the Israelites and their unstoppable God would return to Canaan. The first couple years, especially, he sent patrols south every other month to check on them, devised and revised battle plans, counseled with nearby rulers. He'd never believed Kamose—the one person he'd captured—when he said they wouldn't be coming for forty years, and it nearly drove Keret insane waiting for an attack. Even as a boy Danel had seen him grow twenty years older in just two.

Pouting, Keret raised his hands.

Danel removed the tray and placed it on the pedestal.

"I still miss your mother's cooking, even after twelve years." He took a long drink of wine. "Are the apricots ripe yet?"

"No, and you can't have any even when they are. You know that, yet you ask every season. And you try to eat them every time."

"It's just a little red patch on my face—"

"Your tongue swelled up and you almost choked to death."

"Which one of us is king?"

"Which one of us wants to be dead?"

"No other ruler lets his wazir talk to him like this. Why do I keep you?"

"Because you couldn't find anyone who takes better care of you or your kingdom than I do."

He laughed. "You're right."

Danel signaled to the servant, who gathered the king's dishes and prepared to return to the kitchen.

"How long has it been?" The sovereign spoke without looking up.

Danel turned back. "From the day they left Egypt, 38 years and 11 months."

"It's getting closer."

"Yes, it is."

"Thank you for keeping track."

Danel bowed low. "You are most welcome, my king."

Keret pounded the end of his staff on the floor. "Inform the commander to begin recruiting additional men over the next year. And tell the captain of the guard to double the number of body-guards at my door."

"Yes, Keret."

"Make sure the walls are secure, the reservoir full at all times. Stock enough food to last two months."

"Already done."

Keret smiled. "Of course it is. That is why I made you my wazir."

Danel nodded and left the throne room. The day's work done, he had one last job to do before he could go home. Down another long hall, to the last office on the left. He rapped on the door.

"Enter."

The huge wooden door swung wide. Danel stuck his head in. A

man a few years older than Danel, dressed in soldier's garb, sat at a desk in the sparsely furnished room, putting marks on a sheet of papyrus. His broad frame dwarfed the desk and the chair. He wore his reddish hair loose, and longer than most. Danel waited until he finished, then cleared his throat. The man looked up and smiled broadly. "Danel, what are you doing down here?"

"I came to see you, Aqhat."

~

IT WAS DECIDED.

Zadok told Arisha they were going for a walk around camp, but he was taking her to the pasture. Full of sheep. Animals he found to be calm, trusting, and playful, but which most people thought of as smelly, dirty, and unclean. No one would rather be a shepherd than a warrior. If she had anything against shepherds, or anything else she disliked about him for that matter, he was going to find out now. He would dump her right in the middle of his life, and if she didn't like it, at least he would know before things went any further.

Which probably meant this would be the last time he would ever see her.

He arrived at Miriam's tent. Arisha's back was to him while she talked to Miriam. Her light brown hair tumbled down her back. He couldn't help but notice her soft curves, even under her loose-fitting tunic. She looked over her shoulder and gave him a quick smile, and his breath hitched.

Miriam stepped toward him and handed him Arisha's cloak. Obviously he had Miriam's permission to keep her out until close to sundown.

"Take care of her." She put her hand on his arm, and he got the distinct impression she wasn't talking about just this afternoon.

They strolled through camp to the pasture. Laughing children darted in front of them, and a gentle breeze blew through the rows of tents. At the meals during the last few weeks, Miriam, Aaron or someone else usually helped carry the conversation. Now he didn't know what to talk about. He fidgeted with his hands, and resisted the urge to cross his arms over his chest just to keep them still.

After a mostly quiet walk, they arrived at the rock wall and its gate. He reached down and wiggled the long stick wedged into a niche on each side until it loosened, and then removed it. He straightened and waited for her to walk through.

She tilted her head. "Why is it so hard to get the stick out?"

Zadok's cheeks heated. "Uh, we usually just jump over the wall."

Arisha laughed. The unexpected cheerful sound sent a shiver through him. Her eyes lit up, and her wide, bright smile revealed dimples.

She blinked and looked away quickly—he'd been staring. He swept his arm through the entryway. "Come in."

As she stepped through the gate, a soft scent of mint tickled his nose. He closed his eyes and breathed it in. He'd been around sheep for far too long. He replaced the stick and caught up to her.

They hiked through the lush pasture. He pointed to a young man. "That's Micah." Then he spread his arms and turned in a circle. "And these are my sheep."

Arisha's eyes widened as she scanned the animals surrounding her. Most lay on the soft grass. A few wandered toward the spring for water. Shika trotted near and bumped against her leg. Zadok braced for her to squeal or pull back, but she knelt to touch its fur. The lamb nuzzled her face.

Zadok crouched beside her. "This is Shika. Short for *Neshika*, because she loves to give kisses. I'll move her."

He started to rise, but Arisha put her hand on his arm. "No, it's all right. I like her."

Zadok's heartbeat doubled. She was smiling, not running away, not making disgusted faces.

"They're all yours?"

"Actually, most of them belong to the priests. Only a few are mine."

Arisha petted Shika a few moments longer, then stood. She looked at the lambs lying on the grass, her brows furrowed. "What's that sound? It sounds like one of your sheep is hurt."

He tilted his had to listen. "No, that's one of the ewes getting ready to give birth."

"Why is she making that noise?"

"She's calling to her lamb."

"One of her older lambs?"

"No, the one being born. A ewe will call to her lamb as she is giving birth and after, so he learns the sound of her voice. Even in a flock as big as this one, or bigger, a newborn can always find his imma by sound sooner than by sight."

Arisha grew quiet. Were those tears in her eyes?

He held out his hand. "Come, I want to show you something." She slipped hers into his, and he folded his fingers around hers.

Nearby, one blanket lay on the ground, and another was held up by four tall sticks. Several bowls or baskets lay on the blanket covered by cloths. A couple wet skins hung from one of the sticks.

"I brought some food out here before I came to get you, and made us a shelter from the sun so we could stay a while." He didn't tell her he doubted they'd actually use it.

Her jaw dropped, and she stopped walking. She stared at the blanket.

"Is something wrong?"

She shook her head. "No. Nothing's wrong." She turned to him and managed a feeble smile.

"Come." He pulled her forward.

A yearling lay on the blanket. Zadok scooped up the baby in his arms, rubbed its head. "What are you doing here, Sarah? This blanket is not for you." The lamb baaaed at him. He stroked her neck. "No, I'm sorry. Not today." He set her on the ground and turned to Arisha.

"Not today what?"

"She wanted to stay. I told her today was just for you." He grinned.

Her cheeks flamed, and she tried to hide her face as she lowered herself to the blanket. She tucked her feet to the side, arranging her tunic to cover her legs. "Do you name all your sheep?"

"Yes. Usually just regular names. So far this year Hannah, Sharon, Rachel, Leah, Reuben—my watchman wasn't too sure about that one—and Michael have been born." He uncovered the bowls. One had manna cakes, another had dates, a third—the smallest—had some date honey. Two cups lay next to the bowls.

She raised a brow. "You named one after your watchman?"

He chuckled. "Not really. I just pick names I like." He popped a date in his mouth. "Maybe I should name one Arisha."

Her mouth fell open. "You wouldn't!"

"I like your name."

"But it's *my* name." She placed her hand on her chest.

"All right. I'll let you keep it. For now." He gave her a cup, and stood to retrieve the skins, hung wet to keep cool by evaporation. He sat again—this time closer to her, and poured her a cup of milk, then one for himself.

"You really like being a shepherd, don't you?"

"I do. I love taking care of them. And sheep need a lot of care. They have no way to protect themselves, they wander off, they would follow one another literally off a cliff. Here, in this oasis under Yahweh's cloud, with springs that constantly bubble clear water, the grass never withers for them just like the manna falls for us every day. But otherwise, they would stay in one spot and eat down to the dirt and die of starvation."

"You're not serious."

"I am. They're not very bright. They won't cross even a tiny stream. But I love them. And they will follow me anywhere."

He set the bowl of dates closer to her. "Now, want to tell me what upset you back there?"

"It was the ewe, calling to her lamb."

"Why did that bother you?"

She sucked in a shuddering breath and pointed to Sarah, lying nearby. "Because, this not-very-bright sheep, as you call it, knows its imma's voice, but I don't know mine."

~

S HE CLOSED HER EYES.
        Why couldn't she just keep her mouth shut?
Zadok didn't speak for a long moment.

Now I've done it. Now he won't want me either.

He hooked his finger under her chin and lifted her head to face him. His eyes were dark brown, but soft. They seemed to look all the way into her heart. "You don't remember the sound of your mother's voice?"

"No. I don't *know* it. I wouldn't know it if she were standing here. I left my home when I was about four years old."

"Why did you leave?"

Looking down at the blanket, she picked up a date, rolled it back and forth between her finger and thumb. "I didn't exactly leave. She sold me. As a servant. Then that family sold me. Then at the last house, the master took me to the temple and left me there. They gave him some silver and he just ... left."

"Arisha, I'm so sorry," he whispered.

She jerked her head up to catch his gaze. His face was hard to read. His eyes were full of ... not guilt. He hadn't done anything wrong. It was the look she'd seen in Miriam's eyes when she'd found her at the spring. Compassion, kindness. But at a deeper level.

"So that's when you went to the spring?" He tucked a stray lock of hair behind her ear. His touch made her shiver. "Are you cold?" He grabbed her cloak and settled it around her shoulders.

"Thank you." How could she tell him it wasn't the air that made her shudder? Now what was she saying? "No, I stayed there a few more years until ... Miriam told you about the rites?"

He nodded.

"That's when I left. I went to the wazir. He's the one who

taught me about Yahweh. He went to one of the traders he knew, who also worshipped Yahweh, and asked him to bring me as far south as they could, as close to the Israelite camp as they could, before they headed toward Egypt. He trusted him, but the wazir also warned him they would never be allowed to trade in Arad again if he ever heard anything happened to me."

"So you rode here with the traders?"

"We got pretty close in the caravan. Then I walked for about half a day until I reached the spring. I figured out what manna was and gathered some before anyone else was awake or came to fill their water skins. Slept in the heat of the day under the broom bushes. I don't know how Miriam found me."

He tilted his head. "Yahweh showed you to her."

No. Yahweh would not care for someone like her. Not for the enemy of His people. "Why would He do that?"

He sat back. "What do you think would have happened if you had stayed at the spring alone?"

"I don't know. I never thought about it."

He held up three fingers. "I think one of three things." He folded down his fingers one at a time as he spoke. "You would have died. You would have been found by a less than honorable man. You would have been found by a wonderful family who would raise you as their daughter and find a suitable husband for you. Which do you think is the most likely?"

She scoffed. "Not the last."

"Why? I think you probably had as good a chance at that one as the others."

"Still one out of three."

He nodded. "True." He took her hand in his. "But Yahweh had a better plan."

"Miriam?"

The smile that took over his face sent a frisson of heat throughout her body. She struggled to keep her mind on the conversation at hand. "Miriam says you're part of the plan."

"Whatever His plan, you are safe now. And He will keep you safe." He removed his hand and leaned back on his palms.

She immediately missed the warmth of his touch. Maybe Miriam was right.

She was beginning to hope so.

"I think we should go back. The sun is starting to set. I don't want Miriam to worry, or give anyone reason to talk." He grinned. "But Micah's been here as a chaperone."

She glanced over his shoulder at the boy ambling among the sheep as she gathered the bowls and cups.

"Besides, I have to get back here for night duty."

"Do you sleep out here every night?"

"Until the last couple weeks, I was out here pretty much every day and every night."

Her hand stopped in mid-air. "Why would you do that?"

He took a deep breath. "That story will have to wait for another day."

They folded the blankets and headed for camp. Zadok held her hand until they neared the tents.

At Miriam's, she simply nodded to him and slipped inside. Thank Yahweh Miriam was outside, so she didn't have to explain the smile on her face.

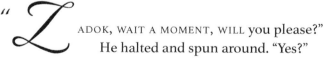

"Zadok, wait a moment, will you please?"

He halted and spun around. "Yes?"

"Have you given any more thought to my question?"

He couldn't stop the grin. "I no longer find it objectionable, if that's what you're asking."

"Good. Then we can set the ceremony for ... next week?"

"Ne- next week?" So many thoughts racing through his head ... He felt dizzy. "Isn't that a little fast? I'm not sure she's ready yet." There had to be another way.

Miriam rolled her eyes. "Zadok, I am dying."

He shifted. "So you've said." Did she have to keep saying that? He didn't want to hear it.

She waved her hand. "No, I mean very soon. A week or two at the most. I know Arisha will insist on being with me to the last. You know that means seven days outside of camp. And I don't want her to have to return to this empty tent when it is over. I want her to have someone to comfort her, hold her."

Zadok rubbed the tip of his thumb over his lip and stared over her head at the mountains to the north for a few moments. "Here is what I will do. I will ask her. If she will not marry me, there is nothing I can do. If she will marry me now, so be it. If she agrees to marry me, but not yet, she can move into my family's tent when she returns. That's where we would live, and I've been sleeping in the pasture, anyway. She would not be alone. I could be with her during the day, and my mother would be there if she awakens in the night until she wishes to wed. Does that meet with your approval?"

Miriam grinned. "No need to worry. From the look on her face just now, she'll marry you."

CHAPTER 4

22nd day of Adar

*A*RISHA GRABBED THE WATER SKINS and set off for the spring, the biggest one northeast of camp, where abundant songbirds made their homes in the broom bushes and in the tops of the date palms. Occasionally a blue-headed agama lizard or spiny mouse skittered away when she buried her feet in the sand.

The late afternoon sun shined on her back—not so hot as to be uncomfortable, just enough to give her a pleasant sense of warmth. After spending most of her life inside as a servant, she loved being outside. Close to the water, the laughing call of doves caught her attention. In a nest in the same broom bush where she'd seen them last month, the male now sat on two white eggs. The *father* warmed the eggs!

Glancing around for the female, Arisha spotted her under a nearby bush pecking at the ground for seeds. She stepped closer to inspect the eggs, but the male raised up on his tiny feet, straining his neck and puffing up his chest. The mother darted out from under the bush dragging a wing as if she were injured, hopping away from the nest, trying to draw Arisha away from her babies.

Such care for their little ones—it was fascinating. Was this how it was supposed to be? How would she know? She'd lived with her masters, the priestesses, Miriam—never a real family. That she remembered, anyway.

She knelt at the spring and sank a skin under the water. The gurgling bubbles—fast and loud at first, slowing until the skin filled—soothed her frazzled mind. She repeated the process with each of the other four, then gathered them up and plodded toward her tent.

Moses and Aaron were expected tonight. They met once a week, taking turns at each other's tents. Miriam said they'd done it ever since they left Egypt, discussing the camp, the elders, plans—anything regarding Israel. She'd also told her they mostly did it because Moses enjoyed spending time with the siblings he'd lived eighty years without.

For the last few weeks, the brothers had come to Miriam's tent so she didn't have to walk so far.

Aaron's wife Elisheba sat by the fire chatting with Miriam as Arisha neared. Arisha slowed, almost turned back. Too late. Elisheba had seen her. She generally remained in the tent as Miriam chatted with her brothers, and whenever visitors came around.

Elisheba jumped up. "Arisha, it's so good to see you. You're always away whenever I come by."

Not away, actually, just inside, where it was safe. But Elisheba didn't need to know that. It would look like Arisha avoided her specifically, and that was not true.

Elisheba put her hand on Arisha's face. "Aren't you pretty? Aaron has mentioned you many times, and I see he does not exaggerate your beauty. I know you've brought Miriam much joy. Anyway, I've brought the manna for Aaron and Moses. He looks forward to these nights so very much. Almost as much as Moses."

She laughed as she set the pot in front of Miriam—didn't she didn't realize Miriam was too weak to cook? Before Arisha could escape, Elisheba wrapped her in a tight embrace. Arisha stiffened as the hug squeezed the breath from her body. When Elisheba released her, Arisha she forced a smile, and tried to make her arms and legs move again. Elisheba knelt and hugged Miriam before she left.

Arisha set the skins by the fire and reached for the manna. "I guess she doesn't know you're no longer cooking."

Miriam looked up. "Of course she does. She didn't want to embarrass me by handing it to you."

Arisha's cheeks warmed—she should have realized Elisheba would be sensitive to Miriam's plight. She stirred the embers in the fire pit into a flame and dumped all the manna, including hers and Miriam's, into a large pottery bowl. When the water was warm, she poured enough into the manna to make a soft dough, and formed it into cakes, which she placed on a wide pan to brown. She had just placed the hot, golden cakes onto a serving platter and risen to retreat into the tent when Moses and Aaron approached the fire.

"Good evening, daughter. Isn't this a lovely evening?" Aaron's deep voice always startled her, even when he stood right before her. But this time she hadn't been paying attention, and now she was trapped, between Miriam and her brother.

She glanced up into his kind face, but said nothing. Why was he so frightening? He'd never said a cross word to her.

"Thank you for looking after Miriam."

She nodded.

Moses stepped near. "Won't you join us this evening?"

Her throat closed—what would she say to them? No, she was better off in the tent. She backed up and shook her head, then escaped into the tent, closing the flaps behind her.

~

*D*ANEL DREW IN THE RAIN-CLEANSED air before he yanked the wooden shutters tight against the spring rains.

The king threw open the door and stomped in. "Can't you leave even one window open? It's not raining that hard yet."

Danel took a slow breath and turned to face his ruler. "Of course I can, but then the floor will be wet in the morning. You know the wind usually picks up at night and blows the rain inside. Which would you prefer: to hear the rain, or a dry floor?"

Keret growled, but gestured at the windows.

A servant lit the three large oil lamps waiting on the shelf in the corner and then placed them around the enormous room, saving the largest for the table by the oversized cedar bed. After pulling a thick blanket from the chest at the foot of the bed and spreading it out, he bowed and exited.

"Would you like some water or something to eat before I leave you for the night?"

"No, I'm not hungry." He stalked to the wall and placed his palm against a shuttered window. He stared at his hand a moment. "What do you suppose they're doing out there tonight?" His voice was low, almost as if he were talking to himself.

"The same thing they've been doing for the last thirty-nine years."

He stood silently a moment longer, then spun and waved a hand at Danel. "That is all."

"Have a pleasant night, then." He bowed and slipped from the room. A guard stood on either side of the door instead of the customary single man, spears in hand and daggers strapped to their hips. They nodded to him as he shut the door, then he strode down the hallway.

His legs felt like weights, and he longed to go home to his wife and grandchildren, but he needed to see Aqhat. He trudged down the stairs, then down the long hall to his friend's office and closed the heavy wooden door, checking twice to ensure it was locked behind him. The thick cedar blocked out sounds from the hall, and kept their conversations private, but did little to keep out the tantalizing smells from the kitchen a few doors down.

Soup that would simmer slowly all night made his mouth water. How could Aqhat possibly get any work done in this office? How many evenings, long ago, had Danel sat in that same kitchen watching his mother? She would cut up vegetables and meat left-over from the evening meal, dropping it all into a huge cauldron of water before setting it over a low flame.

Aqhat stood to greet him. "Danel, it's good you're here. I've been busy since your last visit." He stepped to a small table shoved against the wall and poured a cup of water, then handed it to Danel.

He pulled out a heavy chair and sat. "I hope so. Keret wants to know how the recruiting is going."

Aqhat dropped into a large chair, propping his huge, sandaled feet upon his desk. "I have fifty men beginning training next week."

"Good. He should be pleased."

"Should be. But will he be?"

Danel chuckled and shrugged.

"How's he doing?"

He drained his cup before he answered. "He's calm enough so far. Not like he was the first year or two."

Aqhat groaned. "If he gets that way again, I will not be able to take it."

"You won't have a choice. At least this time you'll be in command of the army. You won't have to make all those scouting runs yourself. You can send the new recruits."

"Maybe you can keep him calm instead."

Danel laughed. "I'm trying."

Aqhat pulled his feet back and leaned forward. "What do you think will happen to Arad? Do you think we'll be destroyed like Egypt?"

Danel let out a deep breath. "I don't know. Yahweh is a mighty God. He cares for His people."

"Yes, we've seen enough evidence of that. He rescued Kamose from our prison. No one else has ever escaped."

Danel raised a finger. "But He didn't keep him from all harm and pain. Kamose suffered mightily before he got away. And the Israelites defeated the Amalekites, but they lost men in the battle as well."

"True." Aqhat paused, drumming his fingers on his desk. He caught Danel's gaze and frowned. "We have spent the last forty years learning about Him, learning His ways. Memorizing all the stories Kamose told you when he was here those long weeks. We no longer sacrifice to the Canaanite gods. Would He destroy us?"

The silence felt like a weight on his shoulders as he thought of how to answer. "I don't think He would want to, but would He save the city just for us? I'm not sure He would do that, either."

~

"*Y*ou want me to do it *today*?" Arisha looked up at Miriam.

"It is just the first of two ceremonies, daughter. You're not marrying him yet. You'll continue to live here with me."

Arisha fisted her hands. "But why? Why we do we have to do it twice? We don't do that in Canaan."

Miriam took Arisha's hand in hers, gently pried it open. "The first is the betrothal ceremony. This is where you are promised to each other. If we were living in Canaan, or anywhere else, the time between the betrothal and the wedding is when the husband would build a house—or add on to his father's house, and prepare everything he would need to take care of you. You would make your wedding outfit, and your headdress of coins. But you would be as good as married even though you still lived apart. You could not separate from each other without a divorce."

Arisha gasped.

"You did agree to marry him, did you not?"

Arisha nodded slowly. The reality of the situation landed on her shoulders with full force.

"Then we will have the betrothal today. You still do not have to marry him until you are ready. Both ceremonies are very simple, just a legal pronouncement."

"All right."

Miriam enveloped her in a warm embrace. "I need to make sure you will be taken care of when I am gone. You understand, don't you, daughter? I know Zadok will be good for you. And you will be good for him as well." The woman who had been closer to her than her own mother in the few short months she had known her, kissed her temple and left her alone in the quietness of the tent.

Arisha sank to the cushioned floor. She could see how Zadok, with his kindness and patience, his calm spirit, could be good for her. What could she possibly offer to him? Why would he agree to marry someone like her? He was strong and handsome—surely he could choose any Israelite woman he desired.

Miriam peeked through the flaps. "Arisha? Zadok is here. Will you come out?"

Her heart began to race, but she closed her eyes. Breathe in, breathe out. Breathe in, breathe out. She could do this.

She stepped outside, and nearly retreated again. Zadok was there, and another man who had to be his father. Slightly shorter, grayer beard, even brighter smile. He looked like he was doing everything possible not to rush to her and embrace her. Instead he simply reached out to touch her shoulder.

"Arisha. I'm so delighted to meet you. I'm Ahmose, Zadok's abba."

She smiled. His voice was soft, like Zadok's, but more ... energetic.

Miriam slipped an arm around Arisha's shoulder. "Ordinarily, your abba would be here. Since he cannot be, Moses has agreed to take his place. Is that all right with you?"

She managed a nod. She had no one but Miriam. That Moses would do that for her when she'd barely spoken to him ...

She glanced at Zadok, deep in conversation with his abba.

Ahmose's hands gestured constantly as he spoke. When Moses approached, Ahmose greeted him with a warm, fierce hug. Did he ever stop moving?

Moses laughed, extricating himself. "Ahmose, my boy. You are still one of my favorite people."

My *boy*? He had graying hair.

"Now, let us start these two on their life together." Moses maneuvered Zadok to face him, and Ahmose stood at his side.

Miriam placed Arisha next to Zadok, hooking her arm around his elbow.

"We have welcomed Arisha among us. When we were at Mt. Sinai, Yahweh told us to welcome strangers, since we were once strangers in a land not our own. She has come to know Yahweh as the only true God, and we count her as our own." Moses faced Zadok. "Now I stand in place of Arisha's abba, and I say to you, today you have become my son-in-law."

Miriam leaned near. "See? That wasn't so bad, was it?"

"I suppose not." Arisha turned to Moses. "Thank you. That was ... unbelievably kind of you."

"I am all too happy to do this for you. It's been a long time since my own children were of the age to marry." Grinning, he turned her toward Zadok. "I think someone else wants your attention." He moved away as Zadok neared her.

"Are you all right?" His soft brown eyes searched her face.

She scrunched up her face a moment, causing him to laugh.

"Don't laugh." She poked his chest, laughing herself. "I'm all right."

"Good. Then I have something to ask you."

～

3rd day of Abib

ZADOK STOOD BEFORE ZIVAH AND Jacob, arms crossed. "She is coming to share the evening meal with us. But hear me: do not ask about marriage. Do not embarrass me, or her. Do not make her talk if she doesn't want to—she is painfully shy. She is so afraid of coming here it's taken me weeks to talk her into it." He took a step toward them and narrowed his eyes. "If you do anything to scare her off or make her uncomfortable, when we do marry I will move to the tents of Benjamin on the other side of camp and I will never come home."

Jacob's eyes widened. Zivah's face lost all color. He'd probably overdone it, and besides, he'd never be allowed to move to Benjamin, and they knew it. He didn't care. He had to make them understand.

He turned and slipped between Moses's and Aaron's tents, and into the walkway. Out of their sight, he stopped a moment and inhaled a long, slow breath. *Yahweh, help this go well. I don't want to scare her.* Why a family meal should be so terrifying he still didn't understand, but to her it was. And he'd promised he would do whatever he could to make it easier.

Arisha waited for him, pacing in front of the tent, twisting the end of her sash. Her lips moved silently—was she praying, too? His heart ached for her. If only he could take away her fear. But the best way to do that was to face it with her.

"Arisha?"

She raised her head to him, and her face softened. It seemed some of her fear dissipated. Did his presence do that? His heart beat faster at the thought.

"Are you ready?" He took her hands in his. "You'll be fine, I promise."

She tilted her head and smiled weakly, and he pulled her into his arms. "I'll be right beside you the whole time," he whispered.

She nodded into his chest.

He stepped away. "Come, then."

Within moments they were at Zadok's tent. She grabbed onto his arm as they stepped from between the tents into view of his family.

Imma was the first to reach them. Instead of hugging her, she simply took Arisha's other hand in both of hers, and Zadok breathed a prayer of thanks.

"Arisha, I'm so glad you've joined us. I'm Zadok's imma, Adi. Zivah is taking care of the food, so why don't you sit right here between Zadok and me and let me get to know you a little better?"

Imma led her to the fire, and Arisha released Zadok's arm but reached for his hand.

"Now I know you've heard about everyone, but I will introduce you." Imma leaned toward Arisha and pointed to each person in turn. "This is Zivah, Zadok's younger sister. The handsome young man next to her is her husband, Jacob. They live a few tents down the row, but they are here all the time."

Adira crawled into Imma's lap and giggled when she tickled her. "This little one is Adira, her daughter. She is named after me."

Zivah pulled the last manna cakes off the fire and dropped them onto a plate. She placed that next to a bowl full of dates.

"Ah, and you know my husband Ahmose, and with him is our grandson, Josiah."

Abba strolled to the fire with Josiah on his shoulders, who proudly proclaimed, "Savta, look! Look how tall I am!"

"I see. You have grown overnight." Imma laughed as Abba placed Josiah on the ground and sat next to him. "Adira, go back to your imma so we can eat." She kissed the girl's cheek and picked her up from her lap.

Arisha gestured to Josiah. "Is he older or younger?"

Zadok was thankful she was making an attempt to join the conversation, but her voice was strained. Was he the only one who noticed?

"He's the oldest, but only by a year. Boy first, girl second, just like Zadok and me." Zivah placed a bowl in Adira's lap.

Arisha smiled. "I always thought an older brother would be nice. Someone to look out for me."

Zivah pointed a finger. "They look out for you, yes, but they also tend to boss you around. And control your life. And act like they're your father instead of just your brother."

"When did I ever do that?" Zadok sat up straighter.

"Every day of my life until I married. You didn't even *want* me to get married."

"What?" Jacob nearly choked on his manna.

"That's not what I said." *Don't start a fight now, Zivah.* He aimed a glare at his sister.

Zivah cleared her throat. "Zadok, how are the sheep? Any new ones this week?

"Yes." He shot her a grateful look. She knew very well how many new lambs he had, but he was thankful she had changed the subject. "I've had more this year than ever. Two yesterday, in fact. We are well on our way to doubling the flock."

"I want to see them! Please!" Adira bounced up and down. Her knee bumped her cup of milk, and it toppled, spilling onto the sand.

Beside him, Arisha gasped softly. She stopped in mid-bite. Holding a date with one hand, she reached for him with the other and squeezed his wrist. What did she think would happen?

Jacob frowned at his daughter. "Adira, couldn't you go even one day without spilling something?" Then he burst into laughter.

"No, she can't." Josiah answered for his sister.

"I'm sorry, Abba." Adira reached for the cup but only succeeded in pushing it further into the sand.

Jacob extricated the half-buried cup, wiped the sand from the rim and poured more milk into it. "She spills something almost every day."

"Which is why we never fill her cup more than half full." Zivah glanced at Arisha as she wiped the sand off the girl's hands.

Zadok felt Arisha loosen her grip on his wrist.

Josiah sat up straighter and looked at Arisha. "She's a baby. I don't spill, ever, 'cause I'm not a baby."

"Josiah! Tell your sister you're sorry." Jacob put his hand on his son's shoulder.

"I'm sorry, Adira." He leaned near and kissed her check. The girl giggled.

Abba chuckled and shook his head. "Now, Zadok, about your sheep. How many lambs so far this year ...?"

Zadok reached for another manna cake. Next to him, Arisha's body relaxed as the conversation changed course.

After the meal, he walked her back. "Was it as bad as you feared?"

"It ended up quite enjoyable, actually. Your niece and nephew are adorable."

"Why were you afraid?"

She looked away. "Meals were never very pleasant, anywhere I lived. I spilled once like that, serving wine ..." Her face clouded.

His heart ached for her. What happened when she spilled? Nothing she wanted to talk about—or remember, apparently. "And with Miriam?"

"No, those are lovely, of course, but there are only the two of us."

"What about when she has visitors?"

"I stay in the tent."

He reached for her hand. "Always?"

She shrugged and nodded.

"You must hear them, at least. What about when Moses and Aaron come over?"

"They seem to have a delightful time. But I assumed maybe it was just because there were no children, or they'd been apart for so long. I thought it was unusual."

They neared her tent. The fire was banked and the flaps pulled shut.

Arisha glanced up and down the row. "I think we're the last ones awake. Everyone has to awaken so early for their morning priestly duties. Ummm, let me check on her." She slipped inside, exiting a moment later. "Miriam has gone to sleep already." She frowned.

"What's wrong?"

"She's just so tired, all the time. I ..." She rubbed her palm with the thumb of her other hand.

"I know she's grateful she has you. You are very precious to her."

She shrugged and dropped her gaze.

"I should go back." He didn't want to. He'd rather talk to her.

He'd shared her all evening, and he wanted some time with her alone. "May I see you tomorrow?"

She looked up. "When?"

He reached to touch her, but pulled his hand back. "As soon as the sun is up."

She smiled. "How about after the mid-day meal? I have many things to do first, and I want to make sure Miriam is doing well."

"I'd like that." He lowered his head and placed a light kiss on her cheek. "I'll see you then."

Morning couldn't come fast enough.

CHAPTER 5

*L*ATER THAT NIGHT ZADOK SAT WITH Abba and Jacob for the first time in almost two years. Not since the Marah debacle had he felt like joining the men around the fire after the evening meal. The cloud above them glowed softly, providing warmth and reassurance of Yahweh's presence.

Zivah had retired to her tent with her children, and Imma had slipped inside her own. A hawk sailed overhead as the western mountains swallowed the last bits of light. A charred palm log crumbled in the pit, sending a shower of flashing red sparks first shooting into the air, then floating down again.

Zadok stared at the ever-shifting flames. His life had altered in ways beyond his comprehension in the last several weeks. Everything he'd planned had been swept away with one simple statement from Miriam. "I want you to marry her."

And he was thankful. Never would he have been brave enough to try to change his life. He would have stayed in the pasture with the sheep forever.

Joshua lowered his lanky frame to the ground next to him. "Zadok. It's been a long time since you have been at your father's fire."

Zadok nodded. "It has. I missed it more than I realized."

Joshua leaned back and stretched out his long legs. The older man had been part of Zadok's life for as long as could remember, living in the tent next to theirs, right behind Moses. As a young man Joshua had shared that tent with Zadok's sabbas, Kamose and Bezalel, and Abba. Joshua had teased Kamose for trading his golden, jeweled armbands, the symbol of his office as captain of the guard in Egypt, for an Israelite tunic when he fell in love with Tirzah, trying to embarrass him. He never succeeded.

And Joshua grieved as deeply as any of them when Kamose died.

The tent flap rustled. A platter of cups full of fresh mint and sage leaves appeared and was placed on the ground to the side, followed by a pot of water. Imma stepped from the tent, then bent to retrieve the items. She knelt next to Abba and set them on the ground by the fire.

"Thank you, *habibti*." He kissed her on the cheek before she disappeared into the tent once again.

Abba returned to his conversation with Jacob, and Joshua turned to Zadok. "I hear you had a guest at your tent this evening."

"Yes, we did. How did you know?"

"I just came from Moses's tent. He's quite fond of her, though she barely speaks to him."

"She barely speaks to anyone."

"So it seems. She speaks to you, though. I wonder why that is." Joshua smirked as he raised a dark brow.

Before Zadok had to answer, Abba spoke. "I believe the water is hot. Does everyone want tea?" He reached for a cloth to grab the handle of the pot, then poured the steaming liquid over the leaves.

A sweet, tangy fragrance filled the air, and Zadok breathed deeply.

After allowing a few moments for the tea to steep, Abba removed the leaves, then passed around the cups. Zadok blew on the tea and took a sip. It tasted of earth and mint and filled him with a sense of familiarity and connection.

Jacob broke the mood by slurping his drink. "Joshua, are you and Moses forming plans to attack Canaan?" His eyes sparkled. Why did talk of war excite him? It always had, even when he and Zadok were children. He'd come over and listen to battle stories from Kamose and Joshua, until they refused to talk of it anymore.

"Not yet. It is not time." Joshua's voice was clipped.

"It won't be long though, will it? Before we enter? It's been almost forty years."

"Thirty-nine next week."

Zadok shifted uncomfortably. Why couldn't Jacob see Joshua didn't want to talk about it? "How many of that generation are left?"

Joshua set his cup on the sand. "Moses and Aaron met with the elders last week. The tribes of Dan and Issachar each have two, Reuben has three, and Asher and Naphtali have one each." He paused. "And Miriam."

Abba cleared his throat. "Joshua, you have another grandchild, yes?"

Joshua smiled. "I do. Micah. That makes seven."

Zadok breathed easier as the conversation took a pleasant turn. Joshua and Abba babbled about sons and grandsons and how much little girls captured their hearts. Even Jacob softened when he mentioned his little ones, until Zadok stopped listening altogether. Would he ever be part of a conversation like this? He had given up on marriage and children, but these last weeks ...

"Zadok?" Joshua's low voice startled him as he placed his hand on Zadok's shoulder. "How is Arisha doing ... with Miriam?"

"Struggling. Miriam is the only person she's ever really felt safe with. Or who's loved her."

Joshua smiled. "Until now."

Heat crawled up Zadok's neck. Hopefully the darkness would hide it. "It will be an enormous loss for her."

"I'm glad you are there to help her through it."

If only he could. Zadok knew the pain of death. He'd lost both sabbas and both savtas in just the last few years. And there wasn't much that could lessen the ache. But he could at least be with her.

If she let him.

~

*T*HE WORK WAS DONE FOR the morning, and Arisha was free to spend the afternoon with Zadok. As she ducked her head inside the tent to put away the clean dishes from the mid-day meal, his voice caught her attention.

"Want to walk to the spring?"

"Sure."

Zadok took Arisha's hand and headed east.

She stopped, pulling on his hand. "It's that way." She removed her hand from his and pointed north.

"Yes, the biggest one is that way, but there's a place I like better this way." He grinned as he walked backward. She pursed her lips, glancing sideways at him for a moment. "All right. We'll see." She caught up to him again, and they strolled to the shallow river that joined all four springs.

"This spot is where my sabba first met my savta almost forty years ago."

"Tell me about it."

They reached the river and Zadok spread his cloak on a fallen date palm and motioned for Arisha to sit. "My savta—actually she's my great-aunt—had two little girls. She was a widow, and she would bring them here in the afternoons."

He sat next to her. "She'd dragged some fallen trunks from the date palm trees into a half-circle so the girls couldn't run too far and she could rest while they played. My abba found them one day, and she had fallen asleep. He was a few years older, and he played with her children, and ended up playing with them almost every day. One day his uncle—Sabba Kamose—came to check on him, ended up talking to her, and eventually they married."

"Sounds like a great story." Arisha sighed contentedly, lifting her face to the sun. "Oh, the sun feels so good."

Zadok laughed and did the same.

"So Zadok, why aren't you married already? You're kind, and handsome. I can't imagine any girl wouldn't be thrilled to be your wife."

Grabbing a handful of sand, he allowed the golden grains to fall through his long fingers. "That's the long story I told you about the other day."

"I think we have time now."

"I was almost betrothed once."

She suppressed a gasp. "What happened?"

The muscle in Zadok's jaw twitched as he stared at the mountains in the distance. Perhaps she shouldn't have asked. But she had. So she waited.

"Her name was Marah. We were days from betrothal when Aaron asked me to be the shepherd for the Tabernacle flock."

"That sounds like an honor. At least a compliment."

"I had already begun raising some on my own. Hardly anyone is raising sheep out here. No one has more than three or four; they're all waiting until we get to Canaan. They think it's too difficult here, that it will be too hard to move them with us." He blew out a sharp breath. "So I said yes. The only problem was, I couldn't participate anymore in the drills to get ready to invade Canaan. It would take all my time to build the flock."

"Why is that a problem?"

"One, I want to. I want to do my part. Two, Marah's father wouldn't let me marry her. He said it was time to let go of the nomadic life of Abraham and Isaac. That I needed to settle down in Canaan and build her a home and be home every night, not out chasing sheep. He didn't think I could provide for her the way he thought I should, was afraid as a shepherd I wouldn't get a proper allotment of land when we reach Canaan. So he wouldn't let her marry me, and to save his reputation he started telling everyone I was a coward, that it was *my* choice not to be in the army."

He sighed. "Joshua and Aaron tried to set the story straight, but her father is pretty persuasive. Now half of Judah thinks I am too afraid to fight for Israel."

Her heart hurt for him. She placed her hand over his. "I'm sorry. That must be very painful."

"I try not to think about it." He turned to her. "Miriam said someone in Arad taught you about Yahweh?"

"Danel. He learned about Yahweh from an Israelite who was captured and held there a long time ago."

He frowned. "Someone who was captured told him about our God?"

"That's what he said. Someone they held as a prisoner and, I gathered, held for quite some time, then escaped."

Emotions flooded Zadok's face—too many for her sort out. "That was my great-uncle." His voice was low.

"The one who met his wife here? At the spring?"

He nodded.

"He was captured? How?"

"When Israel sent scouts into Canaan, they came back with a report not only about how beautiful and fertile the land was, but also about how fierce the people were. My people were afraid, and instead of trusting Yahweh, they demanded to be taken back to Egypt. For that, Yahweh said we would have to wait forty years to enter Canaan, one year for every day the scouts were in Canaan, until all of that generation had died. Only the next generation could enter."

"Oh, how awful!"

"Well, some of the people made it even worse by trying to show Yahweh that they were no longer afraid. They attacked Canaan, but they were soundly defeated, and left behind many wounded. Moses asked my uncle to use his skills as former captain of the guard in Egypt to help retrieve the wounded. He'd only been married a month and didn't want to go, but after a day or so Savta Tirzah convinced him that he should go and bring them home to their wives and children."

"She was very brave. I don't know if I could do that."

"So he went, and was captured by some of Arad's soldiers. The prince held him for days, weeks, trying to find out when we were going to attack again. Kamose kept telling him we wouldn't be coming back for forty years but he wouldn't believe him. A boy there helped him escape."

She grabbed his arm. "That must have been Danel! He said he grew up in the palace."

"And Kamose told him about Yahweh."

"Danel said they talked almost every day." Her words tumbled out. "It's how he learned your history, and he taught the stories to me."

"If you were in the temple, and he was in the palace, when did you see him?"

"I helped count up all the offerings each day, and they sent me to the palace with the report. I gave it to Danel. He was so kind ... he was the only person who ever really talked to me. One day, I was very upset ..."

"Why were you so upset?" He took her hand in his.

"I was sad I didn't have a home, a mother. That I didn't matter to anyone ... and Danel told me about Yahweh, and that I mattered to Yahweh, and to him."

He grinned. "He was right."

"The year I became a woman, it was right before the fertility rites. I would have had to participate. I was terrified. Danel told the priestesses that he needed me to learn a new system for counting and reporting the offerings, and I would need to stay in the palace for several days. He took me to his house and I stayed with his wife until the festivities were over. So I was safe for another year."

He tilted his head and studied her. "It sounds like Yahweh was watching out for you even then."

She paused, rubbing a scar on her hand. "I didn't tell you everything before. I escaped because I wasn't just expected to be part of the rites like everyone else. There was more ... " She didn't want to think about it now. Didn't want to tell him. What would he think of her?

"I just couldn't bear it. Danel helped me. If he were ever to be found out, or I ... "

"Don't worry, that's over now. You're safe here." He flashed that smile that always made her feel secure.

For now, at least, she could put Arad out of her mind.

But some day, Israel would attack Canaan, and what would happen then?

~

*A*RISHA SAT ACROSS FROM MIRIAM before the crackling fire enjoying the evening meal. She handed Miriam the last manna cake just as a cup slipped from the woman's hands and smashed onto a rock placed around the fire. Shards from the pottery cup scattered and milk splashed on Miriam's feet and her cloak.

A chill crawled down Arisha's spine. She grabbed a cloth and dabbed at the wet fabric to sop up the spilled liquid.

"Don't fuss now, I'm fine. Just a little wet." She grabbed Arisha's wrist and caught her eyes, stared her down. "I'm fine. I just spilled a bit of milk. Now stop." She pasted on a smile that appeared forced, but Arisha dutifully stopped.

Tense silence hung between them as they finished their manna. Finally Arisha could stand it no longer. "Miriam, what's wrong? I know something is not right. You sleep more, you are weaker. You say I am a woman and must marry." She drew in a ragged breath. "So do not treat me like a child. Tell me the truth. What is happening to you? Are you ...?" Biting her lip, she tried to bring herself to speak aloud the hated thoughts she'd been avoiding for weeks.

"Yes, daughter. I am dying. I feel it. My heart wants to stay here, stay with you, stay with my brothers ... I am not ready to leave. But my body is finished, I'm afraid." She brushed at the wet hem of her cloak.

Arisha's chest ached. *Stop talking.* Miriam had to stop saying these things.

"It has been betraying me in small ways for over a year. Nothing you would see, but I noticed. In the last few weeks, though, the changes, the deficiencies, have become most dreadful." She sighed deeply. "I am so desperately tired. I can barely hold the smallest item. Even standing takes almost more strength than I have. I fear it won't be long."

She took Arisha's hand, and with her other hand, held up a finger. "And my one wish, before I join our fathers, is to see that you will not be alone. That is why I have been pushing you and Zadok so hard. I know it is a little fearsome at the moment, but he will be good for you when I am gone."

Arisha opened her mouth to speak, but couldn't think of anything to say. She only nodded.

Miriam set her empty cup aside. "I've eaten the manna and spilled the milk. The meal must be over." She laughed weakly. "If you'll help me, I think I'll go to sleep now."

Arisha rose and helped Miriam to stand. Wrapping her arm around Miriam's waist, Arisha noticed the woman was surprisingly light, as if in just two weeks she'd lost half her weight. Arisha guided her into the tent and had barely slipped Miriam's cloak off before she nearly collapsed onto her mat. Arisha pulled the blanket over Miriam's shoulders, and laid her down.

She was asleep in moments.

Arisha cleaned the dishes and left them outside the door of the tent, then sat and listened to the fire pop as the evening breeze drifted by. Her worst fear had been put into words, spoken aloud. Now it all made sense. The reason Miriam had been so insistent she marry.

Because she was going to leave her.

Everyone she'd ever known had left her—or shoved her aside—eventually. Would she ever have anyone who would stay? Ever have a home that would always be hers, or would she continue to be passed around from one unwilling stranger to another?

As the thoughts chased each other around and around in her head, one person kept reappearing, one person who might be able to help her navigate the sea of grief she was about to find herself thrown into.

Zadok.

She found herself walking through camp, nearly to the end of Zebulon and headed toward the pastures. When had she risen and started walking? She didn't remember. As she passed the last tent, thoughts of Zadok didn't erase the heartache that engulfed her, but another feeling sneaked into her heart as well—one she didn't recognize but which was quite pleasant. She almost smiled.

She wrested the branch from the gate and entered the pasture. Holding the hem of her tunic away from her feet, she trudged toward the spring where Zadok kept his flock close to water and lush grass. She watched her step but glanced up now and then, searching for him. There he was—his strong form stood tall among the sheep, his sleeveless sheepskin cloak blowing behind him. His staff hung from his elbow as his arms crossed his chest. His head never still, he scanned the fields, constantly looking after his sheep. She caught her breath. Would he care for her with such determination?

As she neared, it became clear his arms weren't crossed. He clutched a tiny lamb to his chest, swaddled under his cloak. One arm under the small animal, supporting it, one on its back, caressing its head.

He noticed her approach and turned toward her, a smile taking over his face.

She smiled for a moment, then the heated mix of emotions spun out of control and the tears spilled from her eyes.

His eyes widened and he set the lamb on the grass, along with his staff. "Arisha, what's wrong?" He jogged near and placed his hands on her arms.

"It's Miriam ... sh-she ..."

"Is she hurt? Do we need to go tend to her?" He started toward camp but she grabbed his arm.

"No, no, she's not hurt." Her heart felt as shattered as the cup Miriam had dropped. "She's ... she's ... she's dying."

"Wait, y- you ..." His eyes narrowed. "Why do you say that?"

"She told me." Her eyes burned.

"Oh, habibti, I'm so sorry."

"Habibti?"

He grinned. "It's Egyptian for sweetheart. It's kind of unique to my family. Does it bother you?"

She smiled and shook her head and he pulled her into his arms.

Miriam called her daughter, or my child, which was wonderful, but she called many girls that. No one had ever used such a sweet endearment with her. The tears came faster. They soaked through his tunic, and her body shook as she sobbed. His arms felt wonderful around her, so strong. Like he could protect her from anything, like nothing could get to her.

If only that were true.

Zadok stroked her hair as he held her and let her cry. He rubbed her back and kissed her temple, and eventually her sobs calmed. She drew in deep breaths and turned her face to rest her cheek on his chest. After a moment or two, she stepped out of his arms. "I'm sorry. I didn't mean to bother you. I couldn't think of anywhere else to go."

"No, you didn't bother me. I'm glad you came to me. I'm sorry you're hurting so much." He drew her closer, took her hands in both of his. "Arisha, I want to help you."

She frowned, shook her head. "There is nothing you can do. There is nothing anyone can do."

"I may not be able to stop Miriam from dying, but I can try to ease your pain. If you let me."

She looked away.

"I'm not marrying you just because Miriam wanted me to." He placed his hand on her cheek. "That may have been why I met you, but it's not why I want to marry you."

It's not? "Why, then?"

"Because I want to care for you, to provide for you, to love you. Maybe we don't know each other well enough now, but I promise I will never hurt you, or allow anyone else to hurt you."

She thought a moment longer. "All right. But not until after she's gone. I won't leave her."

He smiled, wrapping his arms around her again. "If that's what you want." He pulled her close again and kissed her forehead.

She rested her cheek against his chest. His heart thumped beneath her ear, and she closed her eyes and listened to the strong, steady beat. She'd marry him. She'd promised Miriam, and a woman alone could not survive in Canaan. Zadok was kind, gentle and would take good care of her. He appeared to have genuine feelings for her.

But she would protect herself. She would not expose herself to the pain of loss she was only beginning to feel, a loss that would deepen over the next days and weeks.

So she'd marry him.

But she would not love him.

CHAPTER 6

7th day of Abib

ZADOK PACED IN FRONT OF the tent he shared with his parents. The sun had already set and Arisha should have arrived over an hour ago. His stomach rumbled. He could go ahead and eat without her; Imma had left manna cakes and dates for them. But he hated eating alone anymore. He'd rather wait.

The evening breeze was cool on his bare arms. Would she remember to wear her cloak? She promised she'd return before dark—promised she would let one of the many other women happy to do so spend the night with Miriam so she could get a good night's sleep. Should he go after her? He knelt before the fire and stirred the dying embers, added another log, then rose and stared between the long, straight rows of tents, willing her to appear. After a few more moments, her familiar form ambled toward him. Her head was down, her shoulders slumped, her gait slow.

He moved toward her and pulled her into his arms, and she leaned heavily on him. "You look exhausted. Why so late tonight?"

Her light brown eyes moistened. "Miriam is not doing well. I don't think she has much time left." She brushed away a tear. "She is so weak. I could barely manage to get her to finish a cup of milk. She refused to eat."

He led her to the fire. She sat and reached for the skin of milk but he intercepted it, grabbing the cups with his other hand. He poured her some of the cool liquid and offered her a cake of manna.

"She's dying, Zadok." Her voice trembled.

"I know, habibti." He set the food aside and drew her close, her tears soaking his tunic. "She's been dying for a while now."

"Yes, but I think it will be very soon. Days, maybe. I can no longer pretend it won't happen." She drew in a ragged breath.

He held her tighter, rubbing circles on her back. "All the old ones are dying. She's one of the only ones left."

She nodded against his shoulder.

He kissed her temple and gently pushed her back. "You need to eat if you're to care for her again tomorrow." He returned her food and milk to her lap. "Who's with her tonight?"

"Ruth and Hannah." She nibbled on some manna.

"Have Moses and Aaron been by?"

"Every day. Moses is having an especially hard time."

"He is?"

"He can barely manage. It grows worse each day. He doesn't want to cry in front of her, but ..." She shook her head.

"Do you think she would care if he did?"

"Of course not. She knows she's dying better than anyone." Her voice broke and Zadok reached for her hand. "But I think he wants to be strong for her."

Zadok shrugged. "I think it's natural for men to want to protect women. Younger, older, sister, wife, mother—doesn't matter." He drew circles on the back of her hand with his thumb. *If only I could take this from you.*

"Well, he can't protect her this time. I wish he could." The tears fell again.

They finished the meal in silence. "Can I do anything for you?"

A small smile broke through the gloom. "You're doing it."

He tucked a lock of her long, dark wavy hair behind her ears. "Finish eating and get some rest. You've had a long day." Glancing over her shoulder, he saw Imma step outside the tent. He took the plate from Arisha and helped her to rise. "I'll be back in the morning." He kissed her cheek and allowed Imma to lead her inside.

Zadok stared at the tent flaps, watching the subtle movement as Imma tied the strings from inside. Then the cloth went still. His heart felt as empty as his arms.

He wandered up and down the row of army tents the Israelites had taken from the Egyptians thirty-nine years ago. None of them showed a day of wear. They all looked as good as the night they were first pitched, the night after they had escaped from Egypt. At least that's what he'd been told. Of course, he wasn't alive then. After Israel escaped, they spent the first night at Succoth, the large flat ground the Egyptians used as a staging area, full of tents, water and other supplies. The forty years Moses had spent as a prince had served him well, teaching him not only military strategy, weapons, evasion, and leadership, but secrets like where the tents were kept, and the fact there were eleven forts on the shorter northern route, and that the southern route, though longer, would be safer.

With the death of Miriam, the quiet, safe life they'd been living at the oasis of Kadesh would end—abruptly. Within the next year they would head into Canaan, and then the wars would begin, wars that that he had no guarantee of surviving. How could he do that to Arisha? He too had heard the stories of giants and iron chariots and walled cities, and while he believed Yahweh would give them the land, he knew the Canaanites wouldn't hand it over without a fight.

He rubbed his hand down his face and sighed. He wasn't prepared for this — for any of it. But it was coming, whether he was ready or not.

~

10th day of Abib

*T*HE TENT WAS QUIET EXCEPT for Miriam's labored breathing. Arisha dipped a cloth into the bowl at her side. Squeezing the water from it, she dabbed it on the older woman's brow, cheeks, neck. The water evaporated as soon as she lifted the rag.

Hannah and Ruth sat on Miriam's other side. Occasionally Hannah would take the older woman's hand between her own and softly caress it. Ruth's lips moved silently.

Arisha reached for a clean cloth, using it to soak up some water from a cup. Hovering it over Miriam's mouth, she let a few precious drops fall onto the cracked lips. She tenderly brushed her hair away from her eyes, savoring the feel of her skin beneath her fingers. Wetting the cloth again, she dropped a little more water onto Miriam's swollen tongue.

Arisha's chest constricted, watching the suffering of this woman who had taken the place of her absent mother, this woman who had taught her what it meant to be a child of Yahweh, this woman who had taken the bitterness from her heart and replaced it with love.

The time between Miriam's breaths lengthened, and it seemed as if everyone else held theirs waiting for her to draw another one. When at last she sucked in a noisome, wet chestful of air, then expelled it, the tension in the stuffy tent abated for a brief moment. It slowly built back up as the women surrounding Israel's matriarch nervously anticipated the next one. Fingers were chewed, knees bounced, tunics were twisted.

Arisha's heart was breaking, but she ignored it. Right now, all that mattered was Miriam's comfort. Arisha searched her face. Did she hurt? Her breathing sounded painful, but she actually looked peaceful. Her body was relaxed. When Arisha lifted Miriam's arms to smooth the cool cloth across her skin, they were almost weightless. She offered no resistance. She didn't grimace or groan like so many of the old ones she'd seen—and heard—as they lay dying. If not for the pale quality of her skin, Arisha could almost believe the old woman was sleeping.

Another loud breath snapped her back to the aching reality that Miriam would soon be gone.

A noise from outside drew their attention.

"May I come see my sister?" Moses's soft voice drifted in.

Hannah rose to push aside the tent flaps to let him enter. Arisha was surprised to see the sky was dusky—where had the day gone?

Miriam's youngest brother stepped inside. "And Aaron, or ...?"

"I think he should come now." Arisha tried to keep her voice steady, but she didn't succeed.

Moses's face lost all its color.

"I'll get him." Hannah stepped outside as he knelt next to Miriam.

"Oh, Miriam, my love." Tears gathered in his gray eyes. He stroked her hair, bent to kiss her forehead. "I will miss you so much. As loud, as demanding, as interfering as you could be, I will miss you."

Aaron entered and Arisha scooted into the corner to allow him to sit across from his brother. The other women backed away to allow the men room.

"She did like to interfere, didn't she?" Aaron chuckled dryly.

Moses nodded. "I think she always wished she were a man so she could be truly in charge."

Aaron smiled. "I thought I was the only one who believed that."

Moses took her hand in his. "I will always remember her singing on this side of the *Yam Suph*, lifting her voice to El Shaddai. She was so beautiful that day. More beautiful than usual." Moses's eyes took on a faraway quality, as if he were watching her dance at that very moment. "She spun like she was still a girl."

"She had all the women whirling with her." Aaron laughed softly.

"The whole camp was dancing and singing by the time she was finished." Moses smiled down at Miriam and bent to kiss her again, but a noisy gasp stopped him short. He shot a look at Arisha, his eyes wide.

Arisha shrugged slightly. "She's been doing that all afternoon."

He returned his gaze to Aaron. "Did you think she would be the first?"

"No. She's too stubborn." Aaron reached for her other hand.

Miriam took a shallow breath, then another, and another.

Moses and Aaron turned to Arisha.

"That's new." Tears burned her eyes. Was this it?

"Aaron, you need to go now." Hannah touched his shoulder.

He didn't move.

The quick, quiet breaths continued.

Arisha's hand went to her mouth. Her heart pounded in her chest, in her ears. *Yahweh, please no. Not yet.* And yet, why not? Should she stay here, past her time? Too weak to move, to speak?

Hannah rose and took Aaron's hand in hers. "You know what happens if you are here when ..."

The breaths slowed even more.

"Aaron, now!" Hannah's gaze darted to the doorway and back as she pleaded with the High Priest. "You cannot even be in the tent with her if she dies ... *please* come outside with me."

Aaron slowly rose and followed Hannah out.

Arisha and Ruth left as well. The tent flaps had been tied open, and after a moment Arisha could see Moses fall across her unmoving form, his shoulders shaking. Aaron stood beside her, tears streaming silently down his cheeks.

Hannah leaned in and embraced her. "I'm going to see my children and feed my husband. I'll return to prepare the body in the morning," she whispered.

"I think I will, too." Ruth followed Hannah, leaving Arisha alone with Aaron.

Moses's sobs followed her as she kept guard outside the tent. The wind raced through the camp, moaning, whipping tent flaps and blowing sand. Hopefully it would die down, or tomorrow would not be a good day for a burial.

At length the sobs from within softened, and Aaron turned to Arisha. His face was dry but clouded, his usually bright eyes dark.

"And how are you, daughter? I know you will miss her terribly."

Until then, she had managed to keep her tears in check, but Aaron's soft words unleashed them.

The High Priest drew her close. "She loved you very much, you know that, don't you?"

She knew very well that Miriam had loved her, loved her before anyone else had truly loved her. Arisha had counted on her to show her how to be a wife and mother.

And now she was gone.

~

*A*RISHA'S EYES BURNED AS SHE washed Miriam's body once more. If only she could keep washing her, then it would never be over. But Hannah and Ruth had already stopped, and now they stared at her.

She dropped her cloth into the bowl at her side and dried her hands. Another woman—what was her name?—had come to help prepare Miriam for burial. Arisha reached for the clean tunic, and between them they managed to slip it over her head and draw her arms through. The others waited as she gently combed the thin hair, removing every tangle, arranging it perfectly around Miriam's placid face.

They lifted her a few handbreadths off the floor of the tent, and Arisha and Ruth slid a thin board of acacia wood under the body, then pulled a long, wide cloth over it. They stretched it tight, removing all the wrinkles, and slowly lowered Miriam onto it. Hannah and Ruth pulled the fabric over her to their side and tucked it under, then handed it back to Arisha. She blinked several times, vainly trying to clear her vision, as she placed the edges of the sheet under her.

The scene before her was all too real now, too final. Miriam was gone, gathered to their ancestors.

Arisha wiped the tears from her cheeks. There was nothing more to be done. Preparations were complete. She and the others picked up the bier and slowly rose, lifting the body with them. She weighed so little. Spinning the bier so the head faced the door, in measured steps they carried her out of the tent from which she had not emerged in weeks.

After being inside for so long, Arisha squinted in the late afternoon sun. She blinked rapidly—a good way to hide her tears.

Four men stepped forward to take the body from the women, careful not to come in contact with them. Arisha reached for Miriam one last time; her fingers lingered, refusing to relinquish their hold. Aaron approached his sister once more. His hand hovered over the linen-clad body as he choked back his tears, unable to touch her.

Arisha pulled her hand back, and the men carried her away—away from the tent, away from camp, away from Arisha forever.

The people of Israel joined them as they passed through camp, heading past the springs out to the edge of the desert. The brawny, noisy wind whipped hair, tunics and cloaks. Not yet dangerous, not quite a *khamsin*, but fierce just the same.

The sun hurried to sink behind the mountains, as if even it could not bear to watch Miriam's final goodbye. An almost full moon rose in its place. As rocks began to appear, the men stopped. The people stood in a half-circle, their backs to the wind, heads bowed against the sand the hot air flung at them. The men set their precious load on the desert floor, the crowd blocking the wind. Moses appeared from the east and stepped to the far side of the body and raised his hands. His lips moved but no words came forth.

Arisha and the other women stood aside, keeping away from the others as they were now unclean. "Now she no longer suffers." Hannah's whispers reached her ears from behind.

Miriam had been sick for months. She hadn't eaten, hadn't left her tent in weeks. She'd not really participated in the leadership of Israel's women for the last year or more. Arisha looked at the faces of those around her. Soft smiles, whispers of remembrances, some sniffles and tears. It wasn't that they didn't grieve, but she'd lived a long and good life, and her time here was over. They'd said their goodbyes. Only Arisha, Hannah and Ruth, and a few others had still seen her every day, still needed to bid her farewell.

Moses's voice caught her attention. "Yahweh, you have been our dwelling place throughout all generations. Before the mountains were born or You brought forth the whole world, from everlasting to everlasting You are El Shaddai. A thousand years in Your sight are like a day that has just gone by, or like a watch in the night."

The rest of his words faded as she thought of the time Yahweh had given her with Miriam. He didn't have to give her anything. Miriam was not hers; Arisha had no family, yet Yahweh had placed her in Miriam's tent. Instead of lamenting over what she had lost, she should be grateful for what Yahweh had given her, as little as it seemed.

The men picked up the bier and slid Miriam's body into the shallow depression that had been dug. Sand clashed against the fabric covering her body as they tossed the sand over her. More men came forward to place rocks over her to keep the nighttime animals at bay.

And then it was over.

Arisha waited until the crowd dispersed, remaining with Miriam. Finally she turned to go. She faced east, trudged toward the tent outside of camp. She'd taken only a few steps when a lone figure caught her attention. She stopped.

Zadok.

He stood silently, maybe twenty strides away, pain written across his face. The wind blew through his hair, whipped his sheepskin cloak around his shoulders, tossed sand onto his sandals, but he remained immobile. As solid as the mountains beyond. He couldn't touch her, couldn't come with her, but still he had found a way to let her know he would be waiting when she came back.

She continued to where she would spend the next seven days

with the other women, waiting out her time of uncleanness, her heart heavy. Miriam was gone. Arisha would soon marry Zadok, and though Miriam would not be there to teach her to be a wife, perhaps Adi would help her.

As Arisha turned to tie the tent flaps tight against the wind, she noticed Moses crawling into one of the other tents staked into the desert sand, away from the women. He, too, was now unclean, having embraced his dead sister. He'd been out here last night as well. She hadn't even thought about that. Aaron had refrained; as Israel's High Priest, he was not permitted to defile himself, not even allowed to mourn. Moses would be grieving alone, away from the others, at least for the first seven days. She would be here with three other women, but he would be alone.

At the moment, she couldn't think of anything more agonizing.

CHAPTER 7

13th day of Abib

IRIAM DANCED AND SANG ON the shore of the Yam Suph, surrounded by spinning circles of young women banging tambourines. Older than nearly all the women there, she still exuded an enviable energy. Her strong, clear voice carried above the deafening sounds of the water still swirling from the watery walls Yahweh had collapsed. "I will sing to the Lord for He has triumphed gloriously ..."

Though the celebration had taken place long before Arisha's birth, she'd heard the story so many times she could picture every detail of Miriam praising Yahweh on the shore.

Arisha didn't know everything about Israel's history, but she did know Miriam's. Many nights, as they waited to fall asleep, the woman had told her the cherished tales. Her favorite was the story of when Moses was an infant, and the Pharaoh hatched his evil plan to kill all the baby boys. Miriam hid him in a basket and settled him in the papyrus reeds along the Nile, waiting for an Egyptian to find him. Arisha could only imagine the fear and shock that must have coursed through her when one of the princesses found him. And yet that didn't stop Miriam. She marched right up to her and offered to find a wet nurse, then took Moses home, where his own mother raised him for several years.

Arisha longed for that kind of courage, that wit and audacity. Miriam knew what she wanted and how to get it. She was the unquestioned leader of the women. She was confident and competent—everything Arisha desired to be.

"Arisha?" Hannah touched Arisha's shoulder, rousing her from her daydreams.

"Arisha, why were you caring for Miriam? After her death? Now, we"—she pointed to the circle of women in the small tent—"do that all the time. We're widows. We spend our days caring for the dying and comforting their loved ones. So we have the time to spend weeks out here. But you're young." She sighed. "Why didn't you leave with Aaron? Why allow yourself to become unclean, spend a week away from your betrothed? He cannot be happy about this."

Arisha shifted. How much should she tell these women she hardly knew? They knew she was not Israelite—her name alone revealed that—but how much else did she want to share? "Miriam took me in when I had no one else. I owe her my life."

"I've brought your meal, ladies. A surprise tonight. Manna." The voice outside cackled.

Arisha breathed a prayer, thankful for the interruption.

The women waited to be sure their visitor was safely gone before reaching through the tent flaps for the basket of food.

"Has the wind died down?" Ruth asked.

"Mostly." Hannah placed the basket of manna in the center of the tent and passed the skin of milk to Arisha.

She grabbed the stack of cups from the corner behind her, took one and handed the stack to the woman beside her.

"Where did you meet your betrothed?" Ruth asked, narrowing her eyes.

"Miriam asked Zadok to marry me. Miriam's family has always been close to his, and she chose him for me."

"Zadok?"

"Um ... yes." She squirmed.

"Well, what do you mean *she* asked him?" The third woman—Dinah?—pointed a long finger at her. "You are a marriageable, beautiful woman. Maybe a little older, but so is he. And he's a handsome young man. I'd think the first time he saw you, he'd ask."

Arisha took a long drink of her milk. These women did not let up. Maybe the fact that he'd rarely seen her, that she'd hid from everyone and left Miriam no choice had something to do with it.

"Maybe because—"

"Ruth, be quiet." Hannah glared at her friend.

Maybe Arisha could change the subject. "Is the wind calm enough to open the flaps?"

"Let's see." Hannah peeked out of the tent. "I think we could do that for a while." She rose and tied the flaps back.

Arisha walked to the other end and did the same. A gentle breeze whooshed through, clearing out the stuffiness of the last two days. She exited and let the wind blow through her hair, bringing a sense of calm for the first time since the funeral.

She sat in the sand, and though the evening air around her was cool, the sand's heat seeped up into her body and soothed her weary muscles. How could doing nothing all day be so exhausting?

The sunset splashed bold orange and pink stripes across the sky. A perfect sky for Miriam—audacious and bright. Arisha watched the display until the sun sank below the western mountains, taking all its colors with it. Once again, Arisha felt bereft.

She went inside, and after evening prayers with the others, lay back on her mat.

Two days down, five to go, then she could see Zadok. For the first time since she had agreed to marry him, she actually found herself aching to be near him.

~

17ᵗʰ day of Abib

*T*HE NOISE POKED AT THE edges of his mind, demanding entrance. Zadok had finally fallen asleep in the early hours of the morning after thinking and praying and wondering. It was ridiculous how much he missed her. Did she miss him?

There was no reason to get up. His sheep were well watched, Arisha was gone, and if he stepped outside, Zivah would only harass him. He rolled over, closed his eyes and tried to go back to sleep, but he couldn't ignore the clamor any longer. The mumbling and murmuring continued, growing stronger, finally driving him awake. He sat up and rubbed his temples, trying to dislodge the fog in his head. He lay back down, draping his arm over his eyes.

With no rest coming, he arose, shrugged on his cloak and crawled out of the tent. People rushed past him, shoving and pushing. Where was everyone going?

Jacob banked the fire in front of his tent.

"What's happening?"

"I don't know, but I'm going to find out. I didn't want to wake you." Jacob grabbed a plate from in front of his tent, then stood and waited until he caught Zadok's gaze. "Zivah collected your manna and left you these cakes. She said you haven't been sleeping."

Zadok lifted one shoulder. How did she know? A few nights back in his parents' tent and already everyone knew everything. He gestured to the crowds. "Where are they going?"

"Toward the big spring, I think. Moses returns today. Maybe they're going to see him." Jacob lead them north through the rows and rows of tents, silent until they reached the end, then they angled northeast. "Arisha returns tomorrow?"

"She's supposed to. She and the other women have one more day because they prepared the body."

"Hmmm." Jacob nodded.

The crowd gathered at the big spring was tense and agitated. Cries of "Where's the water?" and "Why did the water dry up?" overlapped each other and grew louder and more insistent.

"There's no water?" Zadok furrowed his brow.

They made their way to the front of the crowd, to the edge of the spring. It was indeed, nearly dry. The day Miriam died it was full. In seven days it had dried up? That seemed impossible, and yet it had happened.

Moses stood in the center of the dry bed. Aaron waited several strides away. No one else had ventured beyond the former edges.

"He looks bad," Jacob whispered.

Moses looked like he hadn't slept since his sister died. His face was drawn, and it even appeared he hadn't washed, although he must have purified himself after his seven days outside the camp. Perhaps the grief had taken such a drastic toll. He simply stood silently, absorbing the shouts and the yelling and the abuse from the crowd.

Jacob spread his hands. "Why won't he say anything? Do anything?"

"I don't know." Zadok shook his head. "It's so unlike him."

"You should have let us die in Egypt!" A large man shoved his way to the front, shaking his fist at Moses. "Almost forty years we've been here, and for what? We're no better off than the day we left. We're back to no water, just like our parents at Meribah!"

A shorter, stockier man joined him. "Benaiah's right. We're all going to die here, us and our children and our animals. We never should have left!"

Never should have left? Zadok, like everyone else, had heard the stories from his father and grandfather of the people demanding to go back to Egypt—more than once on the journey to Kadesh. That very desire, and the refusal to go forward into Canaan when Yahweh commanded it, was the reason for the forty-year delay. Never did Zadok think he would see it for himself. Didn't anyone learn anything?

Joshua sprinted up beside them, out of breath. "What's happening?"

Zadok gestured toward the dry pool. "The people are angry there's no water and demanding to go back to Egypt."

Joshua shook his head. "Looks like they ambushed him on his

way back, caught him before he even made it home." He took stock of the crowd. "I'm going to Moses." He jogged to the center of the pool and huddled with Moses and Aaron.

Moses raised his staff in the air and waited for the crowd to quiet. "I must talk to Yahweh." He strode from the dry pool back toward camp. The crowd parted to let him through, and Joshua and Aaron rushed to keep up with him.

The crowd milled around, edgy, complaining. Miriam's death forgotten, their only thoughts were of water. Benaiah and his friend moved throughout the crowd, keeping everyone agitated.

Zadok frowned. "I don't like this. This sounds just like the time the spies came back and the people threatened to stone Moses."

Jacob glanced around. "How does a crowd become so cruel so fast? Last week everyone's talking about heading into Canaan, now they want to go back to Egypt? *Back* to Egypt—none of these people have ever even been there!"

"I think lack of water or food, or fear can make people do things they wouldn't ordinarily do." Abba spoke from behind them.

"Abba! I didn't see you." Zadok clasped his father's shoulder.

"So they want to go back to Egypt again, do they?" Abba chuckled dryly, although a sadness filled his eyes.

"That's what they say." Jacob huffed. "How could they possibly want to go back to where they've never been?"

Abba looked over the crowd, still milling about. "Egypt is a cruel and hateful place, and my back bears the proof. They speak from fear. Yahweh did not bring us this far to fail; be assured of that. He will take care of His people. He always has. We only need to wait for Moses."

~

ADOK RUBBED HIS THUMBNAIL AGAINST his lower lip as the morning sun beat down on his shoulders. Moses and Aaron had been gone a long time, and the people were growing increasingly restless. There were even a few mentions of stoning—

again. When Benaiah had the men so worked up Zadok feared they would never calm down, Moses and Aaron appeared at the edge of camp, Joshua behind them. They marched through the crowd toward the waterless spring, over the dry ground to the other side, and continued toward the low hills north of camp.

Zadok, Abba and Jacob sprinted to get ahead of the crowd, finally catching up with Moses. When they slowed to a walk, Zadok drew his arm across his brow, leaving a trail of sweat on his skin. "Where do you think he's going?"

Abba shook his head. "I don't know. He seems to be headed for the hills. That's a long way north of camp. Uncle Kamose took me there once when he showed me the trail the spies took." He glanced behind him. "I don't imagine all these people will keep up with him. They'll give up after a bit and turn back."

A hot and uncomfortable walk later the ground became rocky, and finally they came upon the beginnings of the cliffs that later turned into the mountain range that ran the length of Canaan.

Ahead of them lay a flat rock face with a gash in the front. Moses neared the formation, then clambered up on some lower rocks at its base. Aaron followed him; Joshua waited below. Moses turned and waited until the crowd gathered around him.

Zadok's heart hurt for the man—his face still showed remarkable strain, and he appeared utterly exhausted. If only this had happened a few days from now. Moses raised his staff toward the split in the rock. "This is the source of all our water. The water pours out here, runs along the ground, then sinks back under the limestone until it bubbles up at the spring. Yahweh said if I speak to this rock He will—"

"So we get some water." Benaiah shoved his way to the front once again. "How do we know it will last this time? How do we know we're not better off going back to Egypt? We've spent our whole lives here, living on manna, never eating any real fruit or vegetables or bread. And *no one*"—he turned to face the crowd and spread his arms—"except Joshua and Caleb has ever seen Canaan. I'm not sure it even exists!" He laughed. "At least not the way they tell it. Full of grass and water and fruit and wheat and trees of all kinds. We need to g—"

"Now that's enough!" Moses raised both arms and shouted over the man at his feet.

Zadok stepped back. He had never heard Moses raise his voice. Moses had always been the very model of peace and calm. "We are *not* going over that again! The last time someone wanted to go back to Egypt, we had to wait here, in the sand, outside Canaan for forty years! There will be no more talk of Egypt! You will do as I say!" He punctuated his sentence by jabbing the end of his staff into the rock at his feet.

Benaiah raised a fist at their leader. "Just a minute—"

"No!" Aaron lunged at Benaiah. "Leave him alone! Stop talking! Go back to your tent."

Benaiah's eyes grew wide, but he did not move.

"Have you not learned a single thing?" Moses's voice was loud, but shaky. The crowd stilled instantly. Even the birds had fled the mountain. "Must we do everything? Must we bring water from this rock?" He turned toward the face of the mount, raised his staff over his shoulder and slammed it against the rock. An earsplitting crack reverberated through the air. Moses pulled back and then slammed the rod again, releasing another deafening clap. He remained silent and still for a long moment, then fell against the rock, head on his forearms, shoulders shaking. He slowly slid to his knees.

What just happened? "Is he all right?" Zadok moved toward the lower rocks.

"I'm not sure ..." Abba grabbed his tunic and jerked him back. "Stay here."

"But he needs help." Why would Abba keep him from offering aid?

"Aaron's with him."

The stone shuddered and burbled. The people closest to it retreated a few steps. It gurgled louder, and they stepped further to the side. A thundering quake shook the ground under their feet, and water burst from the gash and spewed out, shooting through the air a distance well over the height of three men. It thundered to the ground and flowed about the same distance again before sinking beneath the rocks and eventually disappearing.

The crowd roared its approval and chased after the precious liquid. The few little children that had followed danced in the errant drops before it crashed, until their parents dragged them toward the spring again.

No one gave a second look at the brothers stranded on the rock.

Zadok gestured toward Moses once again. "Should we do something? Look at him."

Moses lay collapsed in a ball where he had stood. Aaron wrapped his arms around him, rocking him like a child. Joshua stood to the side, standing guard over the tragic scene.

Abba took a step forward and waited until Joshua caught his gaze and slightly shook his head.

"No. Time to go." He grasped Zadok and Jacob by the upper arms and started back.

"You're just going to leave him there?" Zadok twisted around to see as Abba pulled him along.

"Joshua and Aaron will take care of him. He doesn't need anyone else watching."

CHAPTER 8

18th day of Ziv

The sun had completed a good deal of its journey through the sky when a young priest strode from the camp, carrying a horn in one hand and a branch of hyssop in the other. An even younger novice, dressed in only the plain linen tunic of his office, followed, carrying a large pot of water. The older man fairly galloped by, staring straight ahead, as if attending to these people in need had interrupted his day.

Arisha quietly called to the others. They lined up in front of their tent.

When the Levites reached them, the priest removed the stopper from the horn, then recited a prayer while pouring ashes into the water. He took the branch from his assistant, dipped it into the water, and sprinkled each of the women in turn. Then he abruptly turned and stalked away without speaking to them, as he had done four days earlier.

"Why does he always seem so sullen?' Arisha whispered to Hannah. This was the fourth time she'd seen him—on Moses's third day, their third, then yesterday—Moses's seventh—and today. Not once had he smiled, nodded or even looked them in the eye.

"He's just angry that after he does his duty here, he's unclean until sundown. Anyone who touches the purification water is."

Arisha looked at the sand. She hadn't realized she would be part of ruining someone else's evening.

Dinah huffed. "What's he got to be upset about? It's just a couple hours 'till then. We've been here a week."

Hannah grinned. "He's young and impatient. Whenever we are here during his week of duty, he acts this way. Some people are just like that. Some people are usually happy, some usually sad, some—like him—usually mad."

Ruth frowned and waved her hand. "Does he think we ask to be set apart from camp for seven days because we wish to help others?"

Arisha tilted her head. "And why is it we have to be out here for seven days?"

"Don't you know?" Ruth narrowed her eyes at Arisha. "No, I guess *you* wouldn't. It is a part of Yahweh's law, part of our lives."

Arisha stepped back. Her shoulders tensed. Had she angered Ruth? She'd only meant to perform one last act of love for Miriam. "I- I ..."

Hannah placed her arm around Arisha's shoulder and turned her away from Ruth. "It's to remind us of the sacredness of life. Anything death touches is unclean, and cannot abide in Yahweh's holy presence. That's why her tent and everything in it must be purified, why we must remain away from camp for one week, why Aaron could not touch his sister at all."

Dinah stepped near and smiled. "We take that burden from the families. We prepare the bodies for them so they can remain in camp, stay together to mourn. It is our gift to the community."

The tension flowed from Arisha's shoulders as she began to understand. Understand why these sweet ladies gave up so much time, why they loved doing it, and why it meant so much to those death left in its wake.

"Let's go, ladies. No need to dawdle." Ruth marched off toward camp.

Arisha gestured toward Ruth. "Where's she going? We can't go back yet, can we?"

Hannah shook her head. "Now we must go to the river between the springs and wash ourselves and our clothes as well. Someone will meet us there with fresh clothing."

Hannah locked her arm in Arisha's as they strolled toward the water. "Ah, here comes Judith now."

Judith shuffled toward them, a bulging bag over her shoulder, leaning heavily onto a cane. Hannah said she used to be one of those who attended the bodies, but the work—and remaining away for a week each time—became too much. Now she ministered to those who ministered, and brought the manna each morning and fresh clothes on the seventh day. "Only until sundown, ladies. Yahweh appreciates your service. I would gladly embrace you if I could." Her bright smile boasted several missing teeth. She tossed the bundle on the ground at their feet.

Hannah knelt to remove the items from the bag and then pushed it toward Judith. "Thank you, my dear. It is never the same without you, you know. We miss you so."

Judith cackled. "I miss you, too, but I don't miss sleeping out here. My bones are too old for that."

Dinah laughed. "Has Deborah had that baby yet?"

Judith beamed so widely Arisha thought the old woman's cheeks would burst. "Yes, she did. And they named her Judith." She groaned as she bent to pick up the bag then tottered off, laughing to herself.

This section of the river was the farthest away from camp, deep enough to bathe in, with a thick stand of date palms providing a screen. The ladies stripped off their clothing and sank under the cool water. Hannah, Ruth and Dinah washed their clothes quickly, stepped back on the bank and dressed, but Arisha relished the feel of the cool water of her skin. The others lounged in the sun chatting while she stayed in the river, only her head above water.

"Toss me your clothes," Hannah said. Arisha wrung the water from her tunic and threw it to Hannah, who draped it next to her own over a rod laid in the crooks of two other tree limbs jammed into the ground.

After she felt completely refreshed, Arisha climbed out of the river. She slipped the freshly washed tunic Judith had delivered over her head, then pulled her wet hair from under the neck. Running her fingers through her locks to remove any tangles, she split the bulk into three sections and began braiding it.

One more meal, then this would almost be over.

Soon the meal was eaten, the dishes washed and stored until next time, the tent swept and tied up. Arisha stared at the western mountains. Why couldn't the sun set any faster? As soon as the orb touched the tops of the rocks, they could return to camp. She could return to ... she wouldn't be *returning* to anything. Miriam was gone.

She would be starting a whole new life.

~

ANEL LAUGHED AS HE TOSSED his grandson into the air. The six-year-old's squeals bounced off the stone walls as he fell back into his grandfather's arms, and his two other grandchildren laughed.

"Danel, be careful."

"You say that every time, Yasha."

"Because I think it every time." Her long, light brown hair was pulled back with a ribbon of cloth that matched her fine linen tunic. Though they'd been married over thirty years, she was still as beautiful as the day he'd met her.

He set the boy on the floor and moved to kiss her on the cheek. "I haven't dropped anyone yet, have I?"

"No." She chuckled. "Come, Duni, time for bed."

"Already?" Duni frowned and stuck out his lower lip.

"Don't whine, little one." She took the child's hand and led him to a room in the back.

Danel turned to the other two. "Izabel, Mika, how about a story?"

Izabel jumped into his arms and placed her small hands on either side of his face. Her wide, brown eyes tugged at his heart.

He stroked her gold-brown hair and pulled her close, breathing deeply. "You look more like your mother every day." The pain was still fresh, though it had been years since Shiba's death.

They settled on the stone bench built into the three walls of the sizable room. His position as wazir afforded him a much bigger house, right outside the palace gates, than most of Arad's residents, although all residences followed the same basic pattern.

Izabel snuggled against Danel's chest, and Danel and her brother stretched out their legs, crossing them at the ankles.

Danel enfolded his arms around Izabel. "Whom would you like to hear about tonight? Abraham? Joseph? Moses?"

"Joseph! Joseph and the coat!" She bounced so hard she hit his chin with her head.

Danel suppressed a groan, holding his chin with one hand and clenching his teeth. When the pain subsided, he spoke. "Again? I've told you that one for the last six nights."

"It's my favorite."

"All right. Abraham had twelve sons—"

"No, not Abraham!" Izabel turned and frowned at Danel.

Danel furrowed his brow. "No? Then who?"

"Jacob!"

Mika laughed.

"Ooohhh. All right then, Jacob had twelve sons, and Joseph was the youngest—"

"No!" Izabel huffed.

When the story was finally finished, with all Danel's "errors" and Izabel's corrections, Yasha appeared from the back room and beckoned to Izabel. The girl placed a kiss on Danel's cheek, leaned over and kissed Mika, and scampered off to bed behind Yasha.

"Why do you do that?" Mika leaned forward, elbows on his knees.

"Do what?"

"Make all those mistakes. It takes so long to tell the story."

"Are you in a hurry?"

"No, but ..."

Danel grinned. "She certainly learns it this way, doesn't she?"

Mika patted his grandfather on the back. "Come, Papa, let's walk in the garden. It's such a nice night." Danel followed his oldest grandchild outside. He often seemed so much older than his eighteen years. Out of necessity, probably.

The pair climbed the two steps, then walked through the stone doorway into their spacious garden. The pomegranate and peach trees filled the air with the fragrance of flower-filled limbs ready to burst with fruit.

"She loves that story," Mika said.

Danel smiled. "This month. Last month it was Moses in the basket."

Mika was quiet for a moment. "Why do you insist on telling her these stories?"

Danel faced Mika. "Aqhat and I have learned everything we could about Yahweh. I want to make sure you—and Izabel and Duni—know everything, too."

Mika rolled his eyes. "I know all the stories, Papa."

"It's more than just knowing the stories. You must know Him, know His character. You must know how He is different from the Canaanite gods."

"Yes, Papa." He sighed.

"But you must also know that it will be dangerous for you to reject the ways and the gods of our people."

"Then why did you do it?"

"Because the weeks I spent with Kamose, and what I learned about Yahweh from him, changed my life. I saw what Yahweh did for Kamose and for all Israel. And everything we have learned since only confirms what Kamose told me: that Yahweh is the only true God. A Living God, not a stone idol, who cares about His people. Kamose left the Egyptian gods for Yahweh, and I have left the false gods of Canaan for Him. Now the choice is yours."

"And if I do, I must keep it a secret?"

Danel nodded. "For a while longer. When he left, Kamose said Israel would be coming to conquer Canaan in forty years. It's been thirty-nine. They'll be coming in less than a year. You can be on Israel's side, or Canaan's."

"Are you asking me to decide tonight?"

"No."

Mika crossed his arms. "Are you even sure they are coming?"

"As certain as I am standing here."

Mika stared at the ground as he dug the toe of his sandal in the dirt. "And you are also certain they will win, aren't you?"

"I am."

He returned his gaze to Danel. "Against all our armies, our trained, well-armed armies with iron chariots. A group of children of former slaves who haven't fought anyone in forty years."

Danel nodded again. "Yes."

"That's incredibly difficult to believe."

"I know."

"But my future ... You've started training me to take over as wazir. Or I can follow my father's path. And what about Demna? If her family knew ..."

"They would never let you marry her. I know it is a huge decision." Danel stepped closer and grasped Mika's shoulders. "But if I am right, and I believe with all my heart I am, then in the end, there will be nothing left in Arad anyway."

"And if I choose Yahweh's side, and you are wrong ..."

"You would lose everything, perhaps even your life."

~

Z ADOK SAT IN FRONT OF the fire, then a moment later jumped back up. He ran his hands through his hair; they came away wet. If he didn't stop sweating, he'd need to wash again.

"Walk with me, son."

Zadok squinted into the setting sun as he glanced up at his father. "What?"

"Take a walk with me. You'll expend some of that energy that has you ready to pounce on everyone."

Zivah started to laugh, but a glare from Abba silenced her.

Served her right. She'd been smirking at him all day.

"Come on." Abba tipped his head toward the pasture. "Let's go."

Zadok sighed and followed Abba south through Judah.

"Why aren't you in your pasture? Why are you stalking around here with nothing to do?"

Zadok huffed. "Jonah said I was upsetting the sheep."

Abba laughed. "You need to settle down." He placed a comforting hand on Zadok's back. "You're as jumpy as a spiny mouse caught outside its hole."

"I feel like one—like a huge hawk is circling over my head ready to swoop down on me, but I just can't see it."

Abba turned his soft brown eyes on him. "Why? Are you afraid to see her? Do you think she doesn't want to see you?"

Zadok shrugged. "Now that Miriam is gone, and no longer pushing her toward me, I have no idea what she really thinks. And I, of course, have let my heart run far ahead of me again."

Abba stopped, pulling on Zadok's bicep to halt him as well. "Habibi, your imma and I have seen the way Arisha looks at you and speaks of you, and I truly believe she loves you."

"But I still don't know if she is ready after such a great loss."

Abba nodded. "True. She's had many terrible losses. And I'm sure she's very much afraid to risk losing again. So, she'll live here with us, and you will be patient, and she will heal."

Zadok sucked in a deep breath. "I don't mind being patient if I believe there is something to hope for."

Abba's eyes twinkled. "There is. Trust me, there is." He began strolling north toward their tents again. "Waiting can be pleasant. I waited fourteen years for your mother."

"Excuse me?" Zadok halted, staring at his father. Fourteen

years? The thought of fourteen more days made his stomach turn somersaults.

Abba chuckled. "Of course, I was only nine when those years began." He smiled, looking in the distance as if at a memory. "I knew your mother was the one I'd marry when she was just a babe, the day she first smiled. And her first smile was for me, though your sabbas never believed it. They said I would hardly leave her alone long enough for her to sleep."

He took Zadok's arm and began walking again. "The four of us grew up together: me, your imma, and Savta Tirzah's daughters, Keren and Naomi. I was six years older than the twins and nine years older than Adi. About the time the twins started attracting boys—even though they were too young to marry yet— Bezalel and Uncle Kamose were asking me who I was interested in. I always said Adi. She was only seven then, and they just laughed at me. They continually suggested other pretty girls. But I never changed my answer. I knew she was the one for me, so I waited."

"That must have been very difficult."

Abba waved a hand. "The first ten years or so I was too young to marry, and obviously so was she, so that wasn't difficult at all. The last few, watching her as she turned from my playmate and best friend into a beautiful, marriageable woman—those were tough. But the waiting was worth it. And you know, I think Savta Meri was always on my side."

"I wish I were as certain as you. I don't seem to have inherited the gift of choosing the right woman."

"Marah's greatest weakness was her own lack of faith. And her abba's as well. For whatever reason they believed your lack of participation in the army's practices now would reflect poorly in your allotment of land in Canaan."

"Is that why he spread those horrible rumors about me?"

"Yes. He was afraid you wouldn't be able to provide for his daughter without land."

"But that's ridiculous. That doesn't even make any sense."

"I know. I consider it a blessing that Yahweh protected you from a father-in-law like that."

"Believe me, I do. But in the meantime, how many people have believed him? Still think I am a coward, prefer to keep sheep rather than fight for Israel?"

"My son, those of us who know and love you know the truth. Trust me, the time to fight will come sooner than you would ever want. Enjoy your peace while you can."

"Thank you, Abba. I will."

Abba squeezed Zadok's arm. "You're welcome, habibi. Now go bring her home."

~

ZADOK STARED WEST, WAITING FOR the sun to drop behind the low mountains that surrounded their camp at the oasis, for once wishing they were as high as Mt. Sinai itself. Or at least the mountains in the north of Canaan.

Not that he'd seen any of them, only heard about them. But they were all higher than these foothills.

Just a little more, a little lower …

He fisted and unfisted his hands, trying to keep from pacing. He'd already received several wary stares from those in the last row of tents, wondering why he was skulking around the edge of camp.

He glanced over his shoulder. Almost. Back to the east, toward the tents of the unclean, barely visible in the distance. No one approached yet.

He'd come too early. He should have waited at his tent. But he was going insane there. Imma wanted him to eat, but he had no appetite. Zivah kept throwing smirks his way. No one mentioned Arisha, but everyone knew that was all he thought about.

At last. A tiny dust cloud kicked up, grew larger as it neared.

It slowly separated into four figures.

His heart stopped, then kicked into triple time. He shook his hands at his sides, but the tingling wouldn't stop. If he couldn't get himself under control, she'd want nothing to do with him. He closed his eyes and forced himself to take deep, slow breaths.

He opened his eyes. He could see her clearly now.

Arisha.

~

"*Y*OUR BETROTHED IS WAITING FOR you." Hannah nudged Arisha as they neared camp.

Arisha sucked in a breath as she watched him pace, then turn back toward camp. Why did he turn away? Had he seen her? Did he not want to meet her? Then why come to the edge of camp? No one asked him to come and wait for her.

He turned again and his gaze caught hers. His face brightened, and warmth flooded her.

A smile took over her face, even though she fought to remain impassive. She didn't want to allow him to affect her so, didn't want to give him such power. But she couldn't resist. His excited grin conquered every defense she had set in place.

He hurried out to meet her.

Hannah squeezed Arisha's shoulder. "We'll see you later, dear. I enjoyed our time together very much. I do hope we can see each other again soon, but I think someone else has a claim on your time right now." She and the others veered off, leaving her to take the last strides toward camp alone.

Her heart fluttered as Zadok strode confidently toward her. Exactly what was he expecting? She was not ready to immerse herself in a new relationship—she was still saying goodbye to Miriam.

She couldn't make her feet move, while he seemed to be gliding effortlessly to her. Her chest ached, until she realized she wasn't breathing. She forced a breath in, then out. She glanced at him, the tents, the mountains, her feet, back to him. His soft brown eyes were locked on hers every time her gaze met his.

Before she was ready, Zadok stood before her.

He skimmed his hands down her arms, his palms barely touching the fabric of her tunic. "I've missed you," he whispered. "How are you feeling?" His gaze searched her face.

"I- I'm not sure."

"I'm sure this is still very difficult for you." His hand touched her cheek. "You know Miriam wanted you to come to our tent, to my family's tent. She didn't want you to be alone."

Miriam had mentioned that. Arisha hadn't thought about it much before now.... Was she supposed to marry him today? Right now?

"I'll sleep in the pasture. I do most of the time anyway. You can sleep in the space that used to be mine. Imma is very excited to have you there. So is Zivah. I think she always wanted a sister." He chuckled softly. "But don't let her boss you around."

Arisha drew in a shuddering breath.

"Are you hungry? Did you eat yet?"

"Ummm ... yes, we ate before we started back."

"Well, you might have to eat again. Imma has dates and milk and tea...."

So many people ... "Oh. All right." She wasn't ready to face them all yet. Could she do this?

Zadok placed his hands on her waist. "Don't worry. Tonight it's just Imma and me."

Arisha released a sigh, much louder than she wanted to. "Oh, good." Oh, no. She looked up at him with wide eyes. Did she really just say that aloud? Had she insulted his whole family?

Zadok laughed and pulled her near. "I know you well enough to know you wouldn't be ready for everyone tonight. Zivah didn't like it, but she'll just have to wait." His arms encircled her and held her close, putting his mouth next to her ear. "Besides, tonight I don't want to share you any more than I have to."

Arisha rested her head on his chest. Why did he feel so good? He was not making her decision to keep her heart safe from him easy.

Zadok took her small bundle from her, then grasped her hand

as they strolled through camp. "Do you still have anything in Miriam's tent? Someone sent over your mat and the dishes Miriam had when they purified her tent."

Arisha shook her head. "No, all I owned was my other tunic." Grief gripped her heart yet again at the thought of an empty tent. "Who is going to live in her tent now?"

"I think a priest who had another baby and is leaving his parents' tent. I'm not sure."

Zadok's imma waited by the fire when they arrived. She jumped up and gathered Arisha into a hug. "Habibti, you must be so tired. It can't be easy sleeping out there all alone."

Zadok sighed. "She wasn't alone, Imma. There were three others."

"Still. No family. It's not the same. Now sit."

Arisha obeyed, and Adi handed her a plate of dates and goat cheese and a cup of milk. "I know you had manna, but that's not enough."

Next to her, Zadok laughed softly. His arm brushed against hers as he leaned in to steal a date, and tingles ran through her body. He glanced at her from the corner of his eye and grinned. Heat stole up her neck and onto her cheeks. Hopefully they weren't as red as they felt.

After the dates and cheese were consumed, Adi sat up on her heels. "I'm going to make sure everything is ready for you inside. We have your mat and blanket. Is there anything else you need or want, anything you're used to?"

Arisha blinked. "Um, no. That sounds good."

"All right then. If you need anything, even if you awaken in the middle of the night, just let me know." Adi patted her knee and disappeared into the tent.

Arisha watched her go. "Your imma is sweet."

Zadok chuckled. "She is delighted to have someone to take care of again."

Arisha turned her gaze from Adi to him. "Are you sure? I don't want to be a burden."

He placed his palm on her cheek. "Never. You could never be a burden to anyone."

Little did he know. She had been a burden to many people.

"I'm so glad you're home."

Home. Was she home? The only place she had ever felt wanted was Miriam's, and even then it was always *Miriam's* home, not hers.

"It's late. I should go." He leaned in, close enough she felt his warm breath on her cheek.

She tensed. Was he going to kiss her?

He placed a lingering kiss on her cheek. "I'll see you in the morning," he whispered. "Good night, habibti."

She missed the warmth of him next to her when he left. Missed his soft laugh, his gentle touch.

She could feel him slowly stealing her heart.

Slowly? She'd only been back a couple hours.

She would have to be very careful from here on out.

CHAPTER 9

13th day of Ziv

ZADOK FORCED HIMSELF TO TRY to concentrate on the words floating around the fire pit, but his mind kept going back to the time he'd spent with Arisha that day in the pasture. Nothing particularly special had happened. He'd simply enjoyed spending the day with her, as he had for most of the last several weeks. Their days had settled into a predictable but enjoyable routine. He joined his family for the morning meal, then he and Arisha took an often longer-than-necessary stroll to the pasture. He usually walked her back before the midday meal, where she helped Imma prepare the food. He joined them for the evening meal, then the women retired inside, and he was left with the men by the fire.

And even though he'd spent most of the day with her, he missed her.

Jacob's voice interrupted his thoughts. "He's not even listening."

Zadok winced when he looked up to see six pairs of amused eyes focused on him. As often happened, Joshua and his son and two grandsons had joined them tonight.

Tobiah nudged him with his shoulder. "What's her name?" Joshua's son had been like another uncle to Zadok, living in the tent next to theirs. He'd grown up with Tobiah's sons Elam and Eliel being his cousins as much as Naomi and Keren's children.

"What?" Zadok tried to keep his voice steady as he accepted a cup of sage-mint tea from Abba, seated on the other side of him. He inhaled the tangy, soothing fragrance.

Tobiah wiggled his brows. "Only a woman can make a man that distracted. What's her name?"

Zadok sipped his tea while he debated whether he should answer.

"Arisha." Leave it to Jacob to stick his nose in where it didn't belong.

"He wasn't asking *you*." Zadok narrowed his eyes at Jacob.

Jacob only laughed. "I know, but you weren't telling."

"Miriam's Arisha?" Tobiah's eyes widened.

"You know her?" Jacob intruded again.

And this was why Zadok didn't want to mention her name. He didn't need any more advice, suggestions, or recommendations.

"Miriam's mentioned her several times over the last few months. Often, the first month. She was quite worried about her."

"So I gathered when she told me to marry her," Zadok said.

Tobiah laughed, a hearty laugh Zadok had always loved. Though loud, the laughter never made him feel insignificant. "Sounds like Miriam. She always cared so deeply, but she did it in such unexpected ways. So when are you going to marry her?"

Zadok took a long drink of his tea, savoring the fresh cool taste of the mint. "When she's ready. I think she is still mourning Miriam."

Tobiah nodded. "Probably a wise move. You don't want her to be sad during your bridal week."

Heat crawled up Zadok's neck at the mention of a bridal week. He hadn't even kissed her yet, except on the cheek. Thought about it—every time he saw that dimple, considered those full lips. But hadn't summoned the courage to do it.

Joshua cleared his throat. "I have something I would like to discuss with you all. As you know, in less than a year, our forty years of waiting will be over. We will enter Canaan. What you do not know,"—Joshua shifted uncomfortably—"is that Moses will not be going."

The others exchanged glances, then Jacob spoke first. "What do you mean Moses will not go? Why not?" His voice was brusque.

"Yahweh told him that because of his disobedience at the rock, when he commanded water to pour out, he cannot enter the land Yahweh has promised us."

Eliel huffed. "I don't understand. What did he do wrong? I didn't notice anything."

Joshua shrugged. "You probably wouldn't, from your point of view. Yahweh told him to speak to the rock, not strike it, and—"

Jacob pounded his fist into his thigh, then rose on his knees. "And that's enough to forbid him to enter? That's ridiculous!"

Abba touched his shoulder, and Jacob sat back.

"Let me finish." Joshua raised his finger. "Do you remember what he said?

Tobiah frowned. "Something about bringing water from the rock."

Abba stroked his beard. "He said 'must *we* bring water from the rock'."

"Yes," Joshua said. "*We*. Not Yahweh. He and Aaron took credit for what Yahweh was about to do. So neither Aaron nor Moses will enter Canaan."

Tobiah closed his eyes and swallowed. "Aaron either?"

Joshua shook his head. "No."

The group was silent for several long moments. The fire popped and crackled as a date palm limb settled in the pit.

Zadok caught Joshua's gaze. "How is Moses?"

"He is actually still far more upset over losing Miriam than about that. I think his despair over her death was partly responsible for his actions at the rock. He wasn't thinking clearly."

More silence.

"So what happens now? What about Canaan?" Jacob looked at the others in the circle.

Zadok waved a hand in the air. "Canaan? Don't you care about Moses? Or Aaron?"

Joshua reached around Tobiah and squeezed Zadok's shoulder. "No, no. It's a good question. Moses's and Aaron's future has been decided, and talking won't change it. Time to look forward and make plans."

Zadok took a deep breath to calm himself. Abba poured fresh tea into his cup.

Joshua continued. "We've talked of many different possibilities. For one thing, it might not be a wise idea to enter from the south again, as we did before." Joshua reached for a stick near the edge of the fire and drew in the sand. "Another way would be to enter from the east. There is a river to cross but the land is flatter. Much easier to camp, to plan battles. But first, Moses wants to send messengers to Edom, to see if we can go through their land when the time comes. Otherwise we'll have to go south around Edom, which will make the journey at least twice as long."

Eliel turned to Joshua. "Is Moses still in charge, or has he turned it over to you now, Sabba?"

Joshua leaned toward Eliel. "Moses will be our leader until Yahweh says he is *not* our leader." Joshua enunciated each word, never taking his eyes off Eliel. "And there is nothing that says I will be the next leader, either. I am his helper, but that does not mean I will necessarily succeed him."

"But that's not right!"

"Eliel, enough!" Tobiah spoke sharply to his grandson, and Eliel frowned and looked away.

Joshua poked his sandy map with the stick he still held. "For now, we need to send messengers to Edom. Each tribe will select its own men, their best emissaries. Good fighters, as well. We have to be prepared for anything."

～

*D*ANEL STROLLED THROUGH THE ORCHARD surrounding the palace walls. Mika was at his side, a large basket hanging from his arm. "I had these trees planted next to the walls years ago, so the fragrance would reach the king's rooms." He laughed. "And mine. Best idea I ever had." He reached up and plucked several ripe, plump pomegranates, peaches and apricots, then placed them carefully into the woven container.

He dropped onto the grass and set the basket next to him, grabbing a couple apricots. Biting into the fruit, he chuckled briefly.

"What?" Mika frowned.

"Keret loves apricots, but he can't eat them. He gets a rash every time he tries. Once he ate less than half of one, and his throat closed up and he couldn't breathe for a moment or two. That was the last time he tried."

Mika huffed. "Don't you have servants to collect this stuff?"

"Yes, but I like doing it. I like being outside, smelling the air, the fruit." He sucked in a chestful of air and closed his eyes.

"We've been here late every night this week. Can't we go yet?"

"Sure. Let's get this inside first." He stood and collected the basket.

Mika rolled his eyes as he rose.

Danel draped his arm around his grandson's shoulder and headed inside. They dropped off the food in the kitchen, but not before placing a few of each kind of fruit in a sack to carry home.

Danel nodded at the soldiers guarding the massive wooden double doors as he left the palace, then headed south toward the small residential district of the palace officials.

He never walked through this area without remembering the single, small room of his childhood. Tucked up against the outer wall, his former house lay far away on the opposite side of the city, where most of Arad's people lived. Once his mother became the palace cook, they moved into the servants' area. Many nights he slept on the floor of the king's spacious kitchen as his mother prepared food for Keret, first as prince, then as king.

As they neared their current, more opulent, home, Mika broke into a jog. Danel frowned, then noticed Demna waiting outside the courtyard. Mika grabbed her, wrapped his arms about her waist, and swung her around. The girl giggled.

Danel breathed deeply. No wonder he was in a rush to leave. Demna had an inexplicable hold over his grandson. Danel feared what she could make Mika do.

Yahweh, protect my family.

He skirted by the couple and ducked into the courtyard. Yasha stood waiting, and he went willingly into her arms.

"Bad day?"

"Not anymore." He kissed her cheek.

"I'll make some tea." She disappeared inside, taking the bag with her.

Izabel and Duni bounced in with Yasha. "Papa!" Izabel clambered into his lap, and he hugged her to his chest. "Did you bring them?"

"Bring what, little one? I don't remember you asking for anything."

"Papa!"

He grinned. "What?"

"The pom'gants."

He burst into laughter. "The what?"

She scrunched her face. "Don't laugh. I can't say it."

"The pomegranates?"

She nodded, clapping her little hands.

"Yes, I brought some."

She scrambled down and bolted for the kitchen, Duni following.

Danel wandered back out to the courtyard, groaning and rubbing his lower back as he took the two steps up. Beyond the wall, Mika still nuzzled Demna. Danel lifted his face to the sky. *Yahweh, please ...*

Mika cast a dark glance to Danel, whispered to Demna, kissing her once more before she left. He locked his hands behind his back and strolled toward Danel, his face solemn. He stopped one step away. "I have decided to take my place in my father's army."

Danel's heart stopped. "You *what*?"

"I am joining the army of Keret. I want to protect the kingdom of Arad, as did my father, and his father before him."

Danel tried to accept everything that statement meant. "So, you will be an officer."

"Of course. I am assured a commission as my father's son."

"But why do you want to do this? You've already begun training with me as the next wazir."

Mika's eyes smoldered. "It will take me years to become the true wazir, not just your assistant. I need something that will get me some respect *now*."

"And you will be forced to worship Canaan's false gods."

"You have shown me no proof that your Yahweh is any more real."

Danel spread his hands. "What has any of these gods ever done for you? For anyone? Can you show me one thing any one of them has ever accomplished?"

Mika pointed his finger. "Can you? All you have are stories from the Hebrews, stories a prisoner told you forty years ago when you were a child."

"I am not the only one who heard those stories. Everyone, every nation has heard them and cowers at the name of Yahweh."

"But what has He done for you?"

"He took a cook's son, the son of an Egyptian trader and made him the highest ranking man under the king in this city. Aqhat, the same thing. A common soldier without the guaranteed commission you have, and yet now he is commander of all the army. We saw what Yahweh did for Kamose. We sought Him out. We worshipped Him. He blessed us."

"I say you earned those positions on your own."

"And how many times have you seen men promoted who don't

deserve it? And those who do, held back because others buy their way ahead? Yahweh looked out for us, put us where He wants us, where He needs us. Of that I have no doubt. Just like He sent Kamose here to teach me about Him."

"So Kamose suffered so you could learn about his God?" Mika threw his arms in the air.

"I am sure of it."

"Again, I find that difficult to believe."

Danel tried to calm himself. "Believe as you wish. But make me understand. Why the army? If not wazir, there are a number of other—"

"Because I want to be like my father!" Mika, red-faced and breathing fast, turned and stalked away.

The words, flung at him like rocks, hurt Danel much as any stones would have. He had spent the last ten years trying to erase the memory of that awful man.

Obviously, he had failed.

⌒

*T*HE MORNING SUN HAD CHASED AWAY the evening's chill and the animals had retreated to their homes to wait out the heat. Arisha scrubbed the pan and handed it to Adi, then reached for another plate.

"Thank you, habibti." Adi flashed her a bright smile.

"Last one."

Adi stacked the plate with the others, then turned her gaze on Arisha. "How are you feeling? It's been a more than a month since you came to live with us."

Arisha shrugged. "Some days are better than others. Some days … I wake up and almost forget. For a moment."

"I remember when my imma died. It was only a few years ago and I was much older than you are. But I remember the pain." Adi's gaze drifted to some distant point over Arisha's shoulder, and she fingered a pendant around her neck.

Arisha had noticed it before. It was always under her tunic, so she wasn't sure what it was exactly, but it hung on a cord made of gold chain. She'd seen the same one on Zivah's neck as well.

Adi returned her gaze to Arisha and smiled. "It may not feel like it now, but it does get better."

"Can I ask you ... what helped?"

"Ahmose. Zadok and Zivah." She paused. "She wasn't the first person I'd lost. Kamose was the first to go—he was never quite the same after he came back from Arad." She brought her hand to her mouth. "I'm sorry."

"Don't be. Keret's competence when it comes to torture is well-known, even beyond Arad. That's why I can never go back."

"I was just a baby when he returned. But Ahmose was nine, and he remembers. Tirzah left us several years ago; Abba a few years after that." Her eyes moistened again. "Imma didn't last long after Abba died. She wasn't old enough to be under the pronouncement —only those twenty and older were prohibited from entering Canaan. But I think she just couldn't face living there without Abba."

She cradled Arisha's hand in both of hers. "No matter how many people one loses, it doesn't get easier. At least not at first. But the hurt? That's actually a good thing. People you knew died in Canaan, right?"

"Of course."

"And did it bother you?"

"No. I didn't care."

"Because they meant nothing to you, and you meant nothing to them. The pain in your heart is because you were a part of Miriam, and she was a part of you. And she always will be."

"But the pain ... it will lessen?"

"Yes. And your memories will remain. And we will be here to help you through it."

Arisha had to admit it had been nice—very nice—being around Zadok's family. Better than she had imagined. They had taken her in and loved her like she *belonged*. She glanced toward the pasture. "I wonder why Zadok didn't join us for the morning meal."

"Probably one of his sheep needed him. Why don't you go to the pasture and see if he's there?"

"Do you mind?"

"Not at all. I'm sure he'd love it." She smiled knowingly.

Arisha kissed Adi on the cheek and raced toward Zadok.

She slowed when she reached the gate. Couldn't be out of breath when he saw her—it wouldn't look good. She found him amongst a group of lambs.

He brightened when she approached. He bent to kiss her cheek, and his touch left heat when he pulled away. "I'm sorry I didn't make it this morning."

"It's all right." *But you have no idea how much I missed you.*

"A couple of my lambs got hurt and I had to take care of their wounds."

"How do you do that?"

"I rub oil on them." He entwined Arisha's fingers in his as they strolled toward the water. He scanned the flock, then stiffened. "One's missing."

"What? How do you know? You didn't even count them."

"I just know. Leah isn't here. She's probably cast again. She's getting too old and too heavy."

"Cast?"

"Come. I'll explain later."

He pulled her along behind him as he jogged toward a copse of trees on the east edge of the spring. He dropped her hand and ran for the ewe lying on her side near the water's edge.

Zadok straddled Leah and grunted as he grasped handfuls of wool, tugging her onto her feet. She baaa'ed and wobbled, and he kept one hand on the wool and wrapped the other around her belly, holding her tightly. He bent so his knees hugged her shoulders, and whispered into her ear. What could he be saying? She swayed against one leg then the other, finally gaining her balance. He patted her neck and straightened. "Good girl. Now go on."

The ewe ambled off toward the rest of the flock, wobbling only once.

He looked over at Arisha and smiled, then frowned. She realized she was staring at him, mouth open. "What's wrong?"

She blinked several times. "Nothing. You were so gentle with her. It was amazing to watch you. You say she does it often, but you acted like it was the first time."

"Well, I really need to shear her. It's not her fault. Her coat's too heavy, and she's getting unsteady on her feet at her age. If she lies down, sometimes her center of balance gets shifted and she can't get up, that's all. I have to help her."

"What did you say to her?"

"I just reminded her she was safe, that I was there to take care of her. Just things to make her feel better. I hope." He chuckled. "I know she doesn't really understand my words, but I think hearing my voice calms her."

Arisha smiled, remembering the times she'd laid her head on his chest, heard his heart beat, and his voice rumble under her ear. Felt strength and care melt from his body into hers. "I know how she feels."

He placed his hands on her waist. "I'd love to take care of you too, if you'll let me." He gazed at her with those soft brown eyes, the ones that seemed to see even the things she didn't want him to see. He drew her closer, kissed her temple. His lips moved to her cheekbone, then to her jaw, then he buried his face in her hair. His warm breath slid over her neck as his arms encircled her, pulling her tight against his chest.

Her stomach did somersaults and her legs turned to mush. Certainly the only thing holding her up—besides Zadok—was the two fistfuls of his tunic she had somehow grasped.

She let go of the cloth she clutched below his shoulders and slid her hands to his waist.

Zadok lifted his face from her neck, sliding his mouth almost to the edge of hers, where he placed a featherlight kiss. Then he straightened.

She tried to think past the fog in her mind and the heat racing through her body.

No matter what she intended, what she wanted, it was settled now. He had her heart and there was nothing she could do about it.

CHAPTER 10

16th day of Ziv

THE LATE MORNING SUN KISSED Arisha's skin as it climbed higher in the sky toward its apex. A breeze rippled the water, sunlight skipping over it like stones. The songbirds in the palms above sang noisily as they chased each other through the brilliant, long green leaves.

She traced circles in the sand, remembering yesterday morning. What had she let happen? Zadok had stolen her heart, the one thing she vowed she wouldn't allow. All her life, whenever she began to trust, whenever she began to feel close to someone, she'd been either sent away or left behind. Somehow separated. Her mother. The priestesses. Danel.

Even Miriam.

Whether intentional or not, somehow or another she ended up alone.

If she allowed herself to love Zadok, it would only happen again.

She needed to take her heart back and lock it up, keep it safely away.

But how could she do that? Because when he held her, whispered in her ear ... when she felt his strength surround her like a warm cloak ...

A gentle trilling off to her left pulled her thoughts away. She glanced at the broom bush beside her. The same pair of Laughing Doves still had their nest there. She studied the birds as the male opened his mouth wide, and the squawking babies dipped their tiny black bills into his and sucked out the food he spit up for them. The mother searched for seeds on the ground beneath them, her soft purple head and neck bobbing up and down with each bite. When Arisha lifted her gaze again to the sloppy but apparently secure nest, she noticed that there were two more shiny white eggs under the father.

Amazing.

She rose and ambled along the edges of the water. She first plucked the plump, broad leaves from the mint plants, then searched for the deep purple flowers of the sage. She pulled the leaves underneath until she had a bulging handful of each, then plodded back to the tent.

Adi sat with Zivah in front of her tent. Arisha set the leaves aside and slapped the sand from her hands before she joined them. "Zivah, are you feeling well? You look a little pale."

Zivah smiled weakly and placed her hand on her belly. "I'm ... I'm expecting a baby. I'm fine, just a little tired."

"Zivah, that's wonderful!"

She winced. "I've known a couple months, but I just told Jacob two weeks ago. He's very excited."

"Why did you wait so long to tell him?"

"I ... I was worried. I wanted to be sure the pregnancy ... would last."

Adi rubbed Zivah's back. "Why did you think it wouldn't?"

"It felt different. Not like the others." She squeezed her eyes shut. "We argued. He wants to go to Edom with Joshua. I told him I didn't want him to."

Adi slipped an arm around her shoulder. "Why don't you want him to go?"

"I'm afraid."

Arisha blinked. Zivah? Afraid?

Adi pulled her closer. "Of what? Losing the baby? Or losing Jacob?"

Zivah brushed a tear from her cheek. "Both." She slumped into Adi and let the tears fall.

Arisha cleared her throat. "Why don't Zadok and I take Adira and Josiah for the afternoon? You can get some rest. We'll take them to the stream to eat and play in the water."

Zivah smiled and nodded.

Adi patted her shoulder. "Why don't you go lie down right now?"

Zivah opened her mouth, but Adi raised her hand.

"Go, now."

Zivah rose and ducked inside her tent.

Arisha waited until she disappeared. "Is she always so stubborn?"

Adi chuckled. "Yes. But it is her strength. Most of the time."

Arisha grabbed the bundles of leaves and carefully spread them out to dry on a long cloth lying in front of the tent.

"More tea leaves? You just brought some yesterday." Adi asked.

"Those were chamomile. These are mint and sage. I want to make sure we have enough to last the winter."

"You do know you don't have to earn your way into the family, don't you?" Adi's voice was soft.

She sat back on her heels. "Old habits, I guess. Part of it is from living as a servant most of my life. But I guess I do want to do nice things ... "

"You can certainly do them if you want to. But not because you think they'll make us love you more. Nothing can do that, habibti." She squeezed her shoulder and stepped inside the tent.

She would try. She longed for the kind of assurance Zadok and his family had, the closeness. She had a taste of it now, and she didn't want to lose it.

~

Z ADOK AND ARISHA HELD ADIRA'S hands as they strolled toward the river east of camp. He'd rather hold Arisha's hand, but ...

They lifted the girl up and swung her back and forth while she giggled with delight.

"Again! Again!" The little girl laughed.

Josiah ran ahead and leaped over the log.

"Don't go in the water yet. We're going to eat first." Zadok dropped Adira's hand and jogged after him. They didn't need muddy feet all over the blanket while they ate.

Arisha stepped over the fallen date palm and settled herself on the sand, thankful for Yahweh's cloud now that spring had fully arrived and the afternoons were heating up, even on the oasis. She untied a knot in a deep red cloth and spread it out, revealing manna cakes and dates.

The boys sat and Josiah grabbed for a cake, but Zadok grasped his wrist in mid-air. The child crossed his arms and pouted. "You are not a hyena, grappling over fallen prey." Zadok said. "There will always be food."

Arisha handed the children each a cake. Then she reached for a skin of goat's milk and poured some into cups.

Zadok leaned back against the log next to Arisha, his arm brushing against hers. The scent of mint lingered on her fingers when she handed him milk. She must have crushed some for tea earlier.

For several moments, the only sounds were the running water of the river, and children noisily smacking manna and slurping milk.

Zadok grinned over the children's heads at Arisha. Her eyes twinkled back at him.

"Look at the lizard!" Adira bounced on her knees and pointed the at the log behind Arisha.

Arisha squealed and jumped away, nearly landing in Zadok's lap. Her back rested against his side. "Make sure your shadow doesn't fall on him or he'll run away," he warned the children, as they knelt on either side of the chameleon. They fixed their attention on the reptile, fascinated by its long tongue darting out to catch insects.

Zadok dropped his arm and slipped it around Arisha's waist, scooting backwards on the sand and pulling her with him. She settled against him and rested her head against his shoulder.

Adira reached for the chameleon's tail and it skittered away.

"Adira! You chased it away!"

"I don't care. It was getting boring." She hopped up and skipped off toward the water, Josiah behind her.

Arisha pulled away from Zadok and sat back against the log, still near him, but not against him, not snuggled into him. His heart ached for more contact.

His niece and nephew played, and he struggled to pay attention, keep an eye on them. Keep his mind off the beautiful woman beside him.

Adira ran up with one hand hidden behind her.

Arisha giggled and reared back as Adira shoved a bunch of wilted red anemones into Arisha's nose. She gently pushed the girl's hand away.

"Don't they smell pretty?" Adira sniffed the flowers herself and grinned.

"Yes, they do. Just like you." Arisha pulled her into her lap, and the girl laughed as Arisha tickled her, held her close for a moment, then set her down in the sand next to her.

Josiah ambled up with a bug in his hand. "Look what I found." He stuck his hand in his sister's face.

"Eeeww. Get that away! Aunt Arisha, make him stop!"

Arisha's breath caught at the word *aunt*.

Josiah apparently caught it, too. He grabbed Adira's hand and pulled her away. "She's not our aunt."

~

*D*ANEL STARED OUT THE WINDOW of his workroom at the fruit trees below. The breeze lifted a sweet fragrance to him, but today it didn't bring him any joy.

He pounded his fist on the window frame. How had he lost Mika? He'd tried so hard to erase the memory of Mika's father. Maybe too hard. Kirtu was a hard and violent man, and he'd beaten sweet Shiba more than once. Of course Mika was too young to remember that. And Shiba had only told him the good things about his father, not wanting him to inherit her own bitterness.

Oh, how Danel missed Shiba. She had her mother's eyes, his own strength, and had somehow managed to hold on to a hopeful outlook throughout her marriage to that prideful man. The blessing in it all was that she had come to worship Yahweh because of her ordeal, and He had given her a wonderful man for her second husband. She was finally happy, until …

And now Danel saw her face every time he looked at Izabel.

His stomach churned. He leaned his palms against the windowsill and dropped his head. *Yahweh, why? Why is this happening?*

Mika thought his father was a great military hero, and now he wanted to follow in his footsteps.

Danel had to stop him. If Yahweh wouldn't do it, he would. He turned on his heel and strode to the door, grabbing the handle and yanking it open. He headed down the hall but before he took many steps, Aqhat rounded the corner.

Danel stopped short. "I was just coming to see you."

Aqhat nodded, took a deep breath. "I thought you might. I didn't want to have that conversation down in my office, so I came up here."

Danel noticed Mepac in the hallway and signaled him. "Could you have Sisa prepare us a tray and bring it up, please?"

"Right away." The servant hurried away.

They entered and Danel walked to the window, tried to calm his breathing and slow his heart rate before he spoke. It didn't work.

He whirled around to face his friend. "Why did you let him join the army? How could you do that to me?"

Aqhat took a step back, arms spread. "*Let* him join? How was I supposed to keep him away? His father was an officer. If he completes the training and passes the test, he is guaranteed a commission. He knows this. You and I know this. I cannot stop him."

"You should have *found* a way!" Danel's voice rose. "If you were truly my friend, you would have. You know what his father was like. You know how important it is to me to keep—"

A knock sounded.

Danel shot his gaze to the door. He closed his eyes a moment, regretting his shouting. He walked to the door and opened it to greet Mepac, who stood with widened eyes, holding a tray of sliced fruit, roasted beef and fresh bread in one hand, and a pitcher of juice in the other. Danel scrubbed his hand down his face. "I'm sorry. Please come in." He stepped aside and motioned to a table in the center of the room.

Mepac stepped wide of Danel and set the refreshments on the table, his eyes never meeting Danel's, then backed out of the room.

Aqhat took two long strides toward Danel, shaking his head slowly. "Danel, what is going on here? I've known you since you were a child, and I've never heard you raise your voice like this. Certainly not to me."

Danel sank into a chair at the table and dropped his head onto his fists. He sat silently for several moments while he tried to sort out the whirlwind of conflicting thoughts chasing one another inside his head. He raised his gaze to Aqhat, who stood calmly before him, waiting. "I am sorry, my dear friend. I guess the fear just overtook me."

"Fear of what?"

"Losing Mika."

"Why would you lose him if he joins the army? I can do many things to protect—"

"It's not just that." Danel blew out a long breath. He stood and poured a cup of pomegranate juice for Aqhat, then water for himself. He carried it to the window and stared out over the trees bursting with ripe fruit, then turned around and leaned against the window sill. "There's a girl."

Aqhat chuckled. "There's always a girl. He's eighteen."

"I know, but I really don't trust her. She has this way of ... of changing him, getting him to do anything she wants him to, and not just in the way all women can make men do things to impress a woman. And her family. He doesn't want to wait to finish his schooling with me. He wants power and position *now*." He paused, the muscles in his neck and shoulders tightening, aching. "And he now says he sees no difference between Yahweh and the Canaanite gods."

"Ooohhh." Aqhat frowned. "No wonder you're so agitated."

"I don't know what to do."

Aqhat placed his cup beside the platter and paced, as was his habit when pondering strategy. "Well, let's think this through. If you let him join, what happens?"

"He sees me as respecting him. Spends less time with her. But is exposed to the Canaanite gods more."

"True, but he can't get married for a while, at least until his training is complete. He wants to earn his commission to impress her family, no?"

"Yes."

"And he spends more time with me." Aqhat grinned.

Danel laughed. "Poor boy."

"And if you try to stop him, what will happen?"

"He'll become angry at me, maybe leave the house—maybe marry her just to get away."

"And then you have lost all influence over him."

Danel nodded, closing his eyes. As much as he hated it, Aqhat was right.

~

"*L*ET'S GO FOR A WALK." Zadok reached for Arisha's hand.

"I have to help clean up." She gestured toward the dishes from the evening meal.

"Go ahead. Zivah and I will take care of it." Adi shooed her away. "Go with Zadok."

Zadok grabbed Arisha's hand and pulled her down the row of tents toward the pasture. The sun was slowly setting, and the sky was a beautiful collage of oranges, pinks and golds.

"I love coming out here at sunset," he said.

"Sunset's always been my favorite time of day."

Zadok stood behind her and wrapped his arms around her waist, pulled her into his chest. "Why?"

"Sometimes it was just because I'd made it through another day." She shrugged. "Other times I was thankful it had been a relatively peaceful day."

"And today?"

"Today was a good day."

"Only good?" He nuzzled her neck.

She giggled. "Very good."

"I saw you flinch when Josiah said you weren't his aunt."

She shifted uncomfortably.

He placed his hands on her shoulders and turned her to face him. "Was that because you don't want to be his aunt ... or because you do?" He tucked her hair behind her ear, left his hand there.

She didn't flinch. Instead, she closed her eyes and leaned into his touch.

"I haven't said anything yet because I was waiting until you were ready, until you were no longer mourning Miriam."

She opened her eyes and looked deep into his. "I'll always miss her. But I think I'm ready to think about the rest of my life now."

"So ... we can have the second ceremony now?"

She nodded. And gave him that smile that melted his heart.

He'd kissed Marah once. His heart beat harder, his breath came faster. But that was nothing compared to what Arisha did to him. Just being near her left him more off-balance than kissing Marah did.

His blood pounded in his ears as his gaze dropped to her mouth. He brushed his lips along her cheek, barely touching her skin. His heart raced when her hands settled at his waist, then slid up his back. Moving his hand to cradle her head, he covered her mouth with his. She tasted of the mint tea she was so fond of. Her lips were softer than he'd imagined, and the heat from the contact spread from his head to his feet. He never wanted to stop.

Completely unprepared for the rush of emotion that overtook him, he pulled back. Hoping she couldn't hear his heart slam against his chest, he fixed his gaze on hers. Was she as affected as he was? Did he move too fast?

She seemed to be breathing as fast as he was, so ... maybe she felt something too?

"Arisha," he whispered.

She stared at him, exacting a promise with her eyes. "Promise me you'll never leave me."

At the moment he'd promise her anything—the moon, the stars, all the milk and honey in Canaan. That he'd never leave her? Easy.

CHAPTER 11

ZADOK TOOK THE FRESHLY WASHED tunic his mother handed him as she emerged from the tent. He inhaled deeply, and the faint but familiar scent of mint filled his nose. He hadn't accompanied her to the spring to wash clothes since he was a small boy, but he could still remember her tossing leaves in the hot water she used to rinse their clothes—a habit their savta Meri had brought with her from her days in the palace in Egypt. Meri favored jasmine, she said, but jasmine didn't grow in the Sinai desert. "Thank you, Imma."

"You're welcome, habibi." She reached up to touch his cheek. "Have you talked to Arisha yet about a time for your wedding?"

Heat crept up Zadok's neck. "Actually, last night."

Imma grinned. "I thought your smile was wider this morning."

"She finally said she was ready. We didn't talk about when, though." He grinned. "Tomorrow would be fine with me."

Imma laughed. "She might need a little more time than that. We have to prepare a robe for her." She put a finger to her lips. "Just a moment ..." She ducked into the tent, and emerged with what appeared to be a tunic.

He pointed to the garment. "What's that?"

"It's the robe I wore. And Zivah wore."

"Ah. I remember."

Imma draped it over her arm, fingered the blue borders. "Still just as blue as the day I married your abba. Hasn't faded at all." Her voice was soft, as if she were speaking to herself more than to him, no doubt remembering every last detail of that day.

"Probably like everything that has remained the same for the last thirty-nine years. Nothing's worn out." He glanced around camp. Not their clothes, their sandals. Only one more year ...

She held up the robe. "She's only a bit shorter than Zivah. It won't take long to alter it to fit her."

"I need to get to the pasture and let Reuben go home. Want to walk with me?"

"Sure. Just a moment." She refolded her tunic and set the soft, blue-edged garment inside the tent, then wrapped her arm around his bicep as they sauntered toward the sheep.

"Abba says he waited for you for fourteen years."

She laughed. "Yes, he reminds me of that often, especially when he wants me to do something for him."

"Do you remember it the same way?"

She shrugged. "Well, of course I was a very small girl for the most of that time. But I will say that before I was attracted to him or even interested in boys, whenever I thought about my future, it included him. I somehow knew he would always be an important part of my life. Like the sun rising every day, or manna falling every morning, I knew my 'Mose would always be there."

"And when did you know you would marry him?"

"My fourteenth summer, when Abba and Imma started mentioning other boys. At that point the vague impression I'd had of him in my life became very clear. I wanted no one else. When I told them, first they were shocked, then they laughed. He'd been telling them that for years. They just never believed him."

"He never showed interest in anyone else?"

"You know your father. He loves everyone, talks to everyone. He is the most compassionate, caring man I know, always has been. So they thought he wasn't ready to pick one and settle down, when he was only being friendly and waiting for me."

"Amazing."

"Yes, he is."

Zadok smiled. Not really what he meant, but his parents' affection for each other was comforting. Could he keep a relationship like theirs for so long?

She stopped walking and pulled on his arm. "Oh, I almost forgot."

"What?"

"You know that Abram across the way died last month?" She squinted against the sun.

Zadok grimaced. "He was a mean old man."

Imma put her hand on her chest. "Zadok! What a horrible thing to say!"

"Well, he was. He yelled at Zivah and me almost every day for doing nothing more than playing."

Imma shrugged. "I think he was sad, and lonely. His wife died many years ago, and they never had children."

"Isn't his nephew living there now?"

She nodded. "He was. But he's moving in with his mother. She is ill and wants them closer. The tent is empty, and no one in his family wants it. I spoke to the nephew and you can have it. If you want it."

Images flashed through his mind—happy, delightful pictures of life with Arisha. "That would be perfect. Just a few tents down ... close enough so she won't be lonely while I'm gone ..."

"Lots of room for babies ..."

Zadok's cheeks flamed. "Imma!"

She laughed.

Averting his gaze, he picked at the hem of the tunic in his hand, but the thought of children with Arisha warmed his heart.

"It will be a week until the tent is cleansed. I took some honeyed manna cakes to the nephew and his wife yesterday after they returned from the funeral. I thought to welcome them, but that's when they said they weren't keeping the tent. They said you could have it, but I think maybe some milk would be appreciated."

"Of course. I'll gather wool for them as well."

"That's very sweet of you, habibi. You know, I think they were just happy to know a family would be there once again. He told me how often they had visited Abram, and that they had asked him several times to come live with them and their children, but he refused. He kept saying he wanted to be left alone."

"Some people are only happy when they're not."

"That's an odd way to put it, but I think you're right."

~

*D*ANEL WATCHED SILENTLY FROM THE edge of the training field as Aqhat put the newest recruits through the drills yet again. The clang of iron on iron rang in his ears as one line of perhaps twenty young men advanced against another. Aqhat had distributed the heavier weapons today, after a couple weeks with wooden swords, and several of the young men were having trouble with the added weight under the burning sun.

Not Mika.

Danel wiped a bead of sweat from his brow with his fingertips and smiled. Like it or not, Mika would make a good soldier.

It wasn't so much that soldiers were bad. They protected Arad, protected their king, their way of life. Aqhat was a warrior. Danel knew many other fine soldiers and was thankful for their services.

So why did it bother him so much that Mika wanted to join the army?

Danel closed his eyes as memories skittered though his brain —of Shiba sitting in his kitchen, tears coursing down her cheek from another blackened eye. The power and prestige had taken over Kirtu's personality and transformed a loving husband into a man who expected to be worshipped at home as he was on the battlefield. And when Shiba and Mika didn't move fast enough, he took out his frustrations first with his words, then with his fists. Since Mika was too little, Shiba received the brunt of them all.

And when she finally had a new and happier life, a gentle and faithful husband who also worshipped Yahweh, an adorable little girl and a baby boy, that horrible accident claimed not only her but her husband as well. Mika was left without a father—again—and Danel and Yasha were left with three grandchildren to raise.

Was Mika strong enough to resist the bad influence the army might have on him, as it had on Kirtu?

Then of course there was the issue of the Canaanite gods. Officers were required to make sacrifices on a regular basis and on all feast days. And the feasts were notoriously decadent. Aqhat managed to avoid them by assigning himself guard duty. And at his age it wasn't suspect. But a young man like Mika? He would be expected to show up and partake of all the feasts had to offer. And Danel doubted Mika would have any problems enjoying the wine, the food, the music ... the girls. Fidelity was not a quality to be admired among Canaanite warriors.

And what about worshipping the false gods? Mika had no regard for Yahweh. He would fall right into line and believe stone idols could protect him, keep him safe in battle, grant him the life he wanted.

Danel knew better. He'd prayed often enough to them as a child, sacrificed grain, watched his mother sacrifice wine, give her last coin. But now he knew the difference between them and the only Living God. Why hadn't he been able to show Mika that difference, make him see, make him believe? He closed his eyes and winced at the thought, pain piercing his heart as fully as one of the swords on Aqhat's training field.

The strident sound of a horn's blast drew his attention back to the present. The recruits brought their swords to their sides, chests heaving. A few had dribbles of dark blood running down their arms where they had failed to block an opponent's blow. The swords must be dulled, as none of the cuts seemed deep.

Aqhat shouted something Danel couldn't make out, and the

men divided into pairs and practiced sparring while Aqhat made his way to Danel.

"He looks good, no?"

"I must admit, he does."

"He can go very far, very fast."

"I pray it doesn't go to his head. That is exactly what happened to Kirtu. And we know how that ended."

Aqhat placed his sword tip down into the soft earth at his feet, resting his hands on the pommel. "I'll keep an eye on him. I'll slow him down as much as possible. The ranks above him are actually overfilled, so it will be easy to keep him back for a while. He won't be quite as powerful and influential as he wants. But he'll still get his commission, and be able to marry, so maybe that will quench his hunger some."

Danel paused a long moment. "But I don't want him to marry her." He spoke almost to himself.

Aqhat chuckled. "You don't really have any say over that now, do you?"

Danel exhaled a long breath. "I know."

"Not that he'd want one, but it's not like there are many Yahweh worshippers around here for him to choose from. And he wouldn't know who they were, anyway." Aqhat glanced up at the sun, now at its highest point. "Tomorrow? Your house?"

Danel nodded slightly. "Sunset."

They watched in silence a while longer, then Aqhat signaled an attendant, who blew the horn again. The men halted, then formed two lines.

"Time for the midday meal. Want to join us?"

"Perhaps. Let me see if Mika wants to talk."

Aqhat nodded and led the line of recruits into the long, low shelter built next to the outer wall of the city. Just a roof held up by wooden poles—barely enough to keep out the sun and rain—it sheltered the men during meals and instruction. A single table lined with benches and set with pottery platters and bowls stretched the length of the shelter. As the men headed for seats, two cooks approached, one with an enormous, steaming pot of what was most likely stew, and the other carrying a massive platter of meat.

The line of sweaty young soldiers-in-training passed him, and Danel reached out to touch Mika's shoulder. His son tensed, stopped. The men filed around him.

Mika turned slowly to face him. "Yes?" His eyes held a coldness Danel had never seen.

Yahweh, help me. Danel stopped himself from flinching and instead smiled. "You looked really good out there."

Mika softened—almost imperceptibly. If Danel hadn't been looking for a reaction, he'd have missed it. "Thank you."

"Would you mind if I eat with you?"

Mika hesitated, stiffened again. "Why? Want to talk me out of staying?"

Danel resisted fighting back. "No. I just wanted to see you. Spend a few minutes with you. I promise I won't try to change your mind."

"All right." He held up one finger. "But one word about the army, or Demna, and you're gone."

Danel noticed four other young men who had not yet taken their seats standing about six long strides behind Mika, arms folded across their chests, eyeing Danel.

Danel nodded. "Sounds fair."

All six walked toward the shelter. Three took seats at the end on one side. The fourth scooted in on the other side, then Mika sat next to him, leaving Danel the last seat.

The cooks moved behind them, ladling the fragrant stew into bowls and adding generous amounts of meat. Danel held up a hand to stop them, but he was too late. He'd never eat that much. "Looks like they feed you well enough." Danel chuckled.

Mika gave a hearty laugh Danel hadn't heard in months. "They do. It's not as good as grandmother's, but there is plenty of it."

A crack in the wall. Not a big one, but a start. *Thank you, Yahweh.*

CHAPTER 12

ARISHA ROLLED OVER ON HER mat. How long had she lain awake? She reached toward the flap, but couldn't stretch quite far enough. She shoved her body forward until she could push aside the tent fabric. The sun had painted the sky a dull gray at this early hour.

She could either keep lying there, or get up. She tossed aside the light blanket and grabbed her sandals. She ran her fingers through her hair, then crawled out, dragging her cloak behind her.

Shivering, she shrugged into her cloak. Spring was nearly over, but the mornings were still a bit chilly, especially in this oasis surrounded by hills and low mountains. The cloud above them kept the air warm enough to sleep comfortably, but the morning still had a bite to it.

She picked up the empty pot left by the fire last night and headed for the sand that lay beyond the tents to collect the day's manna. Only a few other women were out yet, and the quiet allowed her to recount the conversation in her mind over and over. Why did she tell Zadok she was ready to marry him? The smile in his eyes—he was so happy. But was she really prepared?

She told him she was because every time he touched her, or

smiled at her, she lost all rational thought. All she wanted was to be near him, to be protected by him, to be loved by him. To finally have a home. Forever.

But no one could promise forever.

And that was the problem. As soon as she let her life become entangled with his, she would end up alone. Again. Somehow, she always did.

But she had no choice. She had to marry someone, and it may as well be him. The thought of it terrified her.

She finished gathering the manna and took the pot back to the fire pit. No one else was awake yet. She looked south toward the pasture and smiled. Was Zadok up yet? Why did she long to see him so badly?

She headed south, and was almost at the wall when Zadok hopped over. Drawing near, he laid his hands on her upper arms. "You're up early. I was just coming to eat."

"I couldn't sleep, so I thought I'd come see you."

He frowned and stepped back, his eyes skimming over her. "Are you well? Is something wrong?"

How could she tell him the truth? "No, no, I feel fine. I just wanted to see you alone, before the whole family awakened and it became too hard to talk to you."

His face relaxed and a smile took over. "You can always come here to see me. It's just me and the sheep. They won't tell."

She giggled and took his hand. She led him back to the wall and sat.

He perched on the wall next to her, pulling one leg up so he faced her sideways. "Did you want to talk about anything in particular or should I just tell you how beautiful you are?" He pulled her close, almost in his lap, and nuzzled her neck.

She leaned into his chest. "When do you think we should have the ceremony?"

"Tomorrow."

She smacked his arm. "Be serious."

"I am serious. I only say tomorrow because it can't be this afternoon."

"You're hopeless."

"Yes, I am."

She laughed. "No help at all."

"No, I'm not."

"All right, then, what about after the next Sabbath?"

He pulled back, his brows rising. "In three days?"

"That would be after *this* Sabbath. I said *next* Sabbath."

"In a week?"

"Ten days."

He tilted his head. "That's long enough for you?"

"You want to wait longer?"

"No! Of course not. I just thought you would."

She shrugged, then quickly added a smile. *Don't let your fear show.* "Yes. It's long enough."

He narrowed his eyes. "Are you sure?"

She pulled his head toward hers and kissed him the way she should kiss him after they were married. That should convince him. It was enough to convince her.

He moaned and pulled her even closer for another moment while his breathing slowed. "I guess you're sure." He closed his eyes and leaned his forehead against hers. When he looked up, he reached into the bag he kept tied to his belt, and pulled out an object wrapped in lambskin. "Since we've decided on a day, you can have this." Holding it in one hand, with his other he turned hers palm up. He slid the object into her hand and set aside the skin.

She gasped at a carnelian necklace, just like the ones Adi and Zivah wore, glistening in the sunlight. Polished to a brilliant shine, it hung from a gold loop-in-loop chain.

Tears burned her eyes as she fingered the dark red jewel. The warmth of his hand under hers clashed with the chilled metal. A lump in her stomach kept her from speaking, and she lifted her gaze to meet his.

"My sabba Bezalel made them from the armbands Kamose

wore when he was pharaoh's captain of the guard. My imma and sister have one, and my aunts Keren and Naomi. My savtas Meri and Tirzah each wore one. And now you." He moved his hand from under hers and picked up the chain with his fingers. He slid the hook from the last loop and held it up. "May I?"

She nodded, blinking back a tear.

Zadok reached around her neck, and she leaned forward while he fastened it. The play of his fingers on her skin left a trail of heat in their wake. He slid his hands down the chain toward the pendant. "I thought for many days about which one to give you."

"What do you mean?"

"Sabba made ten. The armbands had five carnelians each. Six have been worn. I could have given you one of the new ones, but I finally decided to give you the one Savta Tirzah wore."

"Why is that?"

"You remind me of her. She was quiet, unsure of herself, and at first didn't think she belonged in this family. I wanted you to be absolutely sure you are already part of us, by wearing her pendant, instead of starting from the beginning, with a new necklace. So every time you see it, you'll know you belong."

The tears broke free.

If marrying one man was terrifying, how much more was marrying an entire family?

Yet somehow, he made it seem something very desirable.

At least when she was in his arms.

~

*D*ANEL SLIPPED INTO HIS HOME just as the sun slid behind the city's towering stone walls. The main room was empty, but the aroma of roast beef and vegetables greeted him. He listened for a moment; gentle humming drifted in from the kitchen. He tiptoed through the larger room and peeked into the cooking area. His wife stood at the table, cutting a pomegranate in half. Then she scored the outside of each half another four or five times, popped it inside out, then held it over a bowl and hit it with a large spoon. The seeds fell into the bowl.

He stepped behind her and wrapped his arms around her waist. "I always love watching you do that." He kissed her neck and reached for a small bunch of grapes. "Everything looks delicious, as usual, my sweet."

Yasha smacked his hand and took back the grapes. "Thank you. Who are you expecting tonight?"

"Aqhat and his wife, his daughter and her husband, maybe the two new men."

She turned in his arms to face him. "Banno and Lukii? Are you sure you trust them?"

"Yes. Don't you?" Danel reached behind her and stole a single purple grape.

Yasha shrugged. "I don't know. I guess. It's just that we're getting to be a pretty large group. Don't you think maybe we should split again? Won't it look suspicious to have soldiers meeting regularly in your house for no reason? Aqhat and his family, yes, but random soldiers?"

He ate the grape and stepped away. "I'm not sure Banno and Lukii are ready to be on their own yet. And I don't want to send Aqhat with them because of ... you know ... he needs to stay close to home to tend his wife."

Yasha nodded slowly. "How is Zibqet? I meant to go see her today."

"Getting worse. In fact, it won't be long before she stops coming. And then Aqhat and Bisha will need to take turns staying home with her."

"I don't know how he can stand it. I can't imagine losing you." Her voice broke and a tear escaped.

He neared her again and wiped the tear away with his thumb. "Aqhat never says anything, but I know it's been very hard on him. Bisha is a huge help to him. They rely on each other very much."

A knock sounded at the door.

Danel looked over his shoulder. "That must be Aqhat. I'll get the door."

Yasha placed her hand over his. "Go. I'll bring the food out." She flashed him a tenuous smile and turned back to the table.

Danel opened the door. "Aqhat. Jebir. Where are Zibqet and Bisha?"

Aqhat frowned as he stepped inside, eyes filled with pain. "I had to leave them home. Zibqet was rambling this afternoon, and then her head began to hurt. She was sleeping when we left. I wanted to stay with her, but Bisha insisted I come and she remain instead with her mother."

Danel squeezed his shoulder. "I'm so sorry."

Yasha entered the room and stopped only for a moment, eyes wide at the sight of only the men. She set the food aside and gathered Aqhat into a fierce hug. She gestured to the bench against the wall and them offered them fruit and meat.

Another knock sounded. Danel opened the door to Banno and Lukii. "Come in. It's good to see you again."

The young soldiers took their seats and accepted food from Yasha, who then placed the trays on a low table in the center of the room and sat next to Danel.

"So, what story will we hear tonight?" Lukii stuffed a huge bite of beef in his mouth.

"Which have you heard? I forget which ones we have already told you."

"Tell about the flood again," Banno said. "That's my favorite."

"All right." Danel turned to his friend. "Aqhat? Jebir? Do one of you want to tell it tonight?"

"I'll do it." Jebir slowly lifted a hand. "I may make a mistake or two, though."

Danel smiled. "That's fine. That's how we learn."

∽

"*A*NY MORE FOOD? JUICE?" DANEL moved toward the table. Banno stood and stretched. "I think I need to be going. I have to stand an early watch tomorrow."

Danel walked him to the door and saw him out.

"I should get home to my wife. I promised I wouldn't be too late." Lukii headed for the door.

"Have you decided what to do about the feast day next week?" asked Danel.

Lukii chuckled. "Don't worry. I'll avoid the temple prostitutes."

Aqhat touched the young man's shoulder. "Do you want me to assign you guard duty in another part of the city?"

Lukii's brow furrowed. "Then how will I make my offering?"

Danel's heart slammed against his chest, before it nearly stopping beating altogether. Had he heard Lukii correctly? Did he intend to make a sacrifice to the Canaanite god? "I'm sorry? Why would you make an offering?"

"I always make an offering on feast days."

"But I thought you had joined us in worshipping Yahweh."

"I have."

"And did you not understand that you must now give up all other gods? I thought we had made that abundantly clear."

Lukii shifted from one foot to the other. "Well, I've heard you say that, but ..."

Aqhat put his fists on his hips, stepping nearer. "But ... what?"

"I didn't think that meant giving up *all* the sacrifices. I thought just to Baal. I mean, how will the gods help us if we do not present the proper offerings?"

Beside him, Yasha gasped. Danel grabbed her arm as she began to sway. How had they failed so completely to explain such a fundamental concept?

Aqhat closed his eyes. Jebir slumped onto the bench.

Lukii glanced around. "What?" His eyes widened. "You can't possibly be serious. You really expect me to stop sacrificing to *all* of them? Every one of you has stopped?"

Danel nodded slowly. "Yes. I've not made a single sacrifice at the feasts in thirty-nine years."

"Thirt—" Lukii choked. "You're lucky you're not dead!"

Aqhat continued staring at his soldier, looking far too much like a commander.

Lukii held up a finger in front of his chest. "Look, I only want to make one offering—to Kathirat. My wife and I, we've been hoping to have a baby for over three years ... I promised her I would pray to Kathirat ..."

Aqhat stepped closer to the young man. "Is that the only reason you decided to worship Yahweh? Is he just another god to you? Another possible answer to your prayers you can't afford to ignore?"

Lukii squirmed. "Well, it started out that way. But now, I do believe that He is different. Still, I'm not ready to let everything go yet, either." He looked at his sandals. "My wife, she cries herself to sleep almost every night. I have to do everything I can." He looked up again. "There's not much I can do, but this, at least, is something."

Danel stepped between Aqhat and the young man. "But Lukii, don't you remember the story of Abraham?" He kept his voice low. "We've recited it many nights. Yahweh gave Abraham and his wife Sarah a baby after many years, many more than you have waited, but you must trust only in Him." He paused. "Did Abraham turn to other gods after Yahweh told him to leave his country?"

"No, I suppose not ..."

"Then you too must put your trust in only Yahweh, not the false goddess of Canaan."

"I can try."

Yasha grabbed a handful of Danel's tunic at his back, but said nothing.

"What can I do to help?" said Aqhat, his tone less strident now. "Do you want me to assign you duty elsewhere, or do you want to stay near me at the feast, or ...?"

Lukii expelled a noisy sigh. "With you, I guess."

"Good choice." Aqhat nodded, clapping his shoulder.

"I'm going to go, then." Lukii dipped his head and left.

Yasha dropped onto the bench. "What do we do?"

Danel sat next to her. "Do not worry, my sweet. Yahweh will watch over us." He grasped her hand.

"I'll keep an eye on him." Aqhat glanced at the door. "I'll let you know if I see anything worrisome. But we need to go now, too. I want to get home to Zibqet. Jebir?"

Yasha stood. "Of course. Tell her I'll come by tomorrow with some of this meat and to spend some time with her."

"Thank you. I'm sure she'll love that. And Yasha?"

"Yes?"

"Don't worry about Lukii."

She offered a weak smile. "I can try."

After their guests had left and his wife had retired, Danel sat in the darkness in the empty room and thought through every word of their conversation with Lukii over and over again.

Yahweh, give me strength. Protect us, if You will. I have no idea what the next year or two will hold, even whether all of us will survive.

I know You will not fail us. I ask only for strength, that we do not fail You.

CHAPTER 13

$\mathcal{A}$RISHA WATCHED IN AMAZEMENT AS Adi slipped the needle through the fabric over and over, producing a series of identical stitches along the bottom of the robe. They were nearly invisible on the front side. Would she ever be able to sew like that? "How did you learn to do that? I mean, it's not like there's a lot to practice on."

Adi laughed. "Not according to my mother. She made me practice anyway. She said I'd need to know how when we settled in Canaan." She held the garment out. "Do you want to try?"

Arisha held her hands up, palms out. "No, no. I'm afraid I'd ruin it. You finish."

"All right. I have just a little more, then you can try it on. I've already finished the sleeves, and I'm almost done with the hem." Adi took a few more stitches, then knotted off the thread. "Here you go. Stand up, and let's see if it fits."

Arisha let Adi slip the robe over her shoulders. Her fingers traveled along the soft blue border along the neck and down the front. "It's so beautiful, Adi. Are you sure you want me to wear it?"

"Of course. Zivah wore it, and now you must wear it when you marry Zadok." She placed her palm on Arisha's cheek. "You're my daughter too, now."

As had happened every day—sometimes several times a day— since she and Zadok had agreed on when to marry, tears burned her eyes. She blinked to keep them from falling.

"Oh, habibti." Adi hugged her tightly. "I didn't mean to make you cry."

Arisha laughed as she wiped her eyes. "It seems everything makes me cry lately."

"That's perfectly normal."

Arisha turned at the voice behind her. "Zivah!"

"And now I have the sister I always wanted." Zivah wrapped her arms around her newest relative.

"Oh, let me take off the robe before something happens to it." Arisha shrugged off the garment and folded it before handing it to Adi.

"How about some tea?" Zivah knelt before the fire and poured water into a pot to heat.

Arisha laughed as she sat next to her. "I'm always in the mood for mint tea."

Adi handed her a faded piece of blue linen. "This is the fabric my imma used to teach me to sew. I taught Zivah and I'll teach you if you like."

Arisha's eyes widened. "You would do that?"

"Yes. It's easy to learn the basics, but it does take practice to do it well. Come, watch me." She picked up a fishbone needle with a piece of linen thread, then poked it through the underside of the fabric. "There's a knot at the end to keep it from pulling all the way through. We go a little way away from where we came up, and go back down. Then we come back up next to the first spot, and back down again, and just keep repeating. Want to try?"

It didn't *seem* all that difficult. Arisha took the cloth from Adi. Up, down. Up. Down.

Zivah gestured to Arisha's necklace. "I see he gave you a pendant. Which one did he decide to give you?"

"He said it was his Savta Tirzah's." Arisha continued working the needle.

Zivah smiled. "Good choice. That was my recommendation."

Arisha glanced up at Adi. "And yours?"

Adi grinned. "Mine, too."

Arisha fingered the red stone. "They are exquisite. Each one must have taken days to make. Maybe weeks."

Adi nodded. "I remember Abba working on them. I was very young, so the time kind of blurs, but I remember sitting by him at this very fire pit as he made the chains with the tools he'd brought from Egypt."

"Just the chains?"

"He'd already cut the stones from the bands—which he also made, by the way, during his time as a palace artisan—to make the pendants, then melted the rest of the gold. He formed that into thin sheets, and cut those into wires. He did all that outside of camp since it involved so much fire. Here, he rolled them between two pieces of wood until they were even thinner. He cut them to size, formed them into tiny loops, and sealed them with heat from the fire. Then he squeezed each loop, slipped it onto the previous one on the chain and folded it over until it made a chain of just the right length."

Arisha fingered the chain around her neck. "That must have taken forever."

"He worked on them for many, many nights. Weeks and weeks."

Zivah poured the hot water over the mint leaves in the cups, and gave Arisha and Adi each one.

Arisha blew on the hot liquid and took a sip. Then she continued practicing stitches. Up. Down. "But why ... why did Bezalel decide to make Kamose's armbands into pendants in the first place?"

Adi sipped her tea before she answered. "When Kamose left to retrieve the wounded, he'd only been married to Tirzah a few weeks. He was no longer wearing the bands, so he took them to Abba the night before he left and asked him to keep them, and if he didn't return, to use them to make wedding jewelry for Tirzah if she ever married again—which he doubted she would—or for the girls. He came back, as you know, but when Abba tried to return them, he didn't want them."

"So then what happened?"

"Well, Abba kept them for about eight or nine years. Everyone nearly forgot about them. Then Keren and Naomi were of marriageable age, and he came up with the idea of the necklaces. He didn't tell anyone but Imma what he was doing until he came into camp one day with the ten pendants and the wires."

"That must have been quite a surprise."

"Oh, it was. He let Kamose decide what to do with them. So of course Tirzah and Imma got the first ones, the girls each received one when they married, and the rest were saved for future daughters and daughters-in-law."

"I wish I could have known them."

"Kamose and Bezalel?"

"And Tirzah and Meri—all of them. They all sound like such amazing, strong people." *Not like anyone I'll ever be.* She held up the cloth. "Ugghh!"

"What?"

"Look at these stitches! They're horrible!"

Adi held out her hand. "Let me see." She studied the fabric, turning it over and looking at both sides. "Actually they're not that bad for a first time."

Arisha set the cloth in her lap and picked up her tea.

"Do you know what Tirzah did when Kamose didn't come back with the others?" asked Adi.

Arisha pursed her lips. "Someone like her? I don't know ... looked after the wounded that were brought back? Went after him herself?" She smirked.

"No. Not exactly."

"No? Then what? Waited patiently?"

"Now I was a baby, but she herself told me that she crawled into her tent and wouldn't come out for several days. Wouldn't eat, wouldn't talk to anyone ... finally Rebekah, Bezalel's imma, dragged her out and made her eat."

"But ... she seems so strong from everything you've told me."

"No. She *learned* to be strong. And you will, too."

~

"*D*ANEL!"

DANEL CRINGED AS KING Keret bellowed his name. He was still several rooms down the hall. Thank Yahweh the pitcher of pomegranate juice he carried was covered, or it would have splashed all over the hunk of goat cheese and loaf of bread he'd placed beside it on the tray.

Every day, Danel attended the king before he did anything else. A servant brought him all his other meals, but Danel brought him the first one. That not only kept the king happy but allowed Danel to make sure he knew what the king considered most important that day.

"Danel!"

Another shout. Why was Keret so impatient?

Danel quickened his step to a near jog. He shifted the tray onto one hand and knocked once before entering the king's private room without waiting for a response. "Yes, my king?"

"Where have you been? The day is half gone already!"

There was no use arguing. Or even asking Keret to look out the window to see the sun had barely risen above the mountains in the distance. Danel set the tray on a table and bowed. "I beg your forgiveness, my king."

Keret snorted, but his face softened. "You should."

Danel lifted the pitcher and filled a glass with the deep red liquid. Danel found the beverage sour, but it was the monarch's favorite. He cut off a thick piece of cheese and a slice of bread, then arranged both on a plate, which he set next to the cup.

Keret downed the juice in one gulp but ignored the food. He flipped his long robe around and paced silently.

Danel moved to the window and pushed aside the wooden cover. The dry breeze carried in hints of almond and grape blossoms. Beyond the walls the farmers could be heard harvesting wheat as they worked together to bring in the grain, one farm at a time.

Danel stepped back and waited. The king's sandals slapped against the stone floor as he stalked back and forth, his face pinched into a frown. Five or six times lately Keret had called for Danel but then paced for several long moments before he spoke. It was quite unsettling. And a waste of time. Danel clenched his jaw to keep from sighing, locked his knees to avoid tapping his foot.

Keret stilled and stared out the window, south toward the Israelite camp. "How long?"

"Thirty-nine years, two months. Almost."

Keret paced some more. "We need to begin sending scouts out on a regular basis. Send a patrol out only far enough to see the camp, make sure they are not preparing to move. Have them take care to remain unseen. Once every other week."

"Yes, my king."

Keret raised his brows. "You're not going to argue with me?"

Danel smiled. "Would it do any good?

The king smiled. "Of course not. But you're not going to tell me it isn't time? That they're not coming yet? That *Kamose*"—he sneered at the name—"said forty years, and forty years is still ten months away?"

"No. On the contrary, I think this is a very wise decision."

Keret narrowed his eyes. "You do?"

"Yes, my king."

"Of course. A good commander always knows exactly where his enemy is at all times. You must always be one step ahead."

Keret's face brightened. "Yes! Precisely!"

"And the only way to know where they are, is to go find them. So patrols make perfect sense."

"Then go. Make it happen. I want the first patrol out within three days."

"Of course." Danel bowed again and left the room, closing the door behind him.

Time to see Aqhat.

Danel finished his morning's duties and hurried to the officer's workroom.

"*H*e wants what?" Aqhat furrowed his brow and closed his eyes, as if he hoped the answer might change.

"Patrols. First one in three days."

Aqhat growled.

Danel shrugged. "Think of them as ... training exercises."

"They'll have to be. They won't be good for anything else. It hasn't been forty years."

"I know. But arguing with him about it would only make him that much more determined."

Aqhat walked behind his desk. "I know. What do you think will happen when they do start marching north?"

"North into Canaan?"

"Yes."

Danel shook his head. "I don't know. Yahweh promised them this land. They beat the Egyptian army. They beat the Amalekites."

Aqhat leaned on his palms. "I know. So, if we had a say, what would we do? Would we put up a fight? Would we even try? Would we just surrender? What would be the best plan? I mean, I know Keret would have us fight to the death for his city. But I'm having real problems preparing for a war I know in my heart we will lose." He straightened, crossed his arms over his chest. "How do I as a commander, send my men into certain death? In any other battle, there is at least a chance, no matter how small, that we can win. I study, I strategize, I eliminate every possible risk to try to protect my men as much as possible. But what do I do here?" He dragged his hands though his hair. "Really, what do I do? Some days, I'm ready to resign my commission and let someone else do it."

Danel leaned against the door. "I know. I *know*. Things are starting to get very complicated. Until now, we've been able to hide our worship of Yahweh. Avoid sacrificing to the false gods. Live a life in between. I am afraid that will not be possible for very much longer. Lukii's comments last week were ... unsettling, to say the least, and I fear we may be betrayed. The bigger our number grows, the stronger the possibility becomes."

"I've been watching him, and I've had a few more conversations with him. I don't think we have anything to worry about right now."

"Perhaps not. But I think we need to alert the other leaders that from now on it may be wise to spend time in our meetings praying for strength and wisdom. If we thought it has been difficult until now, I believe the hard part has only begun."

CHAPTER 14

28th day of Ziv

"*H*ER ROBE IS READY. I have the tent prepared. I have cheese and dates and manna and milk inside." Zadok counted on his fingers as he spoke. "What am I forgetting?"

"Nothing." Jacob laughed. "Nothing, except to put on your robe and go get her." He reached for the garment lying on the blanket at their feet. "Did you get any sleep at all last night?"

"I think so. Somewhere toward dawn I must have finally dozed off."

"Nervous? Or excited?" He shook out the robe and held it up.

"Both." Zadok slipped his arms into the sleeves and held them out to the sides. "Abba's robe fits well."

"It should. You're almost exactly the same size. Except for your hair, I can barely tell you apart from the back." He grinned. "You look good." Jacob picked up the blanket and folded it. "Your last night sleeping on the ground. Should I take this to your new tent or to your abba's?"

"Neither. Leave it. I may not be staying here, but someone else will be."

"Really?"

"Yes. I prefer having someone out here with them just in case."

He set the blanket back on the ground. "All right. Ready, then?"

Zadok nodded, then headed toward the pasture gate. "How's Zivah feeling? Any better?"

"Yes, her nausea has stopped."

"Any more news on the mission to Edom?"

"We'll leave once the new moon has passed, so we'll have light on the journey. Joshua says we'll 'just head east.' Bozrah is where their king lives, but he says they will find us long before we reach Bozrah."

"Hmmm." Zadok had heard all Jacob's words, but at the moment their importance was lost on him.

As they reached his family's tent, Zadok's chest tightened. He closed his eyes and inhaled a deep breath. Would he disappoint her? Was she still afraid of him? Had he earned her trust yet?

Would he ever?

He stopped in front of the tent and softly called her name.

His mother stepped outside. "She's almost ready. Just give her a moment." She brushed her hands down his arms. "You remind me of Ahmose on our wedding day."

Zadok glanced around. "Where is he?"

"He'll be here in a moment."

The tent flap rustled. His breathing caught. A hand pulled the fabric back a bit, then retreated. He groaned.

Imma's laugh caused him to scowl at her. "Calm down, habibi." She patted his arm as she glanced over his shoulder. "Ah, here he comes."

Zadok turned his head, shocked to see Abba approach with Moses.

Abba gestured toward the tent. "She still inside?"

Zadok growled.

Abba laughed.

Moses stood next to him and placed his arm around him.

"Zadok, I know you are already married according to the law, and you only need a witness today, but I promised Miriam I would make sure this was completed. Is that all right with you?"

"Yes. Will Arisha object?" Zadok's gaze shot to the tent as the fabric shifted again. A head peered out. He avoided sighing audibly as his sister emerged. A moment passed, his heart beating wildly. Finally, his bride stepped from the tent, and his mouth felt like it was full of sand.

She smiled shyly at him from behind his sister. Her dark hair fell softly out of her head wrap, around her face, curling gently along the border that lined the neck of her robe. She held her hands in front of her chest, the fingers of one hand rubbing the scar on the palm of the other, a clear sign she was nervous, he'd learned.

Abba's hand landed on his shoulder. "I don't think she cares who else is here."

Zadok pulled his stare from Arisha. "Moses?"

"Yes?"

"Would you bless us?"

"I'd consider it an honor." Moses took Arisha's hand in his, grasping Zadok's bicep with his other. "May you learn as your sabba Bezalel did, that it is a blessing to dwell in the shadow of the Most High. May you also learn, as did your sabba Kamose, that if Yahweh is your dwelling, He will be your refuge. Call on His name, and He will rescue you; He will protect you if you acknowledge His name. He will answer you; He will be with you in trouble and deliver you. He will satisfy you with long life." He stepped back and continued. "Care for each other as Yahweh cares for you, and you will enjoy your life together."

After goodbyes and kisses from Abba and Imma, Zadok led Arisha to their new tent just several strides away. He held the fabric back for her and they stepped inside.

"Are you hungry?"

She nodded.

He sat and reached for a plate and skin in the center of the room, poured milk into two cups, then handed her one. The plate held cheese, manna and dates. "Do you just want to talk for a while?"

She nodded again.

After several more moments of silence, he took her hand. "Are you nervous? About marrying me?"

She wiped away a tear. "What if I displease you? Make you unhappy?"

"How could you possibly make me unhappy? You've already made me completely happy by becoming my wife."

"What if I burn the manna? Never learn to sew?"

Zadok burst out laughing. "Learn to sew? Is that what you're worried about? Do you think you have to master those things for me to love you?"

She shrugged.

"Arisha, I love you because I love you. There is nothing you can do to make me love you more. There is nothing you can do to make me stop loving you. I will always love you." He leaned in and brushed her lips with his. "I will tell you every morning that I love you." He kissed her again, then moved his lips to her ear. "Maybe one day you'll believe me."

~

ONCE AGAIN THE KING BELLOWED for Danel. From the anteroom off the hall Danel strode to the throne room, grabbing a cup of juice as he left. No need to rush—no matter how soon he arrived, he would be late.

"Danel!" The king glared down at him from behind his throne. "What took so long?"

Danel remained silent as he ascended the dais, then extended the cup.

Keret ignored the offer. His robe lay tossed over the arm of the throne; his crown teetered on the edge of the pedestal nearby. "Where is the patrol? I heard they have returned."

"Would you like some juice?"

Keret gripped the back of the chair. "The patrol?"

"I hadn't heard that. Would you like me to check?"

"Bring me the commander," he growled.

"I shall. But in the meantime, may I suggest you calm yourself first? Drink your juice. Put on your robe and crown. You'll want to look like the king when you talk to him, not a farmer."

"*You* do not give *me* orders."

"Yes, my king." Danel set the cup down. He picked up the robe and folded it, then laid it neatly on the pedestal before taking up the crown. He stepped nearer to Keret and held up the symbol of his office.

Keret frowned and narrowed his eyes but allowed Danel to place the gold object on his head.

Danel stepped back, eyed the crown, reached out and adjusted it. "Much better."

"If you say so."

"I do. Drink the juice. You'll feel better." He bowed, then left the throne room, shaking his head. The king's obsession with the Israelites was getting the better of him.

Danel headed for the army quarters. Someone there must know something.

A clerk, so young he must have just been hired, ambled from the direction of Aqhat's offices. His tunic was askew; his sandals dusty. He picked at his fingernails as he walked.

"Is your commander in his office?"

The boy looked up, stumbled back a half-step. He glanced over his shoulder. "N- no, I was just looking for him."

"Have you heard whether the patrol is back or not?"

"Word is they just arrived."

"Where would they go first?"

"I believe to the practice field."

"Thank you." Danel turned to go, but stopped to face the clerk for a moment. "And clean yourself up before he sees you. Otherwise you'll be cleaning up after the cattle. Or worse."

The boy frowned. "You're not in the army. How do you know what will happen?"

Danel raised a brow. "I know Aqhat."

The boy's bottom lip quivered for just a moment, then thinned as he pressed his lips together.

Danel turned on his heel and headed right at the first corner, toward the field. A short hallway later, he blinked as he stepped into the bright morning light. He shaded his eyes and scanned the area. Not far from where he stood perhaps twenty men gathered around a long table piled with grapes, bread, cheese, and pitchers. One of the soldiers shoved the grapes aside as a portly, bald cook set a large pot next to a stack of bowls. The older man removed a ladle from his sash and began filling the bowls, which the men greedily snatched up. Sounds of chewing and swallowing and occasional moaning filled the air.

Danel strode up to Aqhat. "Welcome home."

Aqhat smiled and slurped a huge bite of stew into his mouth. "This tastes so good. We haven't had hot food in four days." He took another bite. "Want some?" He gestured with his bowl toward the pot.

Danel grabbed a bowl and filed it with stew, balancing some bread on the edge. "I didn't realize you had gone with them."

"On this first one I did, so I could better plan for the others. And I wanted a look at the camp for myself."

"Good, because Keret wants a report."

"I know."

"Now."

"Can't I finish eating first?" Aqhat spoke around a mouthful of meat.

"Better hurry. He's quite anxious to hear the news."

Aqhat started to set his bowl on the table, but Danel stopped him. "Eat it on the way."

The walk back to the throne room was quick and filled with the sounds of slurping stew. At the door, Danel handed their bowls to a servant. Aqhat was dirty, sweaty and exhausted. Normally he would never be allowed in the king's presence in such condition, but today was different.

Both men walked into the room. Danel moved to stand near the king, while Aqhat stopped in the center of the room, helmet in hand. He dropped to one knee and bowed his head low, waiting to be recognized.

Keret was talking to an attendant, and it was several moments before he called the warrior's name.

Aqhat raised his head. "My king?"

"Stand."

He obeyed.

"What did your patrols find?"

"We saw no move by the Israelites to break camp."

"Nothing to indicate they are preparing to come here?"

"Nothing."

Keret leaned forward. "You must be certain."

"I am. There are no tents being torn down, nothing being packed up, nothing being moved. Livestock are scattered in the pasture. From as close as we could get, I saw not a single sign of departure."

"Very well. You will return in two weeks."

"Yes, my king."

"You may go."

Aqhat bowed deeply and retreated.

Keret watched him leave, drumming his fingers on the arm of his throne. "I don't care what he says. They're coming."

"They can't come if their tents are still staked down. It would take days to pack up that camp. I wouldn't worry about it yet."

Keret slammed his hands down. "I *will* worry about it! I have known this for forty years. They *are* coming, and they are coming sooner than you think." He rose and stalked out of the room, waving his arms and muttering under his breath.

Danel let out a slow exhale. The last year of waiting had barely begun, and the king was already nearly out of control.

It promised to be a long ten months.

And Danel wasn't at all sure he would survive.

~

*I*N THE MIDDLE OF THE night Arisha awoke with a start and glanced around the dark tent. Something was wrong. Her heart beat quickened; every muscle tensed. Where was she? She stared hard at the flap of the tent. Why was it in the wrong place?

Oh. Her heartbeat slowed. Another new tent. How many different places had she called *home* in her short life? Too many to count. None of them ever felt ... permanent. Real.

A soft push against her back reminded her of Zadok's presence. His chest pressed warm against her, expanding with every breath, then withdrawing again. His arm draped over her waist, holding her close.

She closed her eyes again and savored the contact, entwined her fingers with his, pulling his hand to her chest. In the dark of the night, it was easy to imagine a life with him. Pretend he would always be there. See children, grandchildren. A long life, a happy life.

Zadok shifted, burying his face in her neck for a moment before his head dropped back on the cushion they shared.

Arisha waited until his breathing slowed again. Then she pulled the blanket up higher, and sighed contentedly as she drifted back to sleep.

When the warmth of the sun and the aroma of manna cooking over campfires finally invaded their tent, Arisha rolled on her other side and studied the face of the man lying next to her. How could he sleep so deeply? His face seemed so peaceful, so content. As it always did, whenever she saw him. Since the first time, at Miriam's tent. That peace was one of the most attractive things about him. Although his face and form were quite handsome, it was this quiet strength that drew her the most.

She stretched out her fingertips and smoothed his thick hair from his eyes, stubborn curls falling back onto his forehead. She traced his jaw, hidden under his soft beard. Her hand followed the curve of his shoulder, then the muscles down his arm. How could he be so strong and so gentle at the same time?

He was locked in here with her for seven days, but after that ... after that he would leave, and she could never again be certain he would be back. The hope that had burned so brightly in the deep of last night evaporated like smoke in the bright light of morning. Her heart clenched.

His eyes fluttered open. He blinked a few times, then smiled as he drew her closer. His arm still encircling her waist, he leaned forward and kissed her cheek. "Sleep well?"

She nodded. "And you?"

"With you next to me? Of course." He kissed her cheek again, then slid his mouth to hers.

She slipped her arms around his back, his kisses sending heat throughout her body as they became more intense. Every thought in her mind was banished except her delight in the warmth of his body next to hers.

A child's giggle outside the tent drew their attention and she broke the kiss. She furrowed her brow as she glanced at the door. Who would come this early? The day after they married?

Zadok chuckled. "It's just Zivah and Adira delivering our manna for the day." He bounced his brows. "Since it's our bridal week and we can't leave." He kissed her a few more times, then rolled over and sat up. He reached outside and retrieved the food and a skin of milk. "Hungry?"

"Not yet." She shook her head and sat up.

Zadok grinned mischievously and set the food aside.

She laughed. "That's not what I meant!"

He laughed as he grabbed her, laid her back down on the sleeping mat and kissed her passionately. He pulled back to look in her eyes. "I love you, Arisha. I promise you I will prove it to you every day."

She caressed his cheek. *I'm certain you do love me. If only I could say it back.* But that was something she could not risk.

Not yet, anyway.

CHAPTER 15

*1*3th day of Sivan

ZADOK SCANNED THE PASTURE ONE more time, making certain that each of his sheep was happy and well. He trusted his men, especially Jonah, but after being back only one week, he had to be sure himself.

Shika nudged his shin, and he knelt beside the jovial lamb. "Did you miss me, girl?" Zadok rubbed her head, then moved his hands down the animal's neck and back, scratching as he went. "Feels good?"

The lamb responded with a shake of her tail, and nuzzled Zadok.

Zadok patted her head and stood, then signaled Jonah. "I'm going to say goodbye to Jacob before he leaves with Joshua. Take care of my sheep?"

The younger man smiled. "Always."

Zadok jogged to camp. He stopped by his tent and poked his head inside. Arisha wasn't there. Where could she be? He checked Abba's tent. Not there either. And not to the right, at Zivah's. One place left. He cut between Abba's tent and Joshua's. Ah, there she was.

In the walkway in front of Moses's tent a large group milled around Moses, Aaron, Joshua, and Caleb. On the outer edge, Jacob held Adira, who laid her curly head on his shoulder. Josiah stood with his little hand clutched in Zivah's.

Zadok slid in next to Jacob and took Adira from him, who joined the others. Most of the men Zadok didn't know, as the group represented all twelve tribes. He quickly scanned the crowd. Who was from Judah besides Jacob?

Joshua's son Tobiah stood near his sabba. Tobiah's son Eliel as well. But who was that hanging on his arm? Marah? Zadok shook his head.

Next to him, Arisha slipped her arm around Zivah's waist. His sister smiled and chattered, but Zadok knew, and he knew Jacob knew, she was only putting on a brave face. She'd never been alone; she'd always had Imma and Abba, and then Jacob. And though everyone had been expecting this moment, anticipating it, since the pronouncement, no one really knew how she would do on her own.

Moses looked over each one of the emissaries, then turned to Joshua. "You know the message I would like delivered to the king of Edom. Remind them that our ancestors were brothers together in his land, and therefore we are cousins. Then the Egyptians mistreated us, but when we cried out to the Lord, he heard our cry and rescued us. Now we are here at Kadesh, on the edge of Edom's territory, and we need to pass through their country. Assure them we will not go through any field or vineyard, or drink water from any well. We will travel only along the King's Highway."

Joshua nodded. "Do you think they will honor our kinship?"

"I don't know. We can only ask." He tilted his head toward his brother. "Let us bless you before you go."

The group fell silent as Aaron stepped forward and raised his hands over the men. "May Yahweh keep watch over you as you are apart from us. May He bless you and keep you, may He make his face shine on you and be gracious to you; may Yahweh turn his face toward you and give you peace."

"Let us go then, and stop standing around here." Joshua picked up his pack and headed east, his spear resting on his left shoulder.

Jacob grabbed Zivah once more and hugged her tightly. She returned his smile with an uneasy one of her own, and Jacob fell into line with the others. Arisha steered Zivah away from the group, back toward her tent.

"Adira, let's go to the water." Zadok bent to pick her up, but a familiar—and unwelcome—voice caught his attention.

"So, you found another way to avoid the battles now?" Marah's abba sauntered toward him, his four sons in tow. "The marriage exemption. How does it feel to be the first one to claim that?"

Zadok's hands fisted and unfisted. He hadn't *claimed* it. He was told he couldn't go. "I'm not discussing this with you."

"I heard he has an even better reason for not wanting to fight." Malkiel's eldest stood feet wide, his chest puffed out.

"Really?" Malkiel turned to his son in an exaggerated display of curiosity. "And what would that be?"

"I heard his new bride is Canaanite."

The older man's cold eyes drilled a hole through Zadok. "He married a Canaanite? Isn't that forbidden?"

"Not if she worships Yahweh. Which she does." Zadok struggled to control his tone.

"I wonder what our high priest would have to say about this." Malkiel's upper lip curled, while behind him his son cracked his knuckles.

"He knows." Zadok said.

"He couldn't possibly." Malkiel huffed.

"Moses was at the wedding."

"You're lying. I'm going to Aaron. You cannot bring a ... a ... *Canaanite* into our camp without consequences." Malkiel's face was red, his words clipped.

"I already did." Zadok turned to leave.

Malkiel grabbed Zadok's bicep. "She doesn't belong here. And if Aaron won't do anything about it, I will."

Zadok stepped into the man. "Stay *away* from my wife."

Malkiel stormed off, sputtering, trailed by his sons.

They probably never had an independent thought in their lives.

Zadok smiled and bent to pick up Adira. "Let's go to the river, habibti. You too, Josiah. We'll let your imma rest a bit." He kissed Arisha before chasing Josiah, already racing toward the water.

"When will Abba come back, Uncle Zadok?" Adira stared over his shoulder at the retreating figures.

"I don't know, habibti. Not too long. Josiah, too far ahead."

"I miss him."

"I know. No one's ever been gone from us before. It'll be hard for your imma."

Adira sat back on his arm and caught his gaze. "I will be extra good for her."

Zadok chuckled. "That's very sweet of you. I'm sure she'll like that."

She wiggled free and chased after Josiah.

Zadok glanced at the armed scouts marching east. One side of him rejoiced; he wanted to stay home, not sure how Arisha would respond when he finally had to fight on her homeland. The other side wanted do his part, fight for Israel, conquer the land Yahweh had given them.

Not to mention clear his name.

No matter. It would all happen soon enough.

~

ANEL WOUND HIS WAY THROUGH the clamorous throng of worshippers gathered outside the twin temples west of the palace. He twisted and moved to avoid the sweaty bodies that continually jostled him. Songs and chants and instruments competed with each other for dominance over the laughter and shouts of people. His heart ached for the people of Arad, lost in their obscene worship of false gods.

Moonlight bounced off the gold and silver jewelry tied onto the wrists and anklets of the women spinning frenetically in circles large and small, sometimes even alone, oblivious to all else. Girls, some barely marriageable age, dressed in clothing that left nothing to the imagination danced on the round altar that stood nearly as tall as a man, and as wide as five men.

Men and boys waved bundles of golden wheat over their heads, singing and chanting to the god of the harvest. Freshly baked loaves of bread sat on much smaller, square stone altars in the anterooms that served each of the twin temples. Danel breathed in the aroma and his stomach growled. He hadn't eaten since early morning, when he'd awakened the king. All he could force down then was some juice and a bite of cheese. Just knowing what was coming today, what he'd be seeing ...

But the bread arranged around on the altars was for Baal and Asherah, anyway. Not mere humans.

No, the task for humans this day was to encourage the gods to keep blessing Arad with abundance and fertility—for the crops and the people. Because apparently without reminders, the gods might forget how to bestow the fertility, so the people had to show them how. Repeatedly.

A young girl, her long hair flowing down her back, the sash of her tunic looped around her neck instead of tied around her waist, stepped out of the aisle that ran alongside the temples. She clung to an older man dressed in the expensive purple robes of the priesthood of Baal. He kissed her cheek as she left him; another quickly replaced her and he headed back to the room from which he'd come.

Another young woman with a tunic dyed in the same rich violet exited a room, the first of many tucked along the city wall, facing the temple across a dirty and smelly alley. She sauntered into the courtyard, her too short tunic slipping off her shoulder and revealing a good part of what shouldn't be seen in public. "Lotan! Back again?" She wrapped her hand around a young man's neck and pulled his mouth down to hers.

If Danel had had any food in his belly, it would have come up.

The temple consort and her guest retreated to her room.

Danel turned away. Enough. He'd put in plenty of time to be seen, to fulfill his requirement of attendance at the harvest feast in case the king asked him. Or asked others about him. At least Yasha didn't have to witness this depravity, thank Yahweh. Time to go home. But he might have to take the long way to try to erase some of these wicked scenes from his head before he spent time with his wife and grandchildren.

He turned to walk away and slammed into the solid chest of Lukii. "Lukii, wh- what are you doing here?"

Lukii's face turned the color of a pomegranate. He opened and closed his mouth, but no words came out. He paused, then took a deep breath. "Well, I have to come, same as you."

"I know that. I mean what are you doing *here*? By the prostitute rooms?" Danel shoved his thumb over his shoulder. "You said you wouldn't do that." He stepped nearer to the young man. "The altar is here as well. Do you intend to sacrifice?"

"No! No, of course not. I'm just taking a walk to stretch my legs after standing guard for so long."

Danel narrowed his eyes.

"You can check with Aqhat!"

"I will."

Lukii's shoulders dropped. His eyes held no light.

Danel regretted his attack. "Lukii, forgive me. I just wanted to make sure you don't go back to these false gods. But I should have trusted you more." He placed his hand on the soldier's shoulder. "I'm sorry."

Lukii appeared to contemplate Danel's words as a dancer bumped into him. Without speaking again, he stalked away.

Would he forgive Danel?

Or had Danel made a fatal error that placed his life—and his family's—in the angry young man's hands?

~

*A*RISHA STUFFED ANOTHER BRANCH UNDER the huge pot balanced on rocks over their fire. The flame crackled and brightened to a deep orange, then settled down to a nice, hot blue. The bubbling increased, and she stirred the water with a stripped date palm branch, whitened from years of use. The fabric popped up with the bubbles, and she shoved it down, only to have it pop up in another place.

Adi reached over and dropped some more of the weld flower seeds into the pot, and the deep yellow color swirled and frothed. Arisha stirred the water, the fabric clinging to the branch as it circled the pot. Satisfied the color had saturated the cloth, she sat back and picked up her sewing cloth. Up, down. Again. At least her stitches were looking better.

"So, habibti, are you settling into your new tent? Do you need anything?" Adi slapped her hands together to get rid of the color the seeds had left behind.

My husband needs me to tell him I love him. But I can't. "No, we have everything we need. Thank you." She smiled sweetly, hoping Adi wouldn't see she wasn't telling the whole truth.

"It took me a long time to get used to living with Ahmose."

Arisha's head shot up, her eyes widened. Adi sat there eating dates like she'd just stated she wanted more to eat, not that she'd ever been uncomfortable around her husband. Arisha would never have guessed they'd been at odds for a single moment—they seemed to be one person. "Really? I- I thought ..."

Adi laughed. "I know. We get along beautifully, now. But at first, even though I'd never lived alone before, it still felt so ... strange ... to live with *him*, even though I loved him with my whole heart. It is an entirely different thing to share not just your tent, but your life with someone. To share not only your bed, but your thoughts, your dreams, everything you thought was hidden ... I almost felt like he invaded my life."

Arisha's cheeks heated. She bent over her cloth, sewing more quickly. Maybe Adi wouldn't see the pinking of her skin. Or maybe she would think it was because she sat so close to the fire. The bubbling beside her grew louder as the conversation quieted.

"Arisha? Is everything all right?"

She nodded—probably too quickly, since Adi scooted closer and draped an arm around her shoulder.

Arisha dropped the cloth and looked away. She couldn't let Zadok's mother see her face, read her thoughts.

"Let me guess. You're glad you married Zadok, but you are uncomfortable sometimes, perhaps often, and you feel guilty about that, and you are afraid that means you do not love him. But it is too late now, and you are even more afraid you will both be miserable and you will ruin his life."

The breath left Arisha's lungs in a whoosh. How could Adi possibly know that? She swallowed a sob, continued staring into the fire.

"Habibti, Arisha." Adi gently turned Arisha's face toward hers. "You will be fine, I assure you. You both will."

Arisha searched her eyes, desperately hoping for some assurance, some promise it truly would be all right.

"I know you love him—"

Arisha's breath caught. "You do?"

"Of course you do. I can see it in your eyes. The way you look at him. The way you say his name. The way you smile when he says yours." Adi stroked her hair. "You just need time. It takes time to get used to each other."

Maybe Adi was right. Maybe all they needed was time.

"I had it easier with Ahmose, I think. Ahmose is a very confident, very outgoing man. He loves to be around people. He'll talk to anyone. That was a good thing in the first years of our marriage, because it gave me some time alone. But Zadok is quite different from his father. Zadok would always rather be away from people. I'm guessing he is always at home, yes?"

Arisha nodded her head. She didn't trust her voice.

"And is that all right with you? Do you need some time? We can work something out. Ahmose can take—"

"No! I like having him home with me."

"All right." Adi tilted her head. "You just look like you're having a hard time with something, that's all. If I can help you with anything, or Zivah, if you'd rather ..."

"No, it's fine." *Change the subject.* "And Zivah has enough to deal with on her own. How is she doing?"

"Better. She's feeling better, and that helps a great deal."

"Good. Maybe I can take the children to the river again after the noon meal."

Adi nodded, but Arisha could feel her continuing to study her. Did she know? Did she know Arisha was holding back part of herself from Zadok?

Because she could never tell him she loved him. As long as she didn't say it, maybe it wouldn't be real. And if it wasn't real, maybe, just maybe, it wouldn't hurt so much when it finally evaporated like a morning's dew.

~

ZADOK STROLLED UP TO HIS parents' tent. Imma sat outside the door to their tent, sewing a hem on bright yellow fabric.

"Making a new tunic?"

"Yes. This is the last of last year's wool."

"Don't worry. You'll have more in a few days."

She flashed a bright smile. "You just missed Arisha. She took the children to the river with Zivah. But there are manna cakes and dates by the fire there. She pointed with her chin to the plate hidden under a cloth.

Zadok lifted the cloth, removed a cake. "Zivah feeling better?"

"Much. She's in her own tent, resting."

"Good. I never thought it possible, but I miss her teasing."

Adi laughed. "I've been teaching Arisha to sew. She's getting quite good. Better than Zivah, but don't tell your sister I said that."

"I wouldn't dare."

"How are things with Arisha? She seems ... uneasy."

"I'm afraid that's my fault."

"Your fault?"

He nodded.

Adi took a few more stitches. "How is it your fault?"

"I think I make her unhappy."

"Why do you think that?"

"We've been married a little over two weeks. I tell her I love her every morning." He tore apart a date, removed the stone. He continued to rip apart the flesh and toss tiny pieces into the fire. "She has yet to say it to me. I'm afraid I have trapped her in a marriage without love. At least on her part."

Adi set aside the tunic and reached for his hands, stilling them and gently removing the decimated fruit. "Oh, habibi. She loves you. She loves you very much."

"How can you know? How can you say that?"

"I know because I am a woman, and a woman knows these things. And I talked to her."

"And did she say she loves me?" Zadok searched her eyes, hoping for a positive answer.

"She did not have to. I told you, I can tell."

His heart sank. "Then she didn't say it."

"I don't think she can."

"What do you mean she can't? She can't form the words? Doesn't know how?"

"I believe she is afraid."

Air left his chest as if Imma had punched him. What could he have done to frighten her? His memory searched every day they'd spent together, searching for the offending action. "Of what? Me?"

She smiled and squeezed his hands. "No, of course not, habibi. I think she is afraid that if she loves you, you will leave."

Relief warred with confusion. "But I have promised her I won't."

She released his hands and retrieved her sewing. "That's not always up to you, is it? Miriam would not have chosen to leave her. The others, maybe. But one way or another, she's always been left, or sent away. I believe she thinks if she does not love you, you won't leave. Or at least,"—she caught his gaze—"it will not hurt so much when you do."

"But you think she does love me."

Adi laughed. "I know she does. I can see it in her eyes, hear it in her voice." She dropped the cloth again, studied his face. "Are you saying you see nothing in her behavior that says she cares for you? Does she not return your kiss, your embrace?"

Zadok's cheeks heated, and he looked away. "Imma ..."

"Well, there are ways you can tell. Look for her love in ways other than her words. Besides those exact words. Does she try to encourage you? Say kind things? Tell you about her day? Ask about yours? Listen when you talk?"

Zadok recalled the long nights they spent talking about their life here, their life in Canaan ... how much she'd told him of her life before she met Miriam. She'd trusted him with more and more of her feelings and fears almost every day.

"And there are things she can do. Does she do things to try to please you? Make you comfortable? Make you feel important? Does she like to spend time with you?" Adi placed her hand on his cheek. "My son, I know you know all this."

Zadok thought of the times Arisha had come to him in the pasture. Brought him a special snack for no reason whatsoever, just to see him.... His neck heated as he thought of their nights together. She definitely did not shrink from his touch. Many times she kissed him first.

"Zadok?" Imma's voice drew him back to the present.

"I'm sorry. My mind was ... elsewhere." Hopefully his skin had lost its pink.

Adi grinned. "I see that." She touched his arm. "You need to give up on hearing those words. They will come when she's ready. For now, take the rest as a gift. Accept that as her love. If you can't, you may destroy what you have. You have to make her feel secure, and if you are waiting for something that may not come anytime soon, she will feel it and will be even more uneasy. Someone has to give first, and I think it must be you."

CHAPTER 16

"J OSIAH, CLIMB DOWN OFF THAT rock. I don't want you to fall." Arisha shuddered at the thought of her nephew's injured body.

"Imma lets me climb it."

"Then when your imma is here, you can climb it, but not when I am. Come down, please. It makes me nervous."

Josiah made a face. "Aunt Arisha ..."

For a moment, Arisha thought about backing down. She changed her mind, straightened her back. "Josiah, if you can't follow my instructions, I will have to leave you behind next time."

Josiah groaned. "All right. I'll come down."

"Thank you."

Adira, clutching a handful of flowers, laughed.

Josiah halted his descent. "Tell her to stop laughing."

"Adira, don't laugh at your brother."

Adira rolled her eyes.

Arisha needed a distraction, or this would escalate into a quarrel, quickly. "Why don't you see who can find the most dotted bugs?"

"*I* will!" Josiah jumped the rest of the way down.

"No, you won't! You stomp around and make too much noise!" Adira dropped her flowers and rushed for a patch of tall weeds.

Josiah followed her. "This is my spot!"

"Too late! I got here first."

Arisha rose to separate the pair, but Josiah left his sister for another area. Sometimes these two were more than she could handle. At least they were laughing again. Despite the occasional spat, she'd come to love her afternoons with the children at the river. Maybe one day, perhaps next spring, she'd have her own baby with her ....

"You must be Arisha."

Arisha looked over her shoulder to see a young woman. Arisha's gaze skimmed her form, sandals to light brown hair. She was everything Arisha wasn't: tall, beautiful, confident. Her tunic accented her perfect curves, as did the deep red sash she wore low on her hips. And how long did it take to create the elaborate braids piled on top of her head? She couldn't have done it by herself.

Her throat too dry too speak, Arisha merely nodded.

The woman scoffed as she studied Arisha. "I would have thought he could do so much better. He did have me, after all. Almost."

Marah? She'd noticed her when Jacob left, but didn't know the woman clinging to Eliel was Marah.

Arisha swallowed, licked her lips. "Do you need something from me?"

"No, I just wanted to see who he finally settled for. I'd heard about you, but I couldn't quite believe it. I had to see for myself."

Settled for?

"Of course you know whom I will marry, don't you? Someone far better than Zadok. As I deserve."

Arisha nodded again. "Eliel." She wasn't sure exactly what it was Marah deserved, but Zadok certainly didn't deserve this sarcastic, insulting woman.

Marah neared her. "And why are you frowning? You have no right to look down on me. You must know he is only with you because my abba realized Zadok could never be the man I need. I found someone better. And all he was left was ... someone like you." Marah scowled. "A *Canaanite*." She spat out the word.

Adira padded up to Arisha, placing her hand on Arisha's shoulder. "Why is she here?" she whispered.

Arisha stood slowly. "Yes, I am a Canaanite, but I am a worshipper of Yahweh." Arisha's breath came faster and faster. She tried to slow it, to no avail. "And I at least know how to treat all people with respect. I have done nothing to you, and yet you come here and insult me, in front of children who also have done nothing to you. So I want you to turn around and leave us alone."

Marah opened her mouth as if to offer a retort, but instead huffed and stormed off.

Arisha dropped to the sand. The little girl wrapped her little arms around Arisha and held tight. She shushed Arisha and started to rock gently. Like Zivah must do when Adira was upset.

Arisha squeezed her eyes tight. She mustn't let the children see her cry. Gathering her composure, she pulled back from Adira and forced a smile. "Thank you, habibti. I needed a hug. I'm all right, now."

Adira eyed her, but seemed satisfied enough to return to her bug hunt.

Arisha pulled her knees up to her chest and crossed her arms over them, then laid her head down. *"A Canaanite."* Marah's words echoed in her heart. She shoved them down, but the thoughts threatened to push their way back into her mind. She needed something to take her mind off them. "Who has the most dotted bugs? Bring them here, and let's see who won."

Josiah and Adira scrambled toward Arisha, then fell to their knees at her feet, laughing.

"Who's first?"

"Me, me!" Adira slowly opened her hands.

"One, two, three, four ..." Arisha pointed to each bug as she counted, until she reached twelve.

"Now me."

She repeated the process with Josiah and counted sixteen insects.

Adira's lips quivered, and a tear rolled down her cheek.

"Wait, Adira. Here." Josiah placed three bugs on her thumb. "Now you have fifteen. That means you won. See?"

Her face brightened, and she kissed Josiah's cheek. "Thank you!"

"Let's let them fly again, all right?" Josiah opened his hands, and chuckled as the insects flew away.

Adira followed his lead, giggling as she watched the little bugs spread their wings and disappear. "Let's find some more!" She grabbed his hands and they ran back to the weeds.

Arisha chuckled as she shook her head. Arguing one moment, laughing the next.

"Having fun?" Zadok sat beside her, slipping his arm around her shoulder.

Arisha looked at the man beside her.

Did she want to know if he saw her the same way Marah did, or should she just forget about it all?

He tucked a strand of hair behind her ear, traced the edge of her jaw with his finger, sending bolts of heats down her spine.

Oh yes, she did want to know. Had to know. Did he mean what he said every morning?

Or was she just ... someone he settled for?

~

ZADOK'S STOMACH GROWLED AS HE jogged toward their tent. If Benaiah took better care of his animals, came to the pasture more than once every ten days or so instead of letting his goats fend for themselves, maybe they wouldn't always be wandering into Zadok's flock, picking fights with his rams, annoying the lambs. And maybe one of them wouldn't have stolen the food Arisha had packed for him while he was tending to a cut yet another had given one of the younger sheep.

Now on top of missing the midday meal, he was late for the evening meal. He needed food and his belly was letting him know it. The smell of manna cooking over thousands of campfires wasn't helping, either, making his mouth water.

He slowed as he reached home, but Arisha wasn't outside. The dishes were washed and stacked by the tent. A plate of manna, a cloth tossed over it, was set beside them. He picked it up and stepped inside.

Arisha sat on a cushion staring at the wall and rubbing the scar on her palm. She'd been doing that a lot the last couple days. His heart hurt just watching her. Something was bothering her, but he had no idea what. It was time he found out.

He stepped closer. "Arisha?"

She looked up, quickly placing a sweet smile on her face. "I'm sorry. I didn't hear you come in. Please sit. I'll get your food." She rose onto her knees and reached for the plate.

He held it out of her reach.

"Not until you tell me what going on."

She sat back. "What do you mean?"

"Why have you been so quiet the last few days? You've hardly said two words. Have I done something to hurt you? Upset you?"

"Of course not!"

"Then what?

"It's nothing." She looked down, studying her scar again.

"Arisha," he whispered. "I know you better than that."

Her head shot up, eyes widened.

He knelt before her and set the food down, then reached for her hand. "I know you better than you think. Now what happened?"

"Marah came to see me the other day."

Cold fingers wrapped around his heart and squeezed. "What?"

"Marah came to visit me."

He clenched his jaw. "Where? When?"

"At the river."

"At the river?" He thought a moment. "Were the children with you?"

"Yes."

"Did they see her?"

"Yes. I think Adira recognized her."

"Why do you say that?"

"She asked me why she was there."

"What did she say to you?"

"Nothing really. It doesn't matter." She rubbed her scar again.

He pulled her hands apart. "It does. It's obviously upset you. What did she say?"

"She said she wanted to see who you ended up with ... after she left you."

"Anything else?" He fought to concentrate on her words over the blood pounding in his ears.

"She wanted to see who you ... settled for. That all you were left with was someone like me ... a Canaanite."

Zadok took several deep breaths to calm himself before he spoke. Right now he wanted to find Marah and choke her. She could say whatever she wanted to about him, but saying anything about Arisha was going much too far.

"Arisha, I am so sorry. She had no right to come to you, and no right to say any of those things." He took her face in his hands. "And if you have any doubt whatsoever, I did not settle for you. You are worth more than she could ever hope to be. She is nothing but an illusion, outward false beauty, while you are true beauty that goes beyond the surface. And no matter how we came to know each other, or to be married, I thank Yahweh for you every day, and I love you more than I could possibly explain to you. First thing tomorrow I'll go to her and tell her to leave you alone."

"No!" She grabbed his tunic.

"No?"

"No. If she is as shallow as you say, she won't understand, or believe you. It will only make her angry and cause her to say even more hurtful things."

Zadok laughed softly. "And you are as wise as you are lovely.

Come here." He sat up, then reached for her and pulled her to his chest. "You know I love you, don't you?"

She nodded. Wrapping her arms around his waist, she kissed him. She tasted of mint and honey, and she kissed him slowly, her hands roaming his back.

His stomach was empty, but right now a far deeper hunger was being satisfied. He longed to be assured she loved him, and as her kisses became more intense, as her embrace became tighter, as she gently laid him down on the sleeping mat, he knew. At least for tonight.

Manna could wait.

~

13th day of Tammuz
Summer Solstice

*A*NOTHER FEAST, ANOTHER NIGHT OF obligation. The full moon shined her blessing on the city, lighting the streets and the temple's courtyards. The Feast of the Gracious Gods—the twins Shahar and Shalim—was in full swing. Twin sons of Il, one long ago became the morning star and the other the evening star. At least that's what the Canaanites thought. Danel knew Yahweh created everything, but he couldn't let anyone know that.

He wandered through the area around the courtyard long enough to be seen by the priests. Unlike last time, the food was available to everyone and not just the gods. Perhaps if he stayed away from the consort houses, he could keep something down. His stomach rumbled, his mouth watered ... he passed a table full of fruit and reached for a fat, ripe peach. With the first bite the sweet juice filled his mouth. He quickly finished the whole fruit, and grabbed a couple apricots to eat on the way home. He hadn't gone very far when he noticed Lukii just ahead. He quickened his step to catch up with him.

Determined not to make the same mistake as last time, he grasped Lukii's shoulder. "Lukii, talking a break from guard duty?"

Lukii halted and quickly glanced around. "Uh, y- yes. I- I just left Aqhat, as a matter of fact."

"There are quite a few more people here this time, no? Of course this is the most important feast of the summer."

Lukii nodded, but said nothing. He continued to look around as they walked. Maybe a habit left over from guard duty, since his shift had just ended.

"How is your wife?" Danel offered Lukii an apricot.

His face darkened. "She's still very discouraged about not having a baby." Lukii twisted the stem of the orangey-pink fruit. "I don't know what else to do for her."

Danel touched his arm. "I'm so sorry. I don't know either. I can only pray for you both. I know that's a hard thing to bear. We waited a long time for Shiba. And then she was our only child. Our trust in Yahweh was our only solace."

Lukii nodded, but said nothing.

They passed a hastily erected stall roasting meat. Vendors set up all over town during the feast, selling everything from food to jewelry to idols, hoping to attract worshippers. Danel breathed deeply. "That smells delicious. Have you eaten? I haven't, except for this peach. Would you like some?" He turned abruptly toward the vendor.

"No, that's—" Lukii shook his head, but Danel ignored him.

"Nonsense. I won't hear of it. Please let me buy your meal, as an apology for the way I treated you last time."

"I really should get back ..."

He held up a hand, as if to stop him. "No. You must eat with me. I usually don't eat at these feasts, but for some reason I am now exceptionally hungry. Perhaps because I have someone to eat with."

Lukii looked around, shifted from one foot to the other.

Danel turned back to the vendor, a man about his age with a well-worn tunic, stringy hair falling over his eyes, and a young boy assisting him. "Two plates, please."

The pudgy man smiled at the order, several rotting teeth peeking from behind thin lips. He piled steaming hot roast beef onto two pottery plates, added two rounds of bread to each, and handed them to Danel.

Danel held up a finger. "One moment. He reached into the bag tied onto his belt and pulled out four coins, then handed them to the man. "Thank you."

The man examined the payment, and the boy held out a handful of smaller coins.

Danel shook his head. "It's yours."

The child smiled, almost laughing. "Thank you."

"You're welcome." Danel picked up the plates and looked to the spot where they had stood moments ago. No Lukii. He glanced around. Did Lukii leave, after Danel had bought his meal? No, there he was. He had moved to a shady spot off the main path, under a tree. Almost behind it.

Danel handed him a plate, chuckling. "I thought you were playing the child's hiding game for a moment there."

Lukii laughed weakly. He stuffed his food in his mouth.

"Slow down. Are you in a rush?"

"Umm, my wife is waiting for me."

"A few moments more or less won't matter. You'll get a stomachache if you keep eating that fast."

Lukii slowed, but not by much.

"This is very good. The meat is so tender. They must have cooked it very slowly all day."

Lukii nodded.

Danel bit into his bread. Still warm. Either he was very hungry, or the food was extra good.

"Lukii! There you are. I've been looking all over for you!"

Danel jerked his head up, searched for the voice calling Lukii. A female voice. When he found it, his heart sank.

A young girl with a deep purple sash sauntered up to Lukii, a soldier's cloak in her hand. "You forgot this when you left my room. Your head must have been elsewhere." She wiggled her brows at him. "Who's your friend?" She tilted her head at Danel. "I don't think I've ever seen him at feast before."

"*You* never will, either." Lukii took his cloak. "Thanks for bringing me this."

"Don't wait so long next time." She batted her lashes at him, then spun and sashayed away.

"Lukii?"

Lukii closed his eyes.

"Lukii, who was that?"

The soldier remained silent.

"Was that what I think it was?"

Lukii raised his gaze. "I had to. I just had to. My wife, she's so very distraught. I didn't know what else to do."

"But visiting a prostitute?"

"They promise fertility! My wife begged me to. I didn't have a choice!"

"You always have a choice." Danel fought to keep from raising his voice.

"That's easy for you to say. You have a child. Grandchildren. Lots of coin. The king's ear. What do I have? Nothing. I am tired of nothing, and I will do whatever I have to change that!" He threw his plate to the ground, shattering it, and stalked off.

Whatever I have to? What did that mean?

Lukii knew their secret. And he could reveal it. He could destroy Danel. And Yasha, and Aqhat …

Danel's stomach churned and his throat constricted. The meat he'd just swallowed climbed back up his throat. He ducked behind the tree just in time.

CHAPTER 17

UST KICKING UP IN THE east sent a wave of tension through the tribes on the east side of camp. They were used to traders' caravans far to the northwest, but to the east?

"It's the mission to Bozrah. They've returned!" Farther down the row, a young boy ran between the tents shouting.

As word spread, mothers and wives gathered on the sand beyond the edge of camp to welcome their men home. Six days was a long time, for a first mission at least. Once in Canaan, the battles would be far longer, but as of yet no one was used to anything except for drills that lasted only a day. Every man was safely in his tent by nightfall.

Zadok carried Adira, walking beside Zivah and Josiah.

"Do you think they'll all be back?"

Zadok was unaccustomed to seeing worry in his sister's eyes. She was always so strong, so bold. "Of course. This was only a trip to ask permission. If the king said no, they were to return, not start a war with them." He wrapped his arm around her. "He'll be back. Don't worry."

She smiled weakly.

The company of weary soldiers grew closer. Once individual

figures became distinguishable, children and women rushed to greet their loved ones.

Adira squirmed out of Zadok's arms and hopped to the ground, chasing after Josiah. "Abba! Abba!"

Zivah waited quietly.

"You're not going to him?"

"I won't get anywhere near him until the children have finished." She laughed.

In just a few moments, Jacob trudged near. Disheveled and sweaty, he set Adira on the sand and reached for Zivah, who nearly fell into his embrace.

When he released her, he placed a kiss on her cheek and stepped back, one arm still at her waist.

"You look horrible." Zadok chuckled as he took Jacob's pack from him. "Nice and pink."

"Thanks." Jacob grinned. "Six days in full sun will do that."

"I think he looks wonderful." Zivah laid her head on his shoulder, and Jacob kissed her temple.

"What did they say?" Zadok asked.

Jacob shook his head. "It did not go well. At all. It was ... bad. You can talk to Joshua." He looked over his shoulder at the older man striding into camp behind him. "I'm going home." He steered Zivah away from Zadok and lumbered on, his children skipping beside them.

Joshua was surrounded by men from camp, including leaders from each tribe, seeking information from the mission. He raised a hand for attention. "The king of Edom has refused to grant us permission to cross his land."

Loud grumbling and shouts of disbelief shot up from the still-gathering crowd.

Joshua held up his hand again. "We will have to go south, around the Arabah, to avoid crossing their land. It will take much longer, but it is our only choice."

More angry cries, louder than before. Some of the men suggested using force against their distant cousins.

"Right now, we need you to encourage your people, not stir them up." Joshua spoke over the voices raised in dissension. "We will have enough battles to fight in Canaan. We don't need any with Edom, and we certainly don't need any in camp. Yahweh will tell us when we are to go forward." He looked toward the sky. "We move when the cloud moves."

The crowd dissolved, leaving Joshua alone with his grandsons.

Eliel noticed Marah waiting and bolted for her.

Moses appeared at Zadok's side. "Another delay. But after forty years, a week or two is not so bad." He grinned.

Zadok folded his arms and looked out toward Edom.

"You wish you could have gone."

It was a statement, not a question.

"I do. I should have."

Moses's brows quirked. "Why? To prove to everyone you are not a coward?"

"Just to do my part. That is our whole purpose, to take the land we have been given."

"True, but that is not *your* only purpose. We all have many tasks given to us by Yahweh. And right now, you have one that is more important."

"I know, the sheep." Zadok refrained from sighing audibly.

"I was thinking of something a little more important than that."

He blinked. "Arisha?" How could his wife be a *task?*

"Miriam asked you to marry her, to care for her, so Yahweh could heal her heart. She believed, as do I, that was Yahweh's will for you. So for this time, right now, that is what you focus on, taking care of *her*. Perhaps the sheep were only to prepare you for that. To give you the gentle heart you needed."

Once again, Moses's words had turned his thinking upside-down.

"And don't worry about fighting for Israel. Now is not your time, but your time will come soon enough."

～

19th day of Tammuz

*D*ANEL CLOSED THE HEAVY wooden door behind him as he eased into Aqhat's office. "How are you today?"

Aqhat looked up briefly from his position along the side wall. Leaning on his fists, he studied several parchments spread out across a long table. "Hungry. I hate fast days."

Danel chuckled. "Well, Baal's dying. You can't possibly eat. It would be disrespectful."

Aqhat grunted. "No, disrespectful is a stone idol making me go hungry all day. I thought about finding some bread in the kitchen last night to hide in here. But they'd already thrown it all out. Perfectly good food, wasted. I hate that."

"You should be used to it by now."

"It's so pointless. The rains will return whether or not we mourn him enough to bring him back." He returned to his parchments.

"You've got almost three more weeks of this. Better save your frustration. Besides, you can eat as soon as the sun goes down."

Sobering, Danel pulled a chair from the corner to face Aqhat and lowered himself onto it. He cleared his throat. "I have bad news. Last week at the festival, I saw Lukii. I believe he had already completed his guard duty."

Aqhat pulled himself up to his full height. He frowned, remembering that day as he walked toward his desk. "Yes. He seemed to be quite preoccupied that day. How was he when you saw him?"

Danel sucked in a deep breath, rubbed his hand over his face. "That's what I wanted to talk to you about. When I saw him, he had just left one of the priestesses."

Aqhat dropped into his chair. "No ..."

Danel nodded wearily.

"And you saw him?"

"I was there when she brought him his cloak. He'd left it in her room."

"So he *knows* you saw him."

"Yes."

Aqhat shook his head. "What do you think he'll do?"

"I don't know. It's been almost a week, and no one has said anything so far, but ..."

"What did you say to him?"

"I didn't raise my voice, tried to be understanding. He said his wife was beside herself with grief over not having a baby, and begged him to go." Danel thought back to his own struggle. He could still remember the indescribable pain, relive the driving force that seemed to define their existence, recall the numberless nights Yasha cried herself to sleep. "She's desperate, perhaps not thinking clearly."

Aqhat sighed. "He's learned nothing." An awkward silence filled the room. "What do we do if he goes to the king?" When he faced Danel again, his eyes were filled with worry, maybe even fear. It was a look Danel had never seen on Aqhat, not even when he was facing his fiercest battles.

Aqhat knew the answer. It was clear he needed to hear Danel say it.

Yahweh, help us. Danel rose. "You will do whatever the king tells you to do, without revealing yourself. If he tells you to arrest me, you'll do it. You'll put me in a cell, you'll put me in *that* cell, you'll execute me if ordered to. But unless Lukii does, you will not reveal your faith because Yasha and Zibqet, and the children, not to mention the other believers, will need you. Then more than ever."

The muscle in Aqhat's jaw jumped. He swallowed as if he'd eaten a piece of leather, and finally managed a nod. Standing, then rounding the desk, he grabbed Danel in a strong embrace. "You are the best friend I have ever had." His voice was husky with emotion. When he released Danel, his face was again like stone.

Danel grabbed his shoulder. "We've been in this together ever since we helped Kamose escape. We've always known it would come to this point, sooner or later. Frankly, I'm surprised we both made it all forty years."

"Almost."

Danel grinned. "Almost."

"Let's not talk like it's over yet, yes?"

"All right. We'll just wait, and see what happens."

"And pray. Hard."

Danel walked down the hallway and up the stairs to his work-room, concentrating on, counting each step he took. He passed three soldiers and two kitchen workers, each of whom greeted him, but Danel barely noticed them and did not reply. He simply kept putting one foot in front of the other, counting. Right, left, right, left. Twenty-three, twenty-four. Right, left, right, left ... Ninety-eight, ninety-nine ...

He reached his room and pulled the key from the folds of his belt. His hand shook as he attempted to fit it into the slot. The metal bounced against the edges, clanging and banging. *Settle down, Danel.* Someone might hear and ask him what was wrong. He took a deep breath, tried once more, unlocked his door, entered, closed it behind him, and collapsed.

He had made it sound so easy to Aqhat. *Arrest me. Put me in a cell. Put me in* that *cell.* The cell where the worst prisoners were held, where Kamose was held for over a month, where he would have died had not Danel and Aqhat helped him. Danel was probably about the same age Kamose was when he was held there, but he was not nearly as strong. Kamose was a professional soldier, like Aqhat. Not a glorified manager. Danel would never last.

But Aqhat would do it. Not only because he was a good officer who would do as he was told, but because his life depended on it, and the lives of their families, and other followers of Yahweh.

And now those lives hung in the balance, because Lukii knew everyone, and if he wanted to, he could betray them all.

~

28th day of Tammuz

*A*RISHA POURED WATER INTO A pot and placed it carefully on the rocks. She poked at the embers and leaned down, her ear next to the ground, to blow on the red-gray pieces of wood. Gentle whooshes and a few strategic pokes brought the flames back to life, and she sat back on her heels. She grabbed the manna pot next to the fire and shook it. Same as every other day—just enough left for one meal for two people. She smiled. Zadok would be home soon, and they would share the evening meal. He would tell her everything that had happened at the pasture since she had seen him at midday, and she would tell him every outrageous thing Josiah said and every adorable thing Adira did at the river this afternoon. They would marvel at the colors of the sunset and go to sleep. It was exactly the same every night.

And she loved every minute of it. Craved it.

Bubbles appeared around the edges of the water. She reached for the jar and removed the lid. As she tipped it to dump out the manna, a loud sound rent the air. Her ears shut out everything else as the ram's horn blasts resounded throughout the camp. Her stomach clenched.

An assembly. One ... two ... Two long blasts of the ram's horn meant only the leaders. She closed her eyes. *Please no...* One more loud burst of noise made its way through the camp and snaked down her body. Three blasts of the shofar called everyone. The last time all Israel had gathered was to bury Miriam.

She took a deep, slow breath. Nothing could be worse than that. Right?

She sat by the fire, jar still in hand, unable to move, staring, unseeing. What now?

Adi strolled up, a pouting Adira in hand. Zivah followed close behind, scolding Josiah for teasing his sister. "Are you going to the assembly?" Adi tilted her head, studying the boiling water, and the pot of manna in Arisha's hand.

Arisha's gaze darted left and right. She glanced behind her. No Zadok. He was still with his sheep.

His stupid sheep. Now, when she needed him.

Her cheeks heated. That wasn't fair to Zadok. How could he have possibly known Moses would call everyone to assembly? She reached to set aside the water and put away the manna. She tossed sand over the fire. Maybe Adi wouldn't notice her reddened face.

At least she wasn't alone—she had Adi and Zivah. And maybe it was for the best. If Zadok were here he would surely see her unrest, but the children would help her conceal it. Their constant chattering and meandering would draw the women's attention, allow her to hide her unreasonable fears. Her sudden cherished memories of Miriam. Ridiculous imaginings of what could come next.

She followed silently as they strolled through Judah and Issachar, past the big spring, then angled toward the empty expanse outside camp, north of the tents of Dan and Naphtali. After finding a spot where they could see Moses, they waited for the crowd to settle. Arisha stood behind the others, her heart pounding in her ears. She fisted her hands to keep from rubbing her scar. Change was almost never good. This probably wouldn't be good, either.

Moses ascended a small rise. The low hills around them made a perfect amphitheater, allowing his voice to carry to everyone. He raised his hands, waited for absolute quiet. The silence fell on Arisha like a weight, threatening to choke off her air. He just stood there. Why wouldn't he speak?

She opened her mouth, tried to draw in a breath, but her lungs would not expand. Her hands went to her chest, clawing at her tunic, at the air around her.

Zivah turned and frowned, but before she could say anything, Moses began.

"Yahweh has spoken ..."

Arisha tried to ignore the pounding in her head. But then Moses delivered Yahweh's message, and her world collapsed.

~

*A*RISHA STOOD ALONE ON THE expanse of sand north of camp. The setting sun threw long, misshapen shadows across the sand in the distance. The ominous gray shapes crawling over and around the mounds of earth emphasized their uneven contours, making them appear even more formidable. After Moses had spoken, everyone else had returned to their tents for the evening meal, hearts as light as the manna that fell around them each day.

Not Arisha. Her chest felt like a band encircled it and squeezed tight. Her vision blurred and her body was unbelievably heavy. She couldn't move. An Egyptian owl flew over her head. His wings made no sound, but his baleful screech burrowed into her ears, making her wince.

Tear down her home? That's what Moses wanted? Just when she was finally getting comfortable, finally trusting her world could be like everyone else's, it was being ripped apart again.

"Arisha?"

She heard her name but couldn't respond. She opened her mouth but no words would come. She closed her eyes and wrapped her arms tighter around herself against the cooling evening air.

"Arisha?" The voice was closer this time. She forced her eyes open. Zadok stood before her, his hands on her cheeks. When had that happened? She hadn't heard him approach, hadn't felt him touch her.

"It's getting dark. Are you all right? Are you hurt?" His gaze searched her face, traveled down her body, then his ebony eyes locked on hers again. "What's wrong? Have you been standing here since Moses left? Imma told me you said you'd be right behind her, but you never came. I checked the river, the big spring—I was so worried." He ran his hands up and down her arms, studied her from head to sandals again. "I called you several times but you didn't answer."

His furrowed brow and darkened eyes touched her heart. How did she explain this to him? The beginning of the end—what everyone else had waited for, longed for, prayed for, instead brought her agony. Hot tears filled her eyes against her will. She blinked them back.

He didn't push for an explanation. He just waited, as he always did, until she was ready. How did he put up with her, falling apart again and again?

His soft embrace soothed her, gave her strength. After several moments she lifted her head. "I can't stand the thought of tearing down our home." She sniffled, then laughed softly. "I guess that sounds pretty silly."

He wiped away her tears with the pads of his thumbs. "Of course not." He smiled, without a hint of condescension. "But you have to remember, we are only taking it down so we can move it. We're not going very far, and we're not taking it down for good."

"But *why*? Why are we moving? He didn't say. It's not time yet. You said so."

Zadok shrugged. "I don't know. But it's very close to forty years. All the first generation has died. Maybe we are going to move closer to Canaan, a little at a time. Only a day's journey."

She nodded. "I know. It's just that I finally had a home that I thought would be mine forever. I mean, you said we'd have to leave eventually, but I ... well, I don't know why it bothers me so much."

He thought for a moment. "I believe you have to think of home not as a *place*, but a *person*. Or people."

She frowned. "I don't understand."

"Well, whether it's that tent, or another tent, or a house we build in Canaan, I will always be there. We will make a home together—with lots of babies"—he wiggled a brow at her—"and it doesn't matter what kind of house it is."

"Do you promise?"

"If Yahweh allows it, yes."

She scrunched up her mouth. "If Yahweh allows it."

"Yes. I won't make a promise I can't keep. Yahweh is in control of our lives. But if it is in *my* power, I will always be with you."

"I guess that's as good as I can get." She nodded and dropped her forehead against his chest, wrapping her arms around his waist.

He lowered his head so his mouth was next to her ear. "Come on." His voice was low, and his breath was warm on her neck. "We have one more night in our home here."

She giggled, and his chest rumbled when he laughed in response.

Maybe "as good as she could get" would be enough.

CHAPTER 18

1st day of Av

ZADOK STRETCHED OUT HIS STAFF and gently prodded a straggling lamb to keep up with the others. The flock baaa'd and complained and generally made their dissatisfaction known as the tribes marched northeast headed for who knew where. Well, Moses knew where. Maybe Joshua. Maybe Aaron. No one else.

The day had begun almost before the sun rose, but packing up hadn't taken nearly as long as Zadok had imagined. In a very short time, men packed tents, women cooked a day's worth of manna, and the Levites had the tabernacle disassembled and ready to go.

With each man carrying his assigned piece of the tabernacle and its furnishings, the Levites led the way, followed by the clans of Judah, Issachar and Zebulon. Reuben, Simeon and Gad came next, then Ephraim, Manasseh and Benjamin. Dan, Asher and Naphtali brought up the rear.

Trailing the rest of Judah's tribe with the Tabernacle's sheep, Zadok grasped Arisha's hand and entwined his fingers with hers. She lay her head against his shoulder for a brief moment, then looked up and smiled. She'd barely spoken all day, but hadn't complained either. He'd made sure to remain close, even taken her with him to help gather the sheep for the journey.

He shifted the coarse linen pack on his back. The Egyptian army tent folded into its own pack and was light enough to carry. The tent's weight wasn't an issue, but when another pack—with clothes, pots, sleeping mats, and the rest of their belongings, meager though they were—was added, it dug into his shoulder blades.

He glanced above at Yahweh's cloud. It stretched out before them, a hint of flame swaddled in puffy white. It had grown, spread overnight, and was now just the right shape and size to cover the marching tribes. It went before them, carving out a path in the endless sea of sand.

Zadok reached into the bag at his side and pulled out two manna cakes, offering one to Arisha.

"How much farther?" She nibbled on the cake.

Zadok shrugged, his mouth full. He chewed and swallowed. "We stop when the cloud stops." He pointed at the sun, halfway between its zenith and the tops of the mountains in the west. "But I doubt it's much longer. We need enough light to set up camp."

As if Moses—or Yahweh—heard him, a ram's horn sounded once. The procession of people, sheep, and goats slowly halted. Ahead of them, too far ahead to be seen, the Levites would mark off the area of the tabernacle, around which the tribes would make camp.

Josiah tugged at Zadok's sleeve. "Can we watch them set up the tabernacle?"

"I have to set up the tent, and find a place for the sheep away from camp, but maybe Aunt Arisha will go with you." He raised a brow.

"Alone?" Her breath caught.

"You won't be alone. I'll be with you. And Adira." Josiah's wide eyes said he truly could not understand why she would hesitate.

Zadok reached for her arm. "Arisha, you don't ha—"

She squared her shoulders, pursed her lips. "It's all right. We can go."

There really was no one else. Jacob and Abba had tents to erect. Zivah and Imma would get them ready for occupancy. But still— "You sure?"

She nodded, but he wasn't certain she meant it until she laughed—a little—as she picked up Adira and they scampered off.

*T*HE FIRST MORNING AT THEIR NEW camp at the base of Mount Hor, Zadok rose early and slipped quietly from their tent. At Imma and Abba's fire, he was surprised to see Joshua with them.

"Joshua, it's been a long time. What are you doing here so early in the morning?"

"I just got here. I wanted to see your abba. How is your new bride?"

Zadok sighed as he sat next to him. "The move was hard on her. She's still sleeping."

Joshua raised a brow as he poked at the fire. "Oh? I thought we moved at a nice pace for everyone."

"It wasn't the journey. It was the moving. Period. She thought she'd finally found a home, and somehow moving means she might lose it ... She tried to explain it to me, but I can't really understand it."

Joshua laughed. "Never try to understand women. You will not accomplish that task."

Imma smacked Joshua on the shoulder.

Zadok laughed as Joshua rubbed his upper arm. "I understand enough, I think. Miriam said she needs to feel safe. I tried to stay close yesterday. Probably will today, too."

"Good plan." Abba poured hot water into four cups. "What's on your mind, Joshua?"

Joshua rubbed his hand down his beard. "Moses and Aaron and Eleazar left for Mount Hor before sunrise."

Zadok twisted to see the soaring mountain behind them. He turned back to Joshua and pointed his thumb over his shoulder. "That mountain? Why?"

Joshua shook his head. "Said they were going to climb it."

"*That* mountain?" he repeated.

"Yes. And yes, at their age, before you ask."

"Why?" asked Abba.

"They wouldn't say."

"Not even to you?"

Joshua shook his head.

Zadok sipped his tea. This was unusual, but then many of the things Moses did were unusual.

Though what reason they could possibly have for climbing a mountain, he couldn't imagine.

～

"*I*SHAT!" DANEL KISSED THE GIRL on the cheek as he entered the kitchen. Hot air washed over him, carrying the scent of spiced meats and vegetables.

"Danel, don't bother her." Sisa laughed as she passed him, a huge plate of roasted lamb in her hands.

He laughed with her. "I'm only saying good morning."

"You're distracting her."

"Is his food ready?"

"On the table. Mepac!" She shouted for her husband.

"Do you think she yells at him like that at home?" Danel whispered loudly enough for Sisa to hear.

Ishat giggled.

One of the king's personal servants entered and handed Danel a note on rolled parchment, with Danel's name and the king's seal prominently displayed. He frowned. Why would Keret call for him with a royal summons? The king knew he'd arrive with his meal in a few moments.

Then a sickening realization hit him.

The normal sounds of the kitchen disappeared. No sloshing water, no pottery clanking, no gold or silver plinking. Danel looked up. Sisa waited, watching, along with a few others. Ishat chewed her nails, her eyes wide.

He broke the seal, read the note. Felt the blood drain from his face. He turned to answer the servant but he was gone. Danel swallowed and cleared his throat. "Sisa, keep the food warm. Someone will be back for it."

"Someone?" Ishat's voice wavered.

"Maybe me." Danel pasted a smile on his face and stepped toward her. He gave Ishat a kiss and Sisa a quick hug, then spun on his heel and headed for the throne room.

What he had feared for weeks had happened. Why? What had prompted it now? And how much had Lukii told?

Instead of ascending the dais to Keret's side, he stepped to the center of the room and knelt.

"Danel, rise." The king's voice thundered throughout the room.

He stood, kept his head bowed. His breath was shallow, his hands clammy.

"Come closer." This time Keret's voice was as it always was, as if Danel were his closest friend. Which, in many ways, he was.

Danel took several steps toward the throne without raising his head. He worked hard to keep his breathing regular.

The king's robes rustled as he stood and descended the dais. His sandals appeared in Danel's field of vision. "Danel, look at me."

Danel breathed in slowly, then looked up.

"Is it true?"

Danel intended to reveal only what he had to. "Is what true?"

"By the gods, Danel!" The king stalked away several steps, then returned. He folded his arms over his chest. "Do you worship Yahweh, but refuse to honor Baal?" No mention of Aqhat or anyone else.

"It is true."

The king studied his feet for several moments. When he looked up, he shook his head. "Danel, I could have forgiven you almost anything. You must know that. I would not be the king I am without you." He paused. "But I cannot forgive this. The God of the Israelites? If you had only added Yahweh but not forsaken Baal, even that I would have allowed, at least for you!" He stormed away again, staring at nothing for several long moments.

Would it be a lashing? Prison? Death? Danel's head swam with possibilities, none of them good. His throat tightened. He locked his knees to keep from collapsing. *Yahweh, help me.*

Keret returned. He stared at Danel for what felt like an eternity. "Let me ask you something."

Danel vision blurred. His chest refused to do its work. *Don't ask about any others. Please, Yahweh, don't let him ask about anyone else. I beg you.*

"What would you do in my place?"

Danel nearly lost all the air in his lungs when he started breathing again, but he couldn't let the king see his utter relief. But what to say? Should he send himself to prison? He couldn't suggest the king do nothing. That would be absurd. He dipped his head. "My king, I am not nearly as wise as you are and I could not possibly make such an important decision."

Keret laughed out loud. "Ever the gracious servant, Danel, even when your life is in danger." The laugh disappeared as soon as it came. "I cannot kill you, Danel. But until I decide what to do, I must lock you up."

But where?

Keret flipped his robe behind him and returned to his throne. Grabbing his scepter, he sat. He rapped the symbol of his office three times on the floor. A servant hustled in. Keret whispered to him, and he scurried out.

"The worst part is I have no one nearly as competent as you to take your place." Keret frowned.

That's the worst part?

After but a moment, Aqhat entered the room. He walked to the center and knelt.

"Rise."

The soldier obeyed.

"Take this man to a cell ... no, take him to a holding room and lock him in. For now."

"It will be done." Aqhat bowed and approached Danel. He grasped Danel's bicep and led him to the main entry of the throne room and down a hall. Neither of them spoke until they reached a hallway on the east side of the palace against the outer city wall. Aqhat accepted a large ring of keys from a servant, dismissed him, and unlocked the door. He opened it, and Danel entered first.

The room was small and windowless, with only a mat on the floor and a pot in the corner. Danel shrugged. It could be so much worse. "At least it's not a prison cell." Danel turned to his friend. "Do you know what happened?"

"Lukii was on guard duty last night in the king's hallway. Apparently he got drunk before his shift, fell asleep, and the king was going to throw *him* in prison. He traded this information for a pardon. But he lost his commission."

"He didn't mention anyone else?"

"It doesn't appear so." Aqhat surveyed the room. "Looks like you got off as easy as you could."

"For now." Danel repeated the king's last words. "He had you waiting?"

He nodded. "I've known since sunrise, wondering what he would do."

"I'm sorry. That must have been difficult."

"Not as hard as being in here."

"True."

"Well, you have friends in the kitchen, so you'll probably eat well." Aqhat tried to smile.

"You'll go talk to Yasha?"

"As soon as I am off duty."

"We knew this would come. Remind her of that. She can do this."

"She won't be alone."

"Thank you, my friend."

Aqhat left, and Danel heard the metal tumblers fall into place. He turned slowly and studied the room that would be his home.

For now.

Yahweh, help me. Help us all.

~

*Z*ADOK PULLED THE LAST BATCH of dead bushes to the pile. He eyed the pile, then the fold Reuben and Jonah were building. There should be enough bushes to complete it. Thank Yahweh sheep only needed the appearance of a fold, made of nothing more than brush. There weren't any boulders around. He grabbed one of the bushes and dragged it to where Reuben and Jonah were working.

After adding it to the end of the line, weaving its branches with the one before it to ensure it stayed in place, he slapped his hands against each other to remove the dead leaves and twigs. He closed his eyes and stretched his arms above his head. When he opened them, he saw Eliel approaching.

Odd. Why would he come all the way out here?

"Eliel. Everyone all right? Does someone need me?"

"No, ... I- I saw Arisha earlier. I just wanted to see how she was doing."

"Thank you." He picked up his staff and ambled away from Reuben and Jonah. He had no idea what Eliel really wanted, but he should give him privacy just in case.

"I also wanted to see why it is you like doing this"—he swept his hand toward the sheep—"so much."

Zadok blinked. "Being a shepherd?" All he could think of was that Eliel was now with Marah—who hated the fact that he kept sheep.

"I know Marah and her father think this is not ... that it's no longer what an Israelite should be doing. That we should be people of the land now. But my sabba speaks so highly of you, and we have always gotten along ... until now."

Zadok only nodded, unsure how to respond.

"I know Marah's sometimes abrasive, unthoughtful, and I'm sorry for what she said to you and to Arisha—"

"You know about that?"

"Marah told me. Believe it or not, later she often feels quite badly for things she's said. She's never learned to apologize, though."

Zadok smiled weakly.

"Anyway, the problem is, I think I love her."

"Well, then maybe don't give up on her."

"What?"

Zadok shrugged. "Just a thought. I'm not saying accept her behavior, but let her know how you feel. I think her she learned her attitude from her father. Maybe she's willing to change." Zadok considered the hopeful look on Eliel's face. Zadok had never felt like that when he realized what Marah was. He was devastated, humiliated, angry—but never once did he want to try to win her back. "It's worth a try, right?"

"Perhaps. I just—"

A blast from the ram's horn rent the air.

Terror gripped Zadok. His body stiffened as he waited to see whether only one or two more would follow. At the third, he started running. Looking over his shoulder. "I have to go. Arisha will panic." He raced to the tent as fast as his legs could move, leaving Eliel standing there, alone and most likely bewildered.

Arisha stood in front of their tent when he arrived, holding on tightly to Imma's arm with both hands, her eyes staring straight ahead.

Imma leaned in toward Arisha, pointing toward Zadok. He could see Arisha relax. A little.

Arisha left Imma and hurried to Zadok, grabbing his waist, placing her cheek against his chest. He held her close, feeling her relax in his arms. He caught Imma's gaze over her shoulder.

Imma smiled. "We're supposed to meet at the bottom of Mount Hor. That's all I know."

"Maybe Moses has returned." He grasped Arisha's shoulders and gently pushed her back so he could see her face, placing a finger under her chin. He brushed her lips with his. "Are you all right?"

She nodded. Barely.

He turned her so she stood next to him, his arm around her waist.

Imma flashed a bright smile and grasped Arisha's other hand. "Let's go."

Arisha slipped out of Zadok's embrace about halfway to the mount, grabbing his hand like it was her last piece of food.

At the base of Mount Hor, two figures stood on boulders, waiting to address the crowd, which hummed with speculation and gossip.

Two? Didn't Joshua say Moses, Aaron, and Eleazar climbed the mountain? Maybe he misheard. Maybe one of them descended earlier.

Moses raised his hand for quiet. "Aaron has gone to be with our ancestors. He is now with Yahweh. Eleazar is our new High Priest."

Such a simple announcement.

Such monumental repercussions.

Cries and wails filled the air. Shrieks, screams and the sound of ripped clothing surrounded them. Grief and shock settled over the crowd like a wet, woolen cloak, almost as visible as Yahweh's cloud.

Zadok's mind reeled. Aaron gone? Why hadn't Moses told everyone about this before? Why the secrecy? Why the surprise? Why—

Next to him, Arisha collapsed. He dove to catch her before she hit the sand. He gently knelt with her, one knee behind her back, her head in the crook of his arm. "Arisha!" He called softly so as not to create a scene, but his heart raced and he couldn't catch his breath. "Arisha!"

He cupped her face, shook her gently. "Arisha, wake up. Show me you're all right."

Her eyes fluttered open, caught his gaze for the briefest moment, then closed again.

Thank Yahweh.

He slipped his arm under her knees and stood, cradling her to his chest.

"Do you want me to come with you?" Imma grasped his forearm.

He shook his head. "Stay and see what's going on."

As he carried her back to camp, he began to put the pieces together. Aaron was dead. Another loss for Arisha. Miriam. Their home. Now Aaron. It was simply more than she could take at once. And he had no idea how many losses she had suffered before he met her.

He held her closer, resting his cheek on her head. *Yahweh, heal her. I don't know how to help her. I can stay close, but I can't heal her heart. Only you can do that. If there is more I can do, you have to show me.*

He stepped inside their tent, knelt before their mat, and gently laid her upon it. He slipped her cloak and sandals off, and did the same. He lay next to her and gathered her in his arms, praying over her until he, too, fell asleep.

CHAPTER 19

8th day of Av

ZADOK PUSHED ASIDE THE FLAPS and peeked outside. It promised to be a beautiful, sunny day. One that should be enjoyed, outside, with his bride.

The last seven days had been some of the most difficult of Zadok's life. The entire camp was in mourning, with no one to comfort each other. The whole point of the Shiva was that the grieving parties could simply sit, and be taken care of, visited, comforted. But when everyone is bereaved, who comforts whom?

Of necessity, the rules of the Shiva this time were a little different: people gathered their own manna as usual, since there was no one to bring meals to the mourners. There was little talking, since ordinarily only the bereaved could start a conversation. And since everyone was supposed to remain indoors, the camp was eerily quiet.

Now that the first seven days were over, the rest of the Shloshim would be more relaxed. Conversation and going outside were now allowed, but no celebrations—no weddings, no music, no exuberant joy—until the thirty days were completed.

Zadok sat back and reached for Arisha's hand. "Why don't you come with me to see the sheep?" He'd been able to go outside a few times, since the lives of the animals depended on it. He and his men had taken turns checking them and milking them. Since Arisha was not the shepherd, she, like everyone else, had remained inside for the first seven days of mourning the death of the High Priest of Israel.

Arisha had barely spoken, even to Zadok. He had to know she would recover from this latest loss. She needed to go outside, come with him.

"Arisha?"

She raised her gaze to him, blinking. "What?"

"Why don't you come with me to see the sheep?"

"Why are we mourning for Aaron for thirty days, but we didn't for Miriam?"

And there it was. The real source of her pain. "I don't know, habibti. Maybe because everyone had a chance to say goodbye to her before she died. Aaron's death was a complete surprise. Or maybe because he was the high priest. I just don't know." He shrugged. "Maybe you should ask Moses."

She nodded as she rubbed the scar on her palm.

He pulled her hand closer. "You never told me how you got that scar."

She winced.

He wrapped his arm around her shoulders. "Tell me," he whispered.

"The first family I worked for ... One night the mother wasn't around when it was time to eat, so I tried to make the fire. I got it going but when I tried to put the pot on to boil the water, I dropped it and broke it. When I picked up the pieces I cut myself. It bled so much ..."

Zadok's chest hurt. "I'm sorry."

"I got in trouble for breaking the pot."

"Wait—the first family?"

She nodded.

"You were a small child." Why would so young child be expected to handle such tasks?

She shrugged, as if she didn't understand his dismay.

His heart sank. "Why do you rub it when you're upset?"

She lifted a shoulder. "I don't know."

"I don't think it's a good idea. Doesn't it remind you of all the bad things that happened to you?"

"Sometimes."

He reached for the pendant hanging around her neck. "Maybe, from now on, when you start to rub your scar, you should rub this instead, and remember how many people love you."

She smiled. A little.

"I'm serious. You have to stop thinking about all the losses and pain and hurt, and remember the blessings Yahweh has given you now."

"I'll try."

"Good. Now come outside with me. You've been in here too long."

"I just can't yet. But I'll gather and cook the morning's manna for us."

Zadok didn't want to leave her again today, but if she came out of the tent, at least it was a start.

~

*D*ANEL PACED IN THE STUFFY room. A full bowl of stew sat next to an untouched loaf of bread and a bunch of plump, purple grapes on a wooden serving platter. He'd tried to eat. But he couldn't force the food past his throat, no matter how good it tasted, and he could tell Ishat and Sisa had tried hard to see he received the best the kitchen had to offer.

One moment he could be calm, rest in Yahweh's provision, trust that He would ensure that Danel would soon be released. He knew his family would be safe, no one would be harmed. His breathing eased, his chest no longer ached, his muscles relaxed.

Then without warning, thoughts crept into his mind unbidden. Images of torture, memories of Kamose's striped back, which soon morphed into his own wounded body, and stole the air from his lungs. Scenes of his family languishing in prison, Aqhat and Banno and the other believers betrayed and brutalized, or worse ... before he knew it his hands balled into fists, his shoulders hunched, and he could barely catch his breath.

He wrestled his mind into submission and his body into calm, praying for peace. He tried to think about what he would be doing, should be doing, were he not trapped in this room. What items would be on his agenda for today? Anything to distract him from the disturbing possibilities that lay before him.

What day was it? How many days had he been in here? Eight? No, nine. That meant the grape harvest festival would be almost over. Danel chuckled dryly. One good thing, the only good thing, about being locked in here—he was spared from witnessing yet again the most decadent of Arad's festivals. Seven days of celebrating the grape harvest. Seven nights, too, thanks to a full moon. Dancing, wine, food, music, men, women—all the ingredients necessary for an abundance of debauchery. It was traditional for this one week that the girls ask the men to marry them, and for the marriages to take place at the next feast—in one month.

Needless to say, most of them were not successful. At least he wasn't out there this year, watching so many young men and women throwing their lives away. That was his first thought two full moons ago, when he saw Lukii, which led to his being in here ... which could lead to much worse things ... and soon he was breathing hard again, trying to calm himself.

He shook out his hands and drew in long, slow breaths through his nose. Breathe in, breathe out. Breathe in, breathe out. If only he could shake the images from his mind as easily as he shook the tension from his fists.

A rap sounded at the door, shaking him from his reverie. Who would knock? Danel halted in mid-stride, his heartbeat at a standstill as well. The door was locked from the outside. He couldn't let anyone in if he wanted to. Were soldiers coming for him? Had Keret finally decided to send him down to that cell? Or worse? Was he never to see Yasha again?

He stared at the enormous, solid cedar door. Metal scraped on metal as a key slipped into the lock and tumblers fell into place, one by one. The door creaked open.

"Danel?" Aqhat's deep voice reverberated through the room.

Danel suppressed a moan as his heart started beating again and air filled his chest. "Aqhat? What are you doing here?"

Aqhat's grin lit up his face. "Nice to see you, too."

Danel lifted one shoulder. "Sorry. I thought you might be Keret's guards."

"Not a chance. Not this week, anyway. Everyone is far too busy celebrating to be thinking about you." His smile disappeared. "In fact, that's why I've come."

One corner of his mouth tipped up. "You want to celebrate with me?"

Aqhat winced. "I have some ... unfortunate news."

"News? About whom?"

Aqhat sucked in a breath before he answered. "Mika."

Mika. The name hit Danel like a kick in the belly. Aqhat would only risk a visit if he had something of great consequence to tell him. Danel squeezed his eyes shut a moment, a myriad of possibilities racing though his mind. "What?"

"Demna asked Mika to marry her last night."

He stretched out an arm and leaned against the wall, his head drooping to his chest. "And he said ...?"

"He said yes." Aqhat's usually strong voice was nearly a whisper.

Danel's stomach lurched. Mika had succumbed, completely given in to the Canaanite worship of Baal. He was so in love with this girl he'd do anything she asked.

He blinked back tears and stood tall. "Did you speak to him?"

"Only for a moment, when he told me his news. He was looking for you."

Fear gripped Danel's heart. "Did you tell him where I was?"

"No. I wasn't sure you wanted him to know." He glanced at the floor. "And I wasn't sure of what his reaction would be, either."

Danel nodded. Probably a good idea.

"Is there anything I can do for you? Anything you need? Would you like me to bring Mika to see you?"

Danel managed a quick shake of his head.

Aqhat grasped his shoulder and slipped out of the room. "I'll be back later."

Danel's heart constricted, the pain as sharp as if the knife on Aqhat's hip had sliced open his chest. He fell back against the wall, and sank to the floor, his head in his hands.

Did he not want to see his grandson because he was one step removed from prison? Or because he had no idea what he would say to him? He couldn't say. And he couldn't face him. Not yet.

He had lost Mika for good.

~

*T*HE MOON SHONE BRIGHTLY OVER the seemingly unending rows of tents as Zadok neared the edge of camp. His muscles ached and he was exhausted. Micah had been hours late. His sister had a baby and Zadok had given him permission to stay until the babe arrived, which kept Zadok up until the early hours of morning.

He glanced around as his fingers fumbled with the ties on the tent flaps. Still no one was outside, no men laughing around campfires. Only one week of mourning remained. He moved the flap aside as gently as possible, cringing at any noise. He let it fall back into place and tied the two pieces together again. Breathing out a heavy sigh, he pulled off his tunic and slipped off his sandals. He crept to the mat and knelt, then lay down next to Arisha. Slipping under the blanket, he draped his arm around her waist and tugged her close.

She moaned and snuggled closer. "Mmm, I missed you," she mumbled.

"I'm sorry. I had to ..." Never mind. She wouldn't hear him. Or care at this time of night. He kissed her forehead. "I love you."

"I love you, too."

Zadok's heart nearly stopped. Did she really just say that? He listened closely. Her breathing was regular and slow. Either she was asleep—or pretending to be. Either way, some part of her must have meant it.

And maybe regretted it?

The sun came up much too soon after his late night. He felt like he'd just fallen asleep. Giggles pushed their way into Zadok's mind. He tried to force them back out, but more followed. He opened his eyes and shut them again. It was far too bright—he must have overslept. Opening one eye, he sat up. The tent was empty. He breathed in burning wood and cooking manna. At least he hadn't missed the morning meal completely.

He opened his other eye and reached for his tunic. As he slipped it over his head he heard Arisha's voice.

"Finally awake, I see." She laughed.

"Why didn't you wake me?"

"I tried. You must have needed the sleep." She sat next to him and smoothed his hair with her fingers.

I love you, too. Did she remember? "Did I wake you when I came in?"

"I don't think so. I don't remember it, anyway. But it must have been late because I couldn't get you to wake up this morning even when I shook you." She giggled.

"I'm awake now." He placed his hand behind her neck and drew her to him. He kissed her softly. "I love you."

As she did every morning, she only smiled. "Come eat."

He nodded. She didn't seem at all uncomfortable when he said it, so it was likely she didn't remember saying it herself.

But she had said it. And even if she didn't remember, he would never forget.

～

*A*RISHA CUT UP THE DATES into small pieces and stirred them into the hot manna, then poured it into a covered pot. She wrapped the pot in several layers of cloth and carefully placed it into a pouch along with a skin of milk, two cups, and two bowls, then slung the bag over her chest.

She hadn't visited Zadok in his new pasture since they had made camp at Mt Hor. The first week she wasn't allowed to leave the tent, but they were three Sabbaths into the mourning period and she hadn't gone with him yet. He'd asked her to once, but she couldn't bring herself to go anywhere near that dreadful summit, the place that had taken Aaron from her. From Israel.

Today she would surprise him. She would do it.

Arisha straightened her shoulders and headed northeast. It wasn't a long walk. They were camped within a stone's throw of the base of the mountain. But the thought of it was still daunting. She tried to picture the beautiful faces of the sheep she had come to love as much as Zadok did. Especially old Leah. And the adorable lambs.

"May I join you?"

She started at the voice beside her. Moses. She wasn't sure what to say. But since he started the conversation ... "Sure."

"And how are you, daughter?"

Daughter. Aaron always called her that. She blinked back hot tears as she cast a sideways glance at Moses. His cloak was ripped at the neck—he must have torn it in his grief.

"I hear you've had an especially tough time these last weeks."

She nodded.

"I miss him, too. And Miriam."

And Miriam. He had lost both siblings in less than half a year. The pain he must be feeling! She had been so selfish, thinking no one could understand the losses she had been dealt. She stopped short, turned to him. "I'm so sorry. You must miss them even more than I do." She wiped away a tear. "I've been only thinking of myself, and I never thought about you, or ... or Eleazar. How is he? He's not allowed to mourn, is he? As high priest?"

"He's doing better. I'm actually surprised at how well he is doing. He and Aaron said their goodbyes up there." He turned his face to the summit, silent for several moments. "Aaron was so proud, and grateful, to see his son dressed in the High Priest's robes before he died. And Eleazar did look beautiful in them. Still does. Reminds me of Aaron forty years ago. He has his mother's eyes, but the rest of him is all Aaron." He turned his gaze back to Arisha and began moving again.

"The night before we broke camp, Zadok told me something."

Moses nodded. "He can be very wise. What did he say?"

"I was distraught over leaving Kadesh. He told me I should think of home not as a place, but as people. Like him, my new family."

Moses was silent.

"Do you think he's right?"

"I think he's right that home cannot be a place. I lived in the palace for forty years, in the most beautiful house on earth. But it never felt like home. And then I lived in the desert as a shepherd, always moving with my flock. I felt more at home there than I ever did in Egypt. Zadok had the right idea, but you need to go one step further."

"What do you mean?"

"Do you remember what I said when we buried my sister?"

"Not really. All I remember from that day is pain."

"It was a song Yahweh gave me." Moses halted again, closed his eyes and lifted his face to the sky.

Yahweh, you have been our dwelling place
  throughout all generations.
Before the mountains were born
or you brought forth the whole world,
from everlasting to everlasting you are El Shaddai.
You turn people back to dust, saying,
'Return to dust, you mortals.'

A thousand years in Your sight
are like a day that has just gone by,
or like a watch in the night.

His face was almost radiant as he sang to Yahweh. She'd heard Miriam sing often. Aaron sang the High Priest's prayers. She'd never heard Moses. But his voice, although soft, was clear and beautiful.

He turned his gaze back to her, his bright eyes sparkling. He raised one finger. "It is Yahweh himself who must be our home. He has been our dwelling place since before there was time, and will be forever. People, no matter how much they love us, will come and go from our lives, but Yahweh remains faithful forever."

Arisha choked back a sob. "Then why does He give us people, only to take them away?"

Moses chuckled. "You ask the hard questions, don't you? He has a plan, and it does not always make sense to us. He gives us people to love, to be loved, and we do not always know how long we will have them in our lives. But He, He will always be there."

They walked in silence for several moments, the sand crunching beneath their sandals the only sound.

She stopped again. "Would you like to eat with us tonight? I remember you ate with Miriam and Aaron every week. I know it's not the same, but ..."

Moses's bright eyes smiled. "I'd be delighted, daughter."

She touched the rip in his cloak with her fingers. "Maybe I can fix this for you." She giggled. "I've been learning."

Moses laughed with her. "Then I'd be happy to let you try. I'll see you tonight." He turned back toward camp and she almost skipped ahead. Her heart warmed, for the first time in far too many days.

Perhaps it had begun to heal.

~

*Z*ADOK WAS SHOCKED WHEN ARISHA told him she'd invited Moses to join them for the evening meal. Shocked but happy.

The meal had been delightful, with Moses telling them many stories about Aaron and Miriam. Most they had heard, but some he said he had never shared. It was obviously a healing time for him. Afterwards, the women had retired to Imma's tent and Joshua joined them for tea. The full moon shone brightly overhead, and a warm breeze blew through camp. It was a perfect night to sit around the fire, and it had been a very long time since Zadok had joined the others.

"So, now that Edom has refused us permission to travel their land, what do we do?" Jacob accepted a cup from Abba.

"Well, there are only two way to cross the Arabah." Moses took two cups and handed one to Joshua.

"The Arabah?" Zadok sipped his tea, the minty fragrance filling the air around him.

"The Arabah is a huge divide, a desolate and deep valley that runs from the Sea of Salt almost directly east of us, to the gulf in the south." Joshua's hand pointed east, and swept from north to south. "It is controlled by Edom."

"But we didn't cross it on our way to Bozrah." Jacob's brows furrowed.

Joshua grinned. "We didn't go far enough. Their land extends west beyond the Arabah." He drew in the sand with a long finger. "So the only way over it is to go through their land, and walk at the base of the Salt Sea where it is nearly flat, or travel all the way to the south end, near the sea, then turn back north, on the east side of Edom's territory."

"That sounds like it would add a great deal of time to our trip." Abba frowned.

Moses nodded. "Perhaps as much as two Sabbaths."

Zadok shook his head. More travel. Arisha would not be happy. "When do we leave?"

"The Shloshim are over the Sabbath after next. I think we'll wait for another Sabbath, maybe two, to give everyone time to read-just, pack up, fatten the animals, and then we'll head south."

The group was quiet as they contemplated this news. By the next full moon, they would be on their way to Canaan.

"I think I shall retire. The meal was delightful. Thank you all, very much. Zadok, walk with me." Moses pulled himself up with his ever-present staff.

"All right." Zadok set his cup in the sand, and hurried to catch up to the old man.

"I spoke to your Arisha this afternoon."

"I know." They stepped between Joshua's and Abba's tents.

"She is stronger than you know. And far stronger than she realizes."

"She is?"

Moses laughed. "Yes, she is. Miriam was right, she needed you. She still does. But she has strength hidden deep inside. She needs to know that. She needs to know *you* know that."

What was he supposed to say? "All right. But why?"

He laughed again as he opened the ties on his tent. "I have no idea. I just know you both need to be aware of this. Yahweh has told me nothing else."

"That's no help at all."

"It will be." And he disappeared inside, still chuckling.

What an exasperating conversation. Why would Arisha need to be strong? And why would he need to know that? Another one of Moses's famous puzzles.

Just what he needed.

CHAPTER 20

B Y THE LIGHT OF A tiny oil lamp, Danel sat cross-legged on the cold floor and stared at the marks on the inside of the small cedar table's leg. He counted them again. No matter how many times he counted them, it added to the same number. He carefully scratched one more stroke next to the others. The line was getting so long he would soon have trouble hiding it.

He stumbled to the bed pushed into the corner against the far wall, collapsing onto it. He'd been in this room for twenty-four days. Twenty-four days since he'd held Yasha, or heard his granddaughter's giggle, or tossed his youngest grandson in the air. How long was Keret going to keep him here?

He should be thankful he was not in a prison cell. Especially in the one deep underground, where they'd held and beaten Kamose to within an finger's-breadth of his life almost forty years ago.

This room wasn't terrible. An old storage room, it was wide enough for him to lie down. And with the lamp, bed, table and chair Aqhat had managed to get him it was almost comfortable. Almost. Ishat and Sisa sent him food that probably tasted better than the king's.

But it was getting harder and harder to remain grateful. He had little appetite. His clothes draped him like a tent. He slept fitfully. Night and day blended together in this windowless room. Only the noise of busy servants roaming the hallway outside gave him a hint of whether it was morning, afternoon or dead of night.

He stared at the dark wooden beams stretched across the ceiling, tried to remember Yasha's laugh. The sweet sound hovered on the fringes of his consciousness, but it was never quite clear. He could see her face, but he was losing her voice.

And he was losing hope.

Yahweh, why have you left me here, alone?

But had Yahweh really left him? Israel was in Egypt for over four hundred years. At some point, they must certainly have felt like Yahweh had left them. But He delivered them in a way no one could have imagined.

Perhaps He could do the same for Danel.

He just had to hang on.

～

1st day of Elul

*A*RISHA SAT UP ON HER sleeping mat and frowned as Zadok slipped on his sandals in the dusky light of early morning. "Do you really have to go?"

"Arisha, look around you."

She glanced around the tent and raised a brow.

He laughed. "Well, not right now. I mean around the new campsite. There is no water, no grass. The sheep will die."

Sighing, she rested her chin on her drawn-up knees. She'd become used to having him around during the days of mourning. Now that they were over ... "When will you be back?"

"As soon as I find water and ample grass. They've eaten all there is around here. They've been in this one spot for thirty days and the grass does not reappear every morning like it did at the oasis."

"Hurry back?"

He shrugged into his cloak, then stretched out his arm, pulling her up when she grasped it. "I will."

She watched him tie his bag to his belt. "Who's going?"

"All of us—Micah, Ruben, Jonah, everyone. And some new men, too. I'm not sure what kind of animals are out there, so I want as many of us as I can have."

Fear wrapped around her middle like a viper. "Animals?"

Zadok grinned. "Don't worry. They won't go after us when there are fat sheep around." Placing his hand behind her neck he kissed her soundly. "I love you."

She thought for a moment about saying it back ... but she couldn't. Not yet, but she could show him. She nuzzled his neck. "Are you sure you have to leave right now? I mean, the sun is barely up. I haven't even collected our manna."

He moved her face until his mouth met hers, and buried his hands into her thick hair. Her arms slipped under his and around his back as her lips caressed his.

"No, do not tempt me." He pulled away, laughing. "The boys will already be waiting with the sheep."

Arisha grinned. "How do you know they won't be late as well?"

"Because Reuben and Jonah slept with the sheep, and none of them are even married, let alone to you."

She batted her lashes at him.

"Keep it up and we'll starve in Canaan."

"Starve? Why?"

"Because I will never leave this tent and all our sheep will die."

Arisha burst into laughter.

"You laugh now ..."

She threw a cushion at him and he ducked out of the tent.

He peeked back in for just a moment. "You missed." His laughter faded as he walked away.

～

*Z*ADOK WANDERED A HALF DAY farther north before finding enough grass and water for his flock. The lambs were growing every day and needed more and more food. Eight new men accompanied them this time. He wouldn't need them all every night, but this was a good time to begin training them.

While his men set to work on a new fold, Zadok ambled among the sheep munching on the scrub grass near the still water. Neshika rubbed his shins and he gathered the yearling in his arms. "Is this place all right for you?" She nuzzled his chin. He quickly checked her ears, her jaw, her eyes. One tiny scratch behind her right ear. Zadok knelt, placing the animal between his knees, and reached for his horn of oil. Tipping the end onto his extended finger, he dribbled out a few drops of the healing fluid, then rubbed it on the scratch. She grunted her appreciation, and he rose to let her go.

He started as a pair of arms slid around his waist from behind him, turning to see Arisha smiling up at him.

"What are you doing out here?"

"I decided to come with you."

"Good. I was missing you already." He laughed softly and handed her a horn of oil.

"What's this?"

"You can help me check the sheep."

"Check them? For what?"

"Cuts, scrapes, flies. Just watch me. You'll figure it out."

They checked the other sheep, soothing scratches and cuts, reassuring the more skittish among them, and keeping an eye out for predators. They were far enough from the mountain to avoid any leopards or hyenas, unless they were exceptionally bold or hungry.

Zadok studied the horizon again. The setting sun sprinkled bits of pink and crimson on the northern mountains, and threw a large swath of deep purple on Mt. Hor. "Let's get the sheep in the fold before it's too dark."

He called to his flock and stepped through the gate of the newly built enclosure. While Micah counted the animals, Zadok inspected the brush wall a final time, making sure each bush was tightly entwined with the next one, twigs woven together in an unbreakable bond.

"Zadok?" Micah called from the gate.

Zadok straightened and surveyed his flock. "One's missing."

"Yes. I don't know which—"

"It's Leah. Again. I'll go."

"No, let me get her." Outside the gate, Arisha pointed toward the spring. "She's probably still under that acacia tree." She headed for the water.

Zadok pushed the last bush into the opening, leaving Micah and Jonah inside with the animals and the new men. They would be in charge tonight, showing the others to settle the sheep for the night, what to watch for, and how to protect them should any wild animals approach. He walked around the fold, checking its stability as he went. At one point, he grabbed another bush and twisted it into the structure. On his knees, arms elbow deep into the bushes, he heard Arisha approach and glanced quickly over his shoulder into the setting sun to see a figure, but no ewe.

"What took so long?" Zadok squinted into the waning light. "And where's Leah? Wasn't she there? Do we need to help you look for her?"

"It's me, Reuben."

Zadok pulled his arms free and stood, glancing over Reuben's shoulder. "She should be back by now." He brushed the dried leaves from his arms and bent to retrieve his staff. "Come with me. Let's go find them."

He tried to ignore the apprehension building in his gut as he reached the spring. Leah lay contentedly chewing her cud.

No Arisha.

The acacia tree had not been that far from where they'd been standing. She couldn't have gotten lost. Where could she be?

Near the water, something flittered. Zadok stepped to the edge of the spring. The breeze blew whatever it was a few strides further from him. He chased it, picked it up. His heart skipped a beat.

Arisha's headcloth.

And on the edge, a small spot of bright red.

~

*I*T HURT TO BREATHE. WHERE were they taking her? Why? A thousand questions raced through her mind, but no answers followed.

The uniformed man clutched her arm far harder than necessary as he dragged her along. Stumbling, pain.

They reached a copse of trees and came to a halt. In moments more men followed, dragging Micah and Jonah and the other shepherds into view. Melech, Natan, Rafael ... five others. The soldiers shoved the young men toward her.

An older man, obviously the patrol captain, whistled, and they huddled nearby, keeping their voices low.

If they found out she was a Canaanite, she may as well let them kill her right now. She would probably be killed as soon as they reached the city, but as long as she was alive, there was always a chance. A chance of escape. Rescue. Something. She wiped the blood from her jaw where the soldier had held a knife to her throat as he'd grabbed her from behind. The cut wasn't at all deep; he'd only wanted to silence her. It had worked.

She studied the warriors. They were from Arad, of that she was certain. She recognized their uniforms, the symbols on their leather chestplates. Long knives, both sides polished to a razor sharp edge, rested on their right hips, daggers on their left. Their leader also carried a spear.

Jonah put his hands in the air and shouted. "What do you want?"

The captain stormed back toward them and leaned in, his face close to Jonah's. "Quiet!"

Jonah backed up. "If we are on your land, we'll move. We didn't know. I'm sorry." He glanced over his shoulder at Arisha and Micah, then turned back to his attacker.

"I said shut up!" The captain returned to his men, his voice louder now. He wasn't happy with their actions, but now that they'd captured the Israelites there was nothing he could do. He couldn't just release them. He knew they'd run right back to camp and let everyone know Canaanite soldiers were around. He could kill them right here, but he'd be left with bodies to carry or bury. His only choice was to take all of them with him. He sent his men to find water to fill their skins.

What now? Zadok would come for her, surely. He would go back to camp and tell everyone they were missing. He would have no idea where they'd gone, but they'd search for them. Wouldn't they? Even just for eleven of them? Ten shepherds and a woman?

Oh, Yahweh, help me now. I can't go back. It's too dangerous.

Dizziness swept over Arisha. She sucked in a deep breath and tried to remember the words Moses had shared with her the other day.

"It is Yahweh himself who must be our home. He has been our dwelling place since before there was time, and will be forever."

Yahweh was her home, her dwelling place. He would take care of her.

Now all she had to do was remember that, whatever happened next.

~

*Z*ADOK STARED AT HIS DEMOLISHED fold and unprotected sheep. Micah, Jonah, all the new men had disappeared as well as Arisha.

He sucked in a deep breath and tried to slow his raging heartbeat. The images going through his mind ...

"Reuben, I'm going back to camp. Can you ...?" He drew his hand down his face. He couldn't concentrate. What was he going to say?

Reuben squeezed Zadok's shoulder. "I'll repair the fold and stay here. You go. Figure out how we get them back."

The waxing moon gave barely enough light for him to see where he placed his feet as he raced back. He sprinted though camp until he reached his parents' tent, gasping for breath. Only Imma sat outside. "Something happened."

She turned her face slightly to call over her shoulder, never taking her gaze from her son. "Ahmose!"

Abba exited the tent, his usual bright smile absent. Imma's tone must have alerted him.

How did he say this? Deliver news this bad? "Something happened at the fold." The words tumbled out.

Abba gestured to the fire. "Would you like to sit?"

Zadok shook his head, looked away. He felt his chest tighten as he recounted the events that had happened ... how long ago? It felt like a lifetime. "Someone took them away. Arisha, Micah and Jonah. All of them." He felt entirely ... empty. Bereft. Helpless.

"Away where?"

"Who knows. Canaan, probably. There's nowhere else."

"Canaan." Ahmose whispered. "That could be anywhere."

Moses's words sprang to mind. "She has strength hidden deep inside. She needs to know that. She needs to know *you* know that."

Strength? That didn't begin to cover it. She would need that and so much more.

So would he.

Yahweh, help.

～

THE FIRE WAS BIG AND bright enough to keep them warm but Arisha couldn't sleep. Without Yahweh's cloud, the air had a bitter chill at night. Or was that just her fear?

Jonah and Micah and the others made sure to surround her at all times, and despite the circumstances, she felt relatively safe. She'd made this trip once before, going south, in a caravan of camels. She figured it would take two days of hard walking to reach Arad going the same way. Her feet were already sore and they'd traveled only a short way, just enough to be sure to be out of sight of camp.

And then ...? Who knew what would happen once the temple priestesses received word she'd been found.

Let alone the king.

"You have been our dwelling place throughout all generations."

If that is what had to happen, Yahweh would still be her dwelling place.

Wouldn't He? Could He dwell in the temple of a false god?

If she lived that long.

Tears began to flow, but she wiped them away. That wouldn't help now. What she needed was some sleep. No matter what, tomorrow would be a very long day.

~

3rd day of Elul

THE HUGE GATES BEFORE THEM swung open and the little band of prisoners was paraded through the city of Arad just as night began to fall. Thank Yahweh. Another night in the desert would have been ... she didn't want to think about it. The shepherds slept next to her but the soldiers were becoming bolder.

Arisha couldn't see much over the heads of the shepherds—and soldiers—surrounding her, but that didn't bother her. She no longer belonged there.

They were shoved through a few more gates and into a part of the city she was unfamiliar with. The floor was dirt, and high wooden walls comprised two sides of the enclosure, big enough for them to spread out a little.

"Where are we?" Jonah, always by her side, scanned their surroundings.

"I don't know what this is." She shrugged. "That's the palace, though, and that wall"—she pointed north—"is an outside wall. South of the palace is the temple."

The captain left another in charge and left. Moments later, a door from the palace slammed open and an older, angry warrior, with reddish hair stormed out, followed by the captain, scurrying to keep up. The taller one had to be his superior by the way he was shouting. "Whatever possessed you to capture them and bring them here? Were those in any way your orders?"

"They saw us. We had to bring them. They had moved much farther north than they were last time."

"Where were they?"

"Near the mountain peak about halfway between their old camp and here."

The older man surveyed the group. His gaze landed on Arisha and his eyes grew wide. "You brought a *girl* here?" He turned on the captain.

"Commander, I had no choice!"

"If they saw you then you got far too close! You were not following the procedures I gave you." He glanced at Arisha and back at the leader. "A *girl*? What am I supposed to do with her?" The commander paced for several moments.

Jonah wrapped his arm around Arisha and leaned near. "Pretend you're my wife. It might protect you," he whispered.

"Do *not* let them know I am Canaanite."

"Of course."

The commander faced the hostages. "Who's in charge?" He held up one finger. "One person."

Jonah stepped forward.

"What's your name?"

"Jonah." He pointed to himself and then to her. "And this is my wife Ar—"

"Ariel." She interrupted. Her name would surely give her away.

"Ariel," he repeated.

"Very good." The commander stepped back. He looked down on the patrol captain. "You, wait in my office." He pointed to three others. "You. Take them inside. Find a servant and tell him to get them to a room large enough for all of them to let them rest and clean up. Then you're dismissed. The rest of you, to the barracks." He looked over the group once again, rubbing his hand down his face. "I'll go tell the king."

~

4th day of Elul

*D*ANEL RACED DOWN THE NARROW hallway, the sound of sandals pounding the tile floor hard behind him. His lungs burned and his thighs ached, his heart threatened to beat out of his chest.

Fear clouded his mind as he neared the end of the hall. Right or left? Which way? He stopped, looked right, then left. He couldn't remember. Rough hands grabbed him from behind. His tunic chafed at his neck ... he was choking... thrown to the floor.

Danel sat straight up in bed, breathing hard, sweat dripping down his forehead. He wiped it away with the back of his hand.

A nightmare. That's all it was.

He lay back. *Yahweh, calm me.* He continued praying, for himself, for Yasha, for Aqhat and his family, for the other believers, until he fell into a peaceful slumber.

A touch on his arm jerked him from sleep. He clambered away from the unwelcome contact, against the wall, into the corner of the darkened room.

"Danel, it's just me. Calm down." Aqhat backed away, hands in the air.

Danel blinked until his eyes adjusted to the light, and his mind adjusted to the reality of his situation. The door stood wide open, allowing the sunlight that streamed into the hallway to flood the room. His gaze scanned the cell and calm returned. "I'm sorry. I'm a little tense, I guess."

"Understandable. I have good news, though."

Still fighting through the fog in his brain, Danel swung his legs over the side of the bed. Good news? Did he say good news?

"Keret has ordered you released."

"Released? Why?" Not that he wasn't thrilled, but was there an ulterior motive?

"The patrol last night captured some Israelites. Keret wants you to talk to them."

Danel stood and stretched, his muscles aching from too many nights on a too small, too hard bed. "Me? Why?"

"You know the Israelites better. And mostly, he doesn't want to do it."

Danel scoffed. "Of course."

Aqhat looked him over from head to bare feet. "You can't see him like that. I have some fresh clothes being sent in. Are you hungry?"

His stomach rumbled. When had he last eaten a whole meal, not just nibbled on what was sent to him? "I am now. What time is it?"

"Early morning." A rap sounded on the door. Aqhat opened it, allowing one servant to deliver a bowl of water, a comb, and a fresh tunic, and another a plate of bread and cheese and a cup of juice. The soldier held up the tunic, chuckling.

"What's so funny?"

"I was just remembering I did this same thing almost forty years ago for Kamose. Except I wasn't cleaning him up to let him go home."

"Oh?" Danel glanced at the tunic. A little short, but it would do.

Aqhat grinned. "I was bringing Donatiya to him."

Visions of a very well-endowed and scantily clad girl popped into Danel's mind. "I remember her."

"Of course you do. She made herself known to every male over ten years of age in the city. Anyway, Keret thought she might be able to use her ... assets ... to persuade Kamose to give him the information he wanted."

Danel removed his tunic, then dunked the cloth in the water and wrung it out. "I take it she didn't get very far with him?"

"Of course not."

"I wonder what happened to her."

"She married one of the army captains. She had six babies and got fat."

Danel dropped the cloth into the bowl, splashing himself. "You're kidding!"

The soldier smirked. "Yes, I'm kidding. I have no idea what happened to her. Now hurry."

Danel rolled his eyes.

Aqhat gestured toward the clothing. "Get cleaned up and dressed. The king is waiting."

After brushing his hair, Danel slipped the clean clothes over his head.

"Here. Eat." Aqhat handed Danel a piece of cheese.

"Where are they?"

"So far, in a room. Keret wants them to think they're guests."

"That's good." Danel exhaled a long breath and picked up the cheese, biting off a large piece. "What do you know about the captives?"

"Not much. I haven't met them yet. There are eleven, and they're fairly young. Shepherds, I think. I don't know what they can tell us."

"What if they don't know anything?"

Aqhat lifted a shoulder. "I don't know. Keret won't like it, but it's a very real possibility. They don't look much like soldiers. The one that appears to be the leader is named Jonah, and"—he shook his head—"there's a girl."

"A girl?"

Aqhat nodded. "What was her name? Ariel, I think." He tipped his head toward the bread. "Grab that and let's go."

"They often use young men—and girls—to care for the sheep." Danel finished his bread on the way, playing out numerous scenarios in his head. What if they didn't know anything? What if they knew everything? Would Keret launch an attack? What would Yahweh do in return?

At the door of the throne room, he hesitated.

Keret sat on his throne, looking younger than he had in years. He wore his robe, held his scepter straight. His freshly polished crown rested proudly atop his head.

"Danel, enter." He smiled broadly as he extended a hand.

Danel stepped to the center of the room and dropped to one knee.

"Rise, my friend. It's good to see you.""

It is?

"I know you don't believe me, but it is." Keret descended from the dais and stood an arm's length from Danel. "And today I need you. I need your skill and your wisdom. In return, I grant you your freedom."

"For good, or do I go back when I am done with this task?"

"For good."

Danel dipped his head. "Thank you. I am forever indebted to you, my king."

"For good, that is, as long as you do as I ask. Now, go to the captives. Find out their plans. And this time, I want the truth, and I want it fast. Or you *will* lose your freedom, permanently, and this time it won't be to a holding cell."

CHAPTER 21

*D*ANEL KNOCKED BEFORE ENTERING THE room where the hostages were held. He pushed the door open quickly, remembering the fear he'd felt when Aqhat had slowly slipped inside. Doubtless Aqhat had meant not to startle him, but all it had done was allow the fear to build up.

This room was much nicer than the one Danel had just been released from. One of the guest rooms used for visitors, it was comprised of a sitting room with a long table flanked by benches, and a sleeping area in the back with several beds, complete with wool-stuffed mattresses.

He held the door for the servant who entered behind him, carrying a platter of food he'd brought from the kitchen—good food, not prisoner food. The king had made it clear the men were hostages, not prisoners, but Danel wanted them to be certain they would be treated well.

Though for how long, who knew?

"Good morning. I am the king's wazir." *At least I think I still am.* He nodded to the servant who set the food, bowls, cups and pitchers on a table, then scurried out, shutting the door behind them.

The wide-eyed young men backed against the far wall stood as straight as the statues that lined the hallways.

Danel gestured to the table in the center of the room. "Please, come sit and eat. I know you must be hungry. It's a long trek from your camp."

One of the younger ones gasped, his barely bearded jaw hanging open.

Did he frighten them? Or were they just in such bad shape? They looked ready to drop. He glanced at their bloodied feet, scraped shins and ripped tunics. They'd been pushed hard on the walk to Arad. Had they been fed when they arrived last night? Had they been fed at all during their trip? Danel pulled the tray closer and filled cups with pomegranate juice. He gestured toward the benches, then sat down himself and waited. "I thought there was also a young woman."

One of the Israelites stepped forward cautiously and sat. "Ariel is resting."

The others joined him.

"I'm the wazir," he repeated. "The king has sent me to welcome you." *And interrogate you.* He filled the bowls with Ishat's stew and passed them out along with bread. He pointed to the platter of goat cheese and grapes.

They gobbled the food quickly, and Danel poked his head outside to send a servant for more.

"Thank you." The youngest one croaked out his words, his voice hoarse.

"You're quite welcome."

"Why are we here? Were we on your land? We did not mean to trespass, we will not—" The words tumbled from the oldest of the group.

"Hold it, hold it." Danel held up his hands. They had no idea? What did the soldiers say to them? "What were you told?"

"Nothing. They just dragged us away from our sheep and to your city. We asked, but they said nothing."

Danel nodded. "I'm sorry. Others before now could have spoken to you." He exhaled forcefully. "You are being held hostage."

A taller but more slender Israelite, younger perhaps, jumped up, knocking back his chair. "What? Hostage? Why?" His face was red, his hands flailed in the air.

"Micah!" The oldest yanked on Micah's arm.

"Good. You're Micah. And who are you?"

"I'm Jonah. We are shepherds."

"You are Israelites."

Jonah stopped in the middle of a bite of cheese. "What difference does that make?"

"That is why you are here." Danel stood and paced. "The king has kept an eye on your people for forty years now. Well, almost forty years. He has been waiting for you to attack ever since the spies came through here. For the last several months, he has been sending out patrols to check on your movements. They noted your mission east—"

"To Edom." Jonah whispered.

"To Edom?" repeated Danel.

"That was only a mission to ask the Edomites if we could cross their land."

"Successful?"

"They said no."

"Too bad. That would have solved a great many problems."

"It would?"

"Yes, then you wouldn't be coming north, coming here. Anyway, you did come north, and our patrols captured you three. Now the king wants you questioned."

Micah jumped up again. "We came north to bury our High Priest!"

"Micah ..." Jonah pulled him down once again.

Danel sat again. "You came to bury your priest?"

Jonah leaned forward. "Aaron, our high priest, went up to the summit of Mt. Hor with Moses and his son, and did not come down. He went to be with Yahweh."

"And his son is the new high priest?"

They nodded.

"You are not preparing to march on Arad?"

"We are heading south around Edom," Jonah said.

A rap sounded at the door. Danel opened it and stepped aside to allow Mepac and two others to enter, carrying trays laden with fresh bread, bowls of fruit and pitchers of water. "Well, I am not sure what Keret plans to do with you. He says he only wants information, but that's what he said the last time." He chucked dryly. "And look how that turned out," he mumbled to himself.

He picked up a loaf of bread and ripped a piece off, wandering toward the window.

"Danel."

He turned as the servant called to him.

"Sisa said if you need anything more to let her know." He shut the door behind him as he slipped out.

From the other side of the room, another door slammed hard against the wall and a figure stood still in the doorway. She pushed her headcloth back and let it fall around her shoulders.

His breath caught. Could it be ... no ... why??

Could this get any worse?

⁓

THE SUN WAS JUST PEAKING OVER the eastern mountaintops, Yahweh's fiery cloud dimming as the sky brightened. Zadok dragged himself from his mat, then bent to untwist the bushes that were tied together to create the gate, trying hard to keep his mind from the one thing that dominated his every thought, his every breath.

It was the third day Arisha had been gone.

The sheep baaed their way out of the fold, stretching their legs, bumping into each other in their haste. Shika trotted over and stood before him.

Zadok shrugged into his cloak and bent to pick up his staff.

The lamb bleated at him.

"Shika, not today."

She looked at him, bleated again.

He sighed. "I know. I haven't played with you for days. But not today. Just walk with me, all right?" He headed for the front of the flock and set out to find today's grass.

Later as the sheep were grazed contentedly, someone called his name. He stilled at the unwelcome voice. Marah. He straightened and turned, willing himself to show no emotion.

Her face seemed ... different. Softer. Her hair was in a simple braid. She stood with her hands clasped in front of her. Eliel waited behind her, off to the side.

What was happening?

"I would like to help, and I would like to apologize."

What?

"I have treated you, and Arisha, and your whole family quite shamefully." She dipped her head, then raised it, her eyes brimming with unshed tears. "I am very sorry. I had no right to say the things I said to you."

Zadok bit his lip to keep from laughing. Was this a joke?

"Eliel ... helped me realize ... a lot of things. So I would like to help you care for your sheep while we wait for Arisha and the others to come back."

He blinked. Looked at Eliel, who smiled and nodded. Returned his gaze to Marah, who raised her brows.

"You want to help with the sheep?"

"I know what my father thinks. I no longer agree with him. And yes, I want to help until they return."

Until they return. How could she be so confident? "All right." Zadok shrugged. What could he lose?

Eliel joined them. "I'll help too. You shouldn't have to be out here alone. You and Reuben can't do everything."

They led the sheep to the water. He checked the lambs as they came up from the spring, kneeling beside them and inspecting their ears, eyes, heads, legs, anywhere they might have a cut or scrape.

"What are you doing?" asked Marah.

"Checking for any wounds."

Marah watched a few moments, then knelt before the next sheep that wandered up from the water. She imitated him, glancing sideways frequently to make sure she didn't forget anything.

Maybe Marah really had changed. He wasn't giving her credit for it yet, though.

They checked the rest, applying oil when needed, then allowed them to graze. Marah looked over at Eliel and smiled.

"You really love him, don't you?"

"When Eliel said it was over, I was devastated. I cried for two days. Then I asked him how I could fix it. I thought going to him and begging him to take me back would be the most humiliating thing I would ever do in my life, but then he told me what I was like to be around. That was even worse. I sat there and listened to it all. How I made other people feel, how I talked to them. And I vowed I would change."

Neshika bumped against Marah's legs.

Zadok held his breath.

Marah knelt and held the sheep's face in her hands. "And who are you?"

Zadok knelt beside her. "That's Neshika." The lamb licked Marah's face. "And that's why." He waited for Marah's reaction.

Marah laughed, then wiped her face on the sleeve on her tunic. "They are beautiful, aren't they?"

Zadok shook his head. If Yahweh could change Marah, maybe he could bring back Arisha.

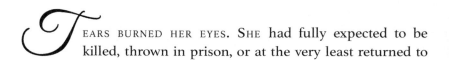

TEARS BURNED HER EYES. SHE had fully expected to be killed, thrown in prison, or at the very least returned to the temple, and with the festival starting soon, she would be expected to end up right where she was a year ago.

Instead, Yahweh sent her to the only ally she had in the entire city of Arad.

Danel ran to her and embraced her tightly, wrapping his arms around her before she had a chance to reach for him. Arms pinned against his chest, sobs wracked her body as relief poured through her. For now, at least, she was safe.

"Let her go! She is my wife! Don't touch her!" Jonah grabbed Danel by the arm and jerked him away from Arisha. He drew his fist back and slammed it against Danel's jaw, knocking him to the floor.

Rafael stepped in front of Arisha and backed her away. "Are you all right? Did he hurt you?"

Natan and Melech formed a barrier between her and Danel.

"He didn't hurt me!" She tried to break through. "He's my friend. He saved my life!"

"What are you talking about?" Jonah shot his gaze from Arisha to Danel, his fist cradled in his other hand.

"He helped me escape from here when I was ... in danger. He taught me about Yahweh. If not for him, I would be dead. Or worse." She shouldered her way back to the older man and helped him rise. "Are you hurt?" She hovered her fingers over his jaw.

"Don't worry about me. Your husband had every right to try to protect you."

"He's not my husband."

Danel frowned, but she ignored it. Time for that later. Right now she only felt relief. "Out of all the people in Arad we could have been sent to, Yahweh sent us here." Her eyes burned with unshed tears.

"I thought I'd never see you again. Thank Yahweh, He has kept you safe. At least until now." His face grew solemn. "And now you are right back in harm's way."

"I'd be dead already if not for you."

One corner of his mouth tipped up into a smile. "You made it to the camp?"

"I did. Moses's sister found me. And I married."

"But not to him?" He glanced at Jonah, who still glared at him.

"To Zadok, Kamose's great-nephew."

Danel's eyes grew as wide as apricots. "I told you Yahweh had a plan for you." He laughed and then clapped a hand over his mouth. "I'm supposed to be interrogating you."

"Ariel, who is this? What's going on?" Jonah neared, scowling.

"*Arisha*"—he chuckled—"and I have been friends for many years. And Kamose taught me about Yahweh, so very long ago. Since then I have learned everything I can about your God. I no longer worship the gods of our fathers and our king, but I must keep it a closely guarded secret. In fact, only this morning I was released from a cell. Keret found out I worship Yahweh. He let me out to talk to you."

"Why you?"

"I know more about the Israelites than anyone else in the kingdom. I'm supposed to get information from you."

"What *information* does he want?"

"I'll get to that. First, there is someone else I want you to meet. Another secret worshiper." He stepped to the door, opened it and whispered to the guard.

"Who is it you want us to meet?" asked Arisha when Danel returned.

"The soldier that helped me and my mother with Kamose's escape. They created a commotion in the hallway, and I led Kamose outside so he could leave the city."

"He's a soldier?" asked Micah, frowning.

"*Was* a soldier. Now he's commander of all Arad's army. So he's in a powerful position to help us try to get you out of here."

Three raps sounded on the cedar door. Danel grinned as he opened it.

A tall, broad-shouldered Canaanite entered—the commander from outside.

"Aqhat, you will never believe who our guests are."

"The hostages?" The warrior raised a brow. "Who?"

Danel pointed as he spoke. This one is Jonah, next to him is Micah, and this one"—he wrapped his arm around Arisha's shoulder—"is Arisha. She is married to Kamose's great-nephew."

Aqhat's jaw dropped for only a moment, then his face clouded. "Yahweh help us. If Keret finds out, he'll kill you both himself."

$\sim$

ADOK SCANNED HIS FLOCK, UNABLE TO tell by sense alone today whether one was missing. His mind was still too occupied.

Yahweh, protect her. Wherever she is, keep her safe.

"Zadok?"

"Moses, what are you doing all the way out here?"

"I came to see how you are doing."

He shrugged. "How would you be doing? If Yahweh had brought you someone, told you to take care of her, and then taken her away?"

"But you do not know that He has taken her from you yet, do you?"

"Maybe not. But I certainly didn't take very good care of her. You yourself said that was my most important job, and I utterly failed. I let her be captured when she was practically right next to me, and I don't even know where she is." He huffed. "No wonder Yahweh doesn't let me fight."

"Those are some pretty serious assumptions."

"How else would you see it?" Zadok threw his hands in the air.

"She wasn't 'right next to you.'"

"Exactly! I should never have let her wander off alone."

"She didn't 'wander off.' She was what, fifty strides away? Retrieving a beloved sheep?"

"Doesn't matter. She was alone."

"And do you think you can be with her every moment of every day for the rest of your lives?"

"If I have to."

"Is that really what Miriam asked you to do?"

Zadok thought a moment, but remained silent.

"Now, as for fighting. No one has been fighting, because we have not yet actually been to war. You have not been *drilling* because you were raising sheep for the Tabernacle as Aaron asked you to. And look around you." He spread his hands as he twisted from side to side. "You started with ... how many?"

"Eight rams and sixteen ewes."

"And now, in five years, you have over five hundred sheep. If you were drilling every day that would not have been possible. And we would not be ready next year to make the sacrifices Yahweh has commanded. *You* are making all that possible. And Joshua and Aaron both knew you would ready to fight when the day comes."

"That's not what everyone else thinks."

"Who cares? Yahweh knows the truth. You know the truth. You have obeyed, and that is all that matters."

"So what do I do now?"

"Be patient. Take care of the sheep. And wait to see what Yahweh will do."

"Just be patient?"

"Take care of the sheep, and be ready for whatever He asks of you next." Without another word, Moses turned and headed back to camp.

Zadok watched him leave.

Wait to see what Yahweh will do. How did Moses always manage to make impossible things sound so easy?

~

*A*RISHA CRINGED. DANEL OBVIOUSLY HADN'T told his friend everything.

The wazir grimaced. "Keret *will* kill her. But not only because she married Kamose's nephew."

Jonah spread his hands wide. "Why would it matter that she married Zadok?"

Aqhat pulled the bench away from the table and sat, grabbing some grapes. "Kamose is the only prisoner who ever escaped, and Keret's never forgotten it. He's held a grudge for forty years. He'd hate anyone even slightly connected to him."

Danel led Arisha to the bench and pushed the bowl of food toward her, but the thought of eating made her stomach turn.

"That's true," Danel said. "But what's worse, is that last year, Arisha was chosen as his consort for the fertility rites. She came to me, and I helped her leave here and get to the Israelite camp. If Keret, or the priestesses, find out she's back …"

Aqhat stood, his eyes narrowed. "You never told me about this."

"I didn't need anyone else knowing, being responsible. Didn't he send you to look for her?"

She'd assumed they sent someone after her, but she didn't know for sure.

Aqhat turned his unreadable gaze to her. He nodded.

Danel sat beside Arisha and poured her some water. "I knew he would. I didn't want you put in the position of lying, or leading patrols away from her. Anyway, I think she was already in their camp by the time he knew she was gone. You'd helped one person escape already. That's enough for the commander in one lifetime, don't you think?" Danel grinned.

"Does he know you helped?" asked Jonah.

"Arisha? or Kamose?" asked Danel.

"Kamose."

Aqhat grinned. "Do you think we'd be standing here if he did?"

"Then I take it he doesn't know you worship Yahweh, either."

Aqhat shook his head, his mouth full of grapes.

Danel rose, ambled toward the sleeping room where most of the youngest shepherds had collapsed onto the beds by now. He turned to face Aqhat. "So now what?"

Aqhat motioned to her. "To begin with, we keep her presence a secret."

"Obviously. Then what?" asked Danel.

"You're supposed to get their plans, right?"

"And report to Keret."

The commander grabbed a chunk of bread. "Then he'll want to launch an attack, which he can't do without me." He ripped a large piece from the loaf and stuffed it in his mouth. After pacing and chewing a few moments, a crooked smile appeared on his face. "We need to stall him."

"For how long? Why?"

"Wait here." Aqhat stood and left the room.

Jonah huffed, pointing at Aqhat. "Where is he going?"

"It's quite irritating when he does that." Danel lifted a shoulder. "You'll get used to it."

"I don't intend to be here that long." He glared at Danel.

A few moments later another three-rap knock sounded, and Aqhat slipped in, glancing behind him as he did. Another soldier followed. "This is Banno."

Danel led the younger man closer. "He's one of the other believers. There are about twenty of us. We meet in small groups, in homes."

Arisha looked him over. He was about the same age as Zadok. A little taller, a little more muscle. His hair was lighter and his eyes were set wider. "And why is he here?"

"He will go to your camp, and inform your people of our plans. If we work together, we can free you." Aqhat sounded quite confident.

Arisha stared back. "How much do you trust him?"

"With my life."

"With ours, you mean."

"With everyone's. If he fails, we all die."

Jonah exhaled a forceful breath. "All right. But how do we get my people to trust him?"

Aqhat pulled an object wrapped in leather from his belt. "Banno takes this as proof he is friendly." He held the object in one hand, and with the other removed the leather, revealing a long gold dagger, in its sheath. Four bands of small red carnelian jewels circled the handle. "This belonged to Kamose."

"I thought it was lost forever." Danel's eyes grew wide as he reverently fingered the weapon.

"I found it hidden in the commander's room when I moved in."

Danel whistled softly. "I assumed someone had stolen it. Guess I was right."

"May I?" Arisha held her hand out.

"Of course." Aqhat handed her the dagger.

It was heavier than it looked. It was spotless, and extremely sharp. "It's extraordinary." She turned it over. "I heard about it. Zadok's sabba Bezalel made this. Before he ever knew Kamose."

"His grandfather made it? The craftsmanship is extraordinary."

"How do we know that's real? That Bezalel made it or Kamose ever owned it?" asked Jonah.

"Because it matches this perfectly." She pulled the pendant from under her tunic and held it out with her thumb. "Bezalel made these from Kamose's arm bands. The carnelians are smaller, but look at the way the stones are set into the gold. Exactly like these are."

Jonah nodded. "All right. I'm convinced. Will anyone in camp recognize it?"

"Zadok's abba would." She tucked her necklace back under her tunic.

"Let's finalize the plans, then we'll send him on his way. It will take him maybe a day and a half to get there, they'll have a day to get organized, and two to get back. It should work out perfectly."

"Perfectly for what?" asked Jonah.

Aqhat's eyes twinkled and a grin took over his face. "You'll see."

CHAPTER 22

6th day of Elul

THE SETTING SUN SIGNALED THE end of another day. Another day without Arisha. In the middle of summer, plenty of sunlight remained, but his stomach rumbled and it was time to return to the tents for the evening meal.

A solitary figure approached from the north. Male, by his gait. He wasn't wearing an Israelite tunic. A nomad would be in a large group. Whoever he was, it couldn't be good.

The man came closer. He wore a leather belt and leather sandals laced to his knees—soldier's sandals.

"Eliel!" He called over his shoulder. Where was he? He ran through the flock, not caring that he might frighten them. "Eliel!"

He found him with Marah behind a tamarisk tree. Eliel pulled away from her, his cheeks reddening. At the moment Zadok couldn't care less whether they were being inappropriate or not. "Eliel, come quickly. Someone's coming!"

"Who?"

"If I knew I wouldn't be calling for you now, would I?"

Zadok ran back, Eliel following.

The stranger saw them and put his hands in the air.

Zadok's hand drifted to the dagger on his belt. Eliel grasped his staff by the end and held it like a club.

As soon as the man was in hearing distance, he shouted. "I come in peace." His words were heavily accented, but understandable. He repeated the phrase.

Zadok relaxed a bit, but his hand remained on the dagger's handle.

The stranger neared, arms still raised.

Eliel raised the staff higher, and the man's face registered alarm. He put both hands in front. "No. No! Please, I bring news of your men."

Zadok eyed the intruder. A strong, young man, he'd apparently been traveling for a couple days. He wore a dagger, only long enough for his own protection. He was filthy, disheveled, and looked exhausted. He held up a piece of papyrus, rolled and sealed. "This is for Ah-mose."

Zadok's heart slammed against his chest. How could he know Abba's name? He turned to Eliel.

His friend shrugged. "Who knows? It's worth a try."

The man nodded and smiled. "Ah-mose," he repeated.

"All right. Let's go then," Zadok said.

Eliel grasped the man's bicep and headed for camp.

*W*hen they reached the fire pit, Eliel shoved the man to his knees. "This man says he has news of our men. He has a note, but it's sealed." Eliel handed the papyrus to Abba.

Abba looked the man over as he unrolled it. When he finished, he looked at him again.

The intruder reached behind his back and withdrew a long object, then handed it to Ahmose.

Abba unwrapped it and gasped.

Zadok stepped closer to see what had drawn such a reaction. A long dagger, with bands of carnelian on the handle.

Abba put his thumb and fingers over his eyes for a moment. He nodded at the stranger. "Let him up."

"What?" Zadok was going to burst with curiosity if he didn't get some information soon.

"Will someone please tell me what's going on?" Eliel looked from Abba to Zadok to the stranger and back to Abba. Apparently he felt the same way. "Where are our men? And Arisha? Is she with them?"

While they were talking, Zivah, Imma and the children approached. Zivah's eyes grew wide. "What's wrong?"

Abba faced the group. "All right. Here's what I know. Arisha, Micah, Jonah and the others were captured by patrolling soldiers from Arad. They've been sending out patrols every two weeks for months waiting for us to attack. Apparently they are holding our people trying to get information on our plans. Now, the king is the prince who held Kamose—"

Adi gasped. "Oh, no."

"Right now, the king plans to get what information he can out of them ... and then probably kill them. But if he finds out that they know nothing, or who Arisha is—that she escaped, or is connected to Kamose—he won't wait even that long. "

Zadok's stomach roiled. This couldn't be happening. He had to do something, anything.

"But, there is a plan." Abba smiled. "Danel, the boy who helped Kamose escape, is now the wazir, and worships Yahweh. The commander of the army also worships Yahweh—"

"But who is this?" Eliel yanked the stranger's bicep.

"Ah, this is Banno. Danel and the commander sent him to us to tell us of their plans. They sent this"—he held up the dagger—"as proof of his identity. You can let him go, Eliel."

"What is that?" asked Zadok.

"This is Kamose's dagger." Abba's voice was thick. "He lost it in Arad forty years ago. Rather, someone stole it from him. Aqhat, the new commander, found it and has kept it safe. Until now. Now, I finally have it back."

"How do we know it's his?" Eliel still wasn't convinced. "This could all be a trick."

"*I* know. He carried it ... Trust me, I know it. Bezalel made it, just like he made this." He slipped a finger under the chain around Imma's neck and lifted the pendant.

"All right, so then what's the plan?" Eliel pointed to the papyrus.

"I assume they didn't want to put too much in writing, in case this fell into the wrong hands. All it tells us is to ready an attack force and get them there three days from now. They'll take care of the rest."

Eliel huffed. "That's asking an awful lot. Send men there with no idea of what comes next?"

"Wait and see what Yahweh will do." Zadok's voice was soft.

Eliel turned to him. "What?"

He lifted a shoulder. "That's what Moses told me. *Wait and see what Yahweh will do.* It sounds like good advice here, too."

Abba wrapped an arm around Zadok's shoulder. "That's excellent advice, habibi. We'd be fools not to take it. Eliel, go to your sabba. We have only tomorrow to ready attackers. Then we must get some rest, so we will be ready for whatever it is Yahweh has in store for us."

Zadok had no idea what Yahweh had in mind, but as far as he was concerned, he'd had enough waiting.

The time had come for action.

∼

*D*ANEL AND AQHAT WAITED OUTSIDE the throne room. The heavy double door was pulled open from inside. Two burly servants stepped aside and the pair stood on the threshold.

Aqhat leaned near. "I do not wish to lie to him, but we'll have to tell him something. It's been two whole days."

"Do what you have to do."

"Enter." The king's voice was gruff. "What have you learned from our ... guests?"

Danel cleared his throat. "As young men, not old enough to be part of Israel's army, they know little, but we believe they know more than they think they do. In conversation they have told us they are headed south, have no plans in place to attack, and are not in training."

"They lie!" Keret rapped the floor with the foot of his scepter.

Danel winced. "I do not believe the men are lying, my king. Whether or not they are informed of their leaders' confidential discussions is another matter."

The king leaned forward in his gilded throne. "They are coming, and soon. Of this I am certain. Commander Aqhat, prepare for imminent attack."

Aqhat dipped his head. "Yes, my king. I shall make all necessary arrangements, though I do not expect any movement for a few days. An experienced army would wait for a full moon to attack. Israel may not be good enough to defeat us, but surely they know that, and since they believe they have the element of surprise, they will wait until there is enough light at night to help, not hinder, which would be at the end of next week's festival of *Ra'shu Yeni*."

Keret paused, exhaled. "If you say so, Commander. Still, I want our city protected."

"Of course, my king."

The pair backed away and exited the throne room. Once safely in Aqhat's office, Danel let out a loud breath.

Aqhat chuckled. "Nervous?"

"Aren't you?"

He shrugged. "A bit."

"Just a bit? 'An experienced army would wait for a full moon to attack,'" he mocked. "What was that all about?"

"I told you we had to stall him."

"That was a complete lie!" Danel threw his arms in the air.

"No, it wasn't. I said *an* army. Not *all* armies. Surely there's an experienced commander somewhere who would wait for a full moon to attack. I've done it myself, in the right circumstances."

"What is your plan, then?"

Aqhat pulled rolls of papyrus from the shelves on his wall. "I need spiced wine. Lots of it. Delivered to the barracks the first night of the festival. Can you do that?" He searched through the rolls until he found one, then unrolled it, scanning it.

"Easily. Why?"

"I'm going to reward some people for their faithful service." He flashed that grin that often made Danel nervous.

"I have no idea what that means."

"Don't worry about it. Just make sure the wine gets to the barracks in three days."

"I hope you know what you're doing. Because one way or another, this will all be over by the time the moon is full."

The commander tossed the parchment on his desk and ran his hand through his hair. "I know. We've known this was coming most of our lives. And I've been preparing for it. You need to trust me. And you need to trust Yahweh. I have no idea what will happen. Who will win. If we will live or die. But I intend to do everything I can to try to ensure that we are on the winning side, that we do live. I'm a soldier. It's all I know to do."

~

*T*HE MORNING SUN REFLECTED OFF the sand north of camp as Zadok paced. What was Arisha doing right now? Had she slept? Had she eaten? Was she injured? Was Jonah looking out for her? Thoughts of her in a cell—or worse—tormented him.

How could Yahweh let this happen?

Zadok was ready to fight. Like every other male, Zadok had been prepared for that since birth. Give his own life for Israel? Absolutely. He had learned to handle a dagger, a sword, even a sling. He knew how to defend himself and how to advance on an enemy. He knew how to take orders and how to lead.

But give up his wife?

That, he was not prepared for.

They weren't even fighting yet. Their battles with Canaan weren't supposed to start for over half a year.

He dropped to his knees.

Yahweh, help me. Give me strength. Help me concentrate.

Keep her safe.

He'd told no one what she'd shared with him about being selected as the king's consort. She'd asked him not to. But now her life was in danger, even more than the others.

How could Yahweh take her, when He had given her to him only months ago?

His throat burned, his vision blurred. He laid his arms on the sand, his head on his arms.

Yahweh, keep her safe. Don't let them kill her. Please.

"Zadok."

Abba's soft voice startled him.

He rose from the sand, brushing the sand off his cloak and the tears from his cheeks.

"I wanted to give you this to take with you." Abba reached into the folds of his belt, and withdrew the carnelian-studded dagger.

"No, you should keep that. That was your uncle's. What if I lose it?"

Abba unsheathed the weapon. "And it was your great-uncle's. I don't believe objects carry luck, or power, but I want you to wear this as a reminder. You come from Hur, and Bezalel, and Kamose. Each of them fought bravely for Israel. You have their passion, their courage, even though you have not had a chance—or a need—to show it yet. Their fire is in you. You need only to release it."

Abba fingered the double-edged blade. "I remember this well. Kamose wore this every day until ... " He slid the dagger back into its holder. "Remember when Moses told you your time to fight was coming?"

Zadok nodded.

"This is it. This is your time."

Zadok reached for the weapon, pulled the gleaming blade from its sheath. Longer than most daggers, it was heavy but well-balanced. It would be a formidable asset.

Was he equipped for this? Could he do this?

Could he not?

His great-uncle wouldn't have hesitated. Or his sabba. Or his abba, for that matter.

Neither would he.

The time for that was over.

Now it was time to fight.

For his reputation, for his wife, for Israel.

$\sim$

*D*ANEL WALKED AMONG THE FRUIT trees outside the walls of Arad. The late morning sun and the scent of ripe apples, pears and peaches floating on the breeze belied the heaviness in his heart.

Three days, that's all he had. Three days until the start of the *Ra'shu Yeni*, the Harvest Festival. Three days to convince Mika that Yahweh was the only true God. He'd spent most of the night praying—praying for Mika and praying for guidance. He was no closer to an answer today than he was yesterday.

He could tell Mika Israel was coming. There would be a battle, and Danel would be on Israel's side. If Israel, a group of children of former slaves who haven't fought anyone in forty years, as Mika called them, prevailed against mighty Arad, it would prove Yahweh was the Living God.

But if Mika's heart was hardened, he would simply run to the king and tell him of Danel and Aqhat's treason, and all would be lost.

What should he do?

He had to try. Somehow he had to try to change Mika's mind about Yahweh. He couldn't let him fight against Israel, against Yahweh, and risk death if he didn't have to.

He changed course, headed inside the gates.

But he couldn't risk the rest of the believers, either. Mika didn't know them all, only the ones who met at Danel's house. But along with Aqhat's family and his own, that was still a large number.

He had to know where Mika's heart was.

Danel waited outside the barracks trying to gather the courage to knock. He raised his hand, dropped it. Raised it again and rapped on the enormous cedar door.

A young soldier—younger than Mika—answered. Behind him an entire company of recruits seemed to be easing the effects of a hard day's training with a jug of spiced wine and several women.

"Is Mika in?"

The man only grunted and slammed the door.

Danel flinched. Ordinarily he would say something about such disrespect, make certain it was punished, but in another day or two, it wouldn't matter. One or the other of them—or both—would no longer be in Arad ...

Moments later Mika appeared. He'd gained some weight, all of it muscle. It looked good on him. "Papa. I wasn't expecting you." His voice cold, he stepped outside and closed the door behind him.

"Should we take a walk?"

Mika shrugged, but started along the worn path that led from the barracks to the training field. "I hope you're not here to talk me out of marrying Demna. You will not change my mind."

The words hit hard. "All right. Maybe I just want to talk to my grandson."

"Why? We have nothing in common anymore. I do not worship your God. I will never worship your God."

That tells me about his heart.

Mika halted, crossed his arms. "Demna is expecting our baby."

Danel felt like he'd been thrown into a stone wall. A baby?

"So you see, I have to marry her."

Danel could only nod.

"But my training will be completed in a few weeks, and I will have my commission. We'll be fine."

Danel tried three times before words actually came out of his mouth. "All right."

Mika stood even taller. "I am the best in my class. I'll command fifty immediately. I'll command a company within a year."

All of which was probably true. Danel's stomach twisted into knots. "Then I guess I should let you get back to your training."

"That's probably best." Mika stared into the distance for a long moment. "Goodbye." He turned and headed back to the barracks.

Danel stared at Mika's retreating back. Somehow, he knew it would be the last time he would ever talk to his grandson.

～

ZADOK SAT AT THE FIRE PIT of his parents' tent, his arms wrapped around his knees, head on his arms. His own tent was far too empty.

When were they going to move? If it were up to him, he'd be halfway to Arad by now.

And dead before he saw the towers, for the city's defenders would surely see him first.

No, all he could do was wait.

Wait and see what Yahweh would do.

The blast of the shofar split the air. Once. Twice. Three times. Zadok jumped to his feet. Abba exited the tent, and the pair silently made their way toward the sound. Imma, Zivah and the children followed.

Joshua, Caleb and Moses stood at the base of Mt Hor, the same place they'd told Israel of Aaron's death. Zadok pushed those memories to the back of his mind.

Moses raised his hands, and when he had everyone's attention, he spoke. "The king of Arad has attacked us without cause, and sent his soldiers to harm us."

A loud cry went up from the people. Questions overlapped each other. "What?" "Who?" "We must go after them."

"He has captured several of our men who were doing nothing more than tending our sheep."

Caleb stepped to the front. "We plan to go after them. Arad is a very small city, but it is heavily fortified, with towered walls thicker than a man is tall. Double gates that are guarded day and night. Armed men patrol both the city and the country around it."

Zadok's heart beat double-time. Why was Caleb so doubtful? Was he suggesting they leave Arisha and the others there? He'd go alone if necessary.

A tall young man shoved his way to the front. "Yahweh will help us. He has helped us time and time again, whenever we have asked Him." He climbed on a boulder, then turned to face the crowd. "I say we ask for Yahweh to lead the way! We go after this wicked king. And if Yahweh will return our men to us, we promise we will destroy this evil city!"

The Israelites cheered. Men all around Zadok pumped their fists in the air, yelling, shouting and roaring. Faces were red, voices became hoarse, shoulders were slapped. Had they not been calling for Arisha's rescue, it would have frightened him.

Moses raised his hands for silence. "As we said, the city is small. Since it was men of Judah who were taken, Joshua will lead the men of Judah against Arad. The rest of you can return to your tents, and ask Yahweh for his blessing and protection. Caleb and his men will distribute arms and tell you what little we know, and some training will take place today before we leave tomorrow at dawn."

Women, children and old men immediately returned to their tents. The younger men of Judah stayed. Joshua dispatched some to the weapons stores, divided the rest into their companies. Zadok set out to find Caleb. Finally he spotted him, at the front with Moses and Joshua, deep in conversation.

Zadok drew close enough to tap Joshua on the shoulder. The former spy turned and tried to include him in the conversation, but he declined and pulled him aside. "Joshua, why is Caleb so against rescuing Ar—, the men?"

"What do you mean? He's not against it at all." He glanced over his shoulder at Caleb.

"Didn't you hear him? All he talked about was how hard it would be."

"Zadok, he was only trying to get the people behind him. The passion, the enthusiasm for this, has to come from everyone, not only the few who know the ones abducted. This has to be about more than them. This has to be about *Israel*. By this action, Arad has attacked all of Israel."

Zadok had not thought of it that way. It was true, of course, but all that mattered to him was Arisha.

"The shepherds. Were any of them old enough to begin drilling yet?"

"Some. But they were all big and strong and they can take care of themselves, or I wouldn't have picked them to protect my sheep from leopards and hyenas. They'll be able to wield a sword, trust me."

"Good. Go to the weapons cache and make sure you take enough swords and daggers for them as well as yourself. Get some others to help you carry them over."

Zadok nodded as he headed for the weapons. He'd only gone about twenty strides when he noticed Marah's abba marching toward Joshua, his jaw set.

Not again.

Zadok reversed course. He was not going to let Malkiel interfere.

Malkiel stomped up to Joshua. "Surely you're not letting him go?" Pointing at Zadok, he spoke without waiting for Joshua to even acknowledge him.

Joshua turned around slowly. "Malkiel. Thank you for coming to offer your support. And yes, I am. He's one of my captains, actually."

"He's the biggest coward in all of Judah!" He waved his arms, as if he could scoop up all Judah and put it at Joshua's feet to prove his point.

"He's not. I've told you before, Aaron instructed him to spend his time growing the flock."

"A convenient excuse."

"Malkiel, I am the commander of Israel's army and I don't have to explain anything to you." He stepped away. "Zadok? The weapons cache?"

Malkiel followed. "You cannot let him go! I have four sons going and he will put them all in danger!"

Joshua halted and faced the angry man. "Do you really believe that?"

Malkiel folded his arms over his chest. "I do."

"Very well. Then *your* sons may stay home."

Joshua left Malkiel fuming and muttering.

As Zadok picked out the weapons, all he could think about was bringing home Arisha, but Joshua was right. There was far more at stake here than some shepherds and his wife. Malkiel proved that.

At least that's what his head said.

What his heart felt was altogether different.

CHAPTER 23

Z ADOK VISITED HIS SHEEP ONE last time. Would he ever see
them again?

Reuben touched his shoulder. "I'd really like to go with you, but
I'm assuming you want me to stay here." His eyes spoke the disap-
pointment he couldn't express.

Zadok glanced over the growing flock. "I need you here,
Reuben. No one else knows them like you do. If I don't come back
..."

"Don't say that."

"You're the only one left. They took everyone else." His gaze was
drawn uncontrollably north.

"I know." His voice was soft.

"You know them, you know how to protect them, know what
they need. Not as well as I do, of course." He attempted a smile.
"Take care of them for me?"

"Of course."

Zadok blinked back the moisture gathering in his eyes and
turned to go. Hopefully he could get a little sleep before dawn.
They faced a long two days of hard marching before they attacked
Arad. Thank Yahweh Banno had told Joshua of the trade route so

they didn't have to climb the cliffs the spies climbed when they entered Canaan. The way was longer, but they could move faster, and far more easily. Still, it would take two full days without stopping.

"Zadok!"

Eliel and Tobiah strode toward them, with a handful of cousins trailing them.

"Eliel. Tobiah. What are you doing?"

"We've come to help. We'll watch the sheep for you until you return. We're Ephraimites, and only Judah is fighting." He glanced at his cousins. "I know they are very young and inexperienced, but I've helped the last several days, and with Reuben's help, we can do it. Besides, you won't be gone that long." He flashed a wide grin.

Zadok couldn't decide whether his confidence was encouraging or unnerving.

"Reuben can't stay here every day and every night, like you do."

Zadok swallowed hard, his throat burning. "I-I don't know what to say. Thank you."

Tobiah squeezed his shoulder. "Just bring her back. Bring them all back."

～

*A*RISHA AWOKE IN THE GUEST ROOM, the darkness like a weight on her chest. She sat up, let her eyes adjust to the meager light shining in the windows above their beds. Micah snored on her left; Jonah slept soundlessly on her right.

How much longer would they be in this room? What would happen once they left? The king had promised they would be treated well, but Danel had expressed doubt. Without a doubt she would be killed if the king learned she had returned to Arad.

She lay back, draped an arm over her eyes. Aqhat and Danel had not shared the specifics of their plans, simply saying they had everything under control. That word had been sent to their camp, to Zadok, and a rescue would be soon underway.

Zadok. Her heart ached for his strength, his peace. His comfort.

She had never told him she loved him, though he told her every morning. Her thoughts returned to their last morning together, the way she'd tried to convince him to stay with her ... thank Yahweh she'd gone to him, even if it led to her capture. If her last act meant he could believe she loved him.

If only she'd said the words.

Maybe she should have stayed home. But then maybe they would have taken him. Maybe ...

Enough maybes. What happened, happened, and she was here in a "guest room" in Arad, waiting. Waiting for Danel, waiting for the king, waiting for Yahweh.

Waiting was not easy.

~

9th day of Elul

*D*ANEL DESCENDED THE STAIRS, THE light growing dimmer with each step. At the bottom of the staircase was a hallway. To the right lay the room where Kamose had been held, where Keret threatened to, and probably would throw not only the Israelites, but him as well if their plan went awry. To the left, his destination.

He turned left, took eleven steps. He'd made this trip many times, never thinking much about it. Then again, he'd never thought much about living out his days at the other end of the hall. He turned the key in the lock, pushed open the door, and entered. The sweet scent swirled in the air. He inhaled deeply, letting the fragrance calm him. He walked along the wall, looking down row after row of shelves running the length of the throne room, floor to ceiling on both sides, each shelf lined with huge pottery jugs of spiced wine.

He inspected the jugs, checking the tags tied to the necks with linen cord. Honey and cinnamon. Honey and mint. Juniper and mint. He chose twenty-four jugs for the festival, carrying them one by one to a table in the hallway, then closed and locked the door behind him.

Danel chuckled. These should be very helpful tonight.

~

ADOK, JACOB, CALEB, JOSHUA AND the other Judahites waited on a hill outside Arad as the waxing moon rose. There was just enough light for them to see the walls of the city. A full moon would have been better, but that's when they would have been expected.

"Wait," said Banno. "I'll bring back our contact." He slipped silently down the hill.

Zadok's breath caught. What if this was all a setup? What if Banno brought back an entire city full of soldiers? Had they made a fatal error trusting him?

But there was the dagger. Ahmose believed it was Kamose's. But it could truly be Kamose's, and they could still be in danger.

Zadok breathed deeply, closed his eyes. He needed to calm down. Getting himself worked up so he couldn't think straight would only put him in more peril once the fighting started.

If it started.

Banno appeared with an old woman and a huge smile. A woman? What kind of contact was that?

"I am Yasha." Her calm face put Zadok at ease. "Yahweh has sent you to us." She clasped Joshua's hand with both of hers, then Caleb's.

"And you to us," responded Caleb. "Now, what are we to do?"

She gestured toward the gate. "The commander, Aqhat, will be guarding the gate alone some time later tonight. He has made sure there are no guards on the walls or towers or anywhere in the city."

Zadok gasped. "How did he manage that?"

"He is the commander of all Arad. He told every unit another unit was on duty. This is the first night of the Festival of the Harvest, and the men have been celebrating most of the day, so they were quite willing to believe that. He will light a small fire at the right side when the revelers have returned to their homes and the streets are empty. That is your signal to enter." She spoke with amazing clarity, almost authority.

"He will take you to your men. Once you reach your men, there is no guarantee what will happen. Even after his preparations, you may still encounter serious resistance."

Caleb nodded. "We are prepared."

"There is one more thing."

"Anything. After what you have done for us. Anything."

"My family and Aqhat's family left the city earlier today. We want you to take us with you." Her voice softened and her eyes pleaded with Caleb.

"Of course, if you wish."

Yasha swallowed, looked at the ground.

Caleb touched her shoulder. "Is there something else? What is it?"

"My husband would never ask you, but will you do your best to bring him out? Keret has already punished him for worshipping Yahweh. He doesn't know about any of the rest of us. But someone betrayed Danel, and Keret locked him up for over a month." A tear made its way down her wrinkled face.

"Of course, we will do whatever we can do."

"Thank you." She grasped his hands again and turned to go, but Zadok stopped her.

"Kamose was my uncle. He taught my wife about Yahweh. I especially owe Danel. I will protect him with my life."

"Thank you, my dear." Yasha grabbed him and embraced him. Then she pulled away and pointed a bony finger at him. "But I must tell you, if you give your life for his, he will never forgive me." She spoke sternly.

"What if I do my best to return us both to our loved ones?"

She smiled. "I think he would like that. We're waiting on a hill over there. We will be out here praying for all of you, all night, until you make it back here." She gestured toward a group of about twenty people, seated on the ground some ways away. "Those are my two youngest grandchildren, and Aqhat's wife, daughter, her husband, and three children. All of us trust in Yahweh."

For the first time all night, Zadok relaxed. "I feel safer already."

It was closer to dawn than the middle of the night when a light finally blazed at the right side of the gate. Zadok inhaled deeply. *Yahweh, go with us.*

"Let's go." Caleb whispered loudly from the front. The men crept down the hill toward the walls of Arad. Caleb raised his fist and they stopped a stone's throw away. At the entrance, they made their way to the center of the double gate. Banno called out in a low voice.

Another voice answered, then one of the doors swung outward. The Canaanite officer stood waiting, hurrying them inside the city's massive walls. Once inside, the officer shut the enormous door and turned. "I'm Aqhat, commander of Arad's army. I'll take you to your men. After that ..." He raised a hand, palm up, let it drop against his leg, then moved forward again.

The waxing moon shed only enough light for Zadok and the others to follow without stumbling over each other.

At the palace walls inside Arad, Aqhat turned. "I need only two of you inside."

Caleb pointed to Zadok. "You and I. Yes?"

Zadok was thrilled and terrified at the same time. After all the years of waiting, wanting to prove to everyone that he was indeed a warrior, now he wondered.

"And Banno and I. The rest of you, find a place to hide and wait. If we can, this will be a rescue mission. If not, be prepared—for war." Aqhat unlocked one of the two cedar doors and slipped inside, the others behind him.

~

*D*ANEL JUMPED AT THE SOUND of heavy footfalls in the hall. *Please be Aqhat.* He pressed against the wall, making himself as small as possible, knowing it would not help at all if they were Keret's soldiers coming to arrest him, and not Aqhat. Even though at this time of night—more accurately, morning—that was highly unlikely.

"Danel?"

The loud whisper eased Danel's fears, and he exhaled the breath he had been holding. "Aqhat?"

"Yes." Rounding a corner, his friend came into view, along with Banno and two lightly armed Israelites. "This is Caleb and Zadok."

"I'm Danel, keeper of all keys." He grinned weakly as he jangled a large ring of keys, then turned back to the commander. "And your soldiers?"

"I checked as inconspicuously as I could. They should be quite drunk by now."

"Twenty-four jugs of wine will do that." He grinned.

"Very well. Let's go rescue them." Aqhat pointed down the hall.

The group of five turned left and stole down the hall, to the section of the palace reserved for entertaining guests. One more turn, a key in the lock, a door pushed open.

∼

*T*HE SOUND OF SANDALS SLAPPING against tile in the hallway woke Arisha from a light sleep. She jumped out of bed and raced to the door, the shepherds on her heels. Placing her ear against the wood, she strained to hear voices, footfalls, anything.

The footsteps drew nearer, stopped. A key was placed in the lock. Arisha's breathing sped up, her hands shook. Who would be entering their room this early in the morning?

The door pressed inward.

She stepped back.

Danel peeked in, and Zadok slipped in behind him, a huge grin dominating his face.

Arisha gasped, her body rigid for a moment. Then she threw her arms around his neck. "Zadok! You came for me."

He returned the embrace, nuzzling her neck. "Always. I will always come for you."

Jonah headed for the other room. "I'll wake the others."

Micah was already up, shaking the younger men. "Natan, Rafael, let's go. Asher, Seth."

The group followed Aqhat, his sword now in hand, and the others back down the hall. At every corner, he stopped and glanced each way before continuing, but they soon reached the palace doors. The commander pulled the doors open and the group filed outside.

Straight into a company of Arad's finest warriors.

～

*D*ANEL'S HEART STOPPED. FOR A moment.
Until Mika pushed to the front.

Then it sped up and beat much too fast.

"I told you I was the best in my class." He glared at Danel, arms crossed. "I knew you would do something like this."

"But ... how did you even know there were captives in the palace?"

"I have a lot of friends. Everywhere."

Danel's gaze darted from side to side, looking for an escape. The soldiers flanking Mika were young and inexperienced, but well-muscled and grim-faced. They were spoiling for a fight. "Mika, please don't do this. These young men have done nothing wrong. Let them go, then you can do what you want with me."

Mika reared back, laughing. "Are you joking? This is my best chance for a fast promotion straight to the top. I've got you *and* Aqhat."

Aqhat scoffed. "You think they'll make you commander over this?"

"Probably not. Even I admit I'm too young. But I'll skip a *lot* of steps." Mika drew his sword. "Now, you can surrender, or we can fight it out."

Danel's stomach soured as one of the other Israelites stepped out of the shadows. "We fight it out."

Mika turned, momentarily surprised. Then he grinned. "Have it your way." He lunged at the man, and within moments every soldier was locked in combat with an Israelite, clashing in a sea of skin and swords. Footsteps pounded, blades clanged, orders were shouted.

Danel unsheathed his sword, tried to remember the training all palace officials had to undergo when hired, and again each year during the rainy season. *Aim for the heart, defend yourself.* Sounded simple enough, but he was an old man with bad knees who couldn't move nearly as quickly as these boys.

Maybe the best thing for him was to get Arisha to safety. He spun around. Where was she? There. Behind Zadok. Danel tried to make his way to her, but a burly warrior blocked his way. The youngster swung his sword. Danel blocked the blow with the flat of his blade. The soldier swung again, and Danel jumped back to avoid the strike, raising his weapon. When the blow fell to the ground, Danel brought his sword hard down on the young man's arm, exposing muscle and bone. Blood gushed and the enemy sword clattered to the ground.

Danel grabbed it and bolted for Arisha. Grasping her arm, he tugged her back toward the palace. "Come with me." He shouted over the noise of the clanging iron and grunting men. "I'll get you some place safer until this is over."

She looked at Zadok, fending off blows. He cast a glance over his shoulder and nodded. "I'll find you."

Breathing fast, heart pounding, Danel hurried for the door, pulling perhaps a little too hard on Arisha's arm. But better a sore limb than ... almost anything else that could happen. He dropped her arm long enough to open the door, then placing his hand on the small of her back, almost pushed her inside. He yanked the door shut behind them.

The hallway led to the kitchen, which at this hour should be deserted. "Follow me." He whispered, not daring to take any chances.

They crept down the hall. If they could make it past the kitchen, there were a number of rooms he could lock her in that no one would be able to enter until he came back for her, rooms no one would suspect anyone would be in, let alone a girl. Ten more steps. Six, five ...

"Stop. Not one more step. Mika told me you would try something like this."

One of the soldiers from Mika's group stepped into the hall from the darkness of the kitchen, a smirk on his face and a sneer in his voice. He stood in their path and leered at Arisha, eyeing her from sandals to head. "So the rumor was true. You were hiding a girl in there."

Danel's blood ran cold. Arisha's face lost its color.

"What's your name?"

"Her name is Ariel."

"That's not what I heard." The soldier glared at Arisha.

Danel pulled her closer.

"I heard ... she is the runway consort of last year's Ra'shu Yeni."

Arisha's body leaned heavily against him.

Danel gripped her tighter. How could he possibly know that? Mika said he had spies everywhere but ... could one of the servants bringing food have overheard something? Surely they wouldn't have discussed it ... but maybe someone recognized her.

"In fact, I think we'll just take her to the king right now."

～

*Z*ADOK FOUND HIMSELF QUICKLY OUTNUMBERED. The techniques he had learned in the drills returned to his memory easily, though it had been years since he actively participated. *Keep moving. Protect your chest.*

A Canaanite came at him. He lifted his sword with both hands, brought it down straight toward Zadok's head. Zadok held his sword parallel to the ground, handle in his right hand, blade in his left, careful to avoid the polished edge. He blocked the blow, then pulled his sword back. The enemy's blade fell. Zadok swung his weapon to the left then toward the soldier, slamming the end of the handle into his face. He could hear the bones crush as the man shrieked in pain.

The Canaanite dropped, but another took his place. Taller and stronger, this one swung his sword over his left shoulder and brought it down hard—slicing into Zadok's right side under his leather chest plate. A gash—shallow but long—opened in his tunic, then his skin. Pain he had never known raced from the wound throughout his body. Warm liquid flowed down his hip, drenching his tunic.

His vision blurred, but he could see well enough to thrust his sword into the chest of the gloating soldier standing before him. He tightened his grip on the blade and pushed down as crimson soaked the man's uniform. He collapsed and Zadok jerked the sword free.

Breathing fast, he reached down and sliced a long piece of cloth from the soldier's cloak, wrapped it around his middle to stanch the flow of blood. It immediately soaked through. He cut one more, wrapped it around himself.

He had barely tied the knot when yet another soldier approached. For what felt like a lifetime, but what was surely only a few moments, they blocked one another's blows. When the enemy drew back to swing his blade from side to another, Zadok saw his chance. He ducked low and let the weapon slice the air above him. As the enemy stood twisting to the side, slightly off balance, Zadok rose, stepping forward, and jabbed his blade deep into his belly. The Canaanite fell face down into his own blood.

Over the clanging of clashing swords and daggers, the sound of sandals against stone caught Zadok's attention. He looked up.

From beyond the palace came more soldiers.

This was not going to end soon.

CHAPTER 24

*I*F ARISHA HAD ANY FOOD in her stomach, it would have come up. Since it was barely dawn, her belly was empty. That didn't stop the nausea.

"No! Let her go!" Danel lunged at the soldier. It did little good.

Twice as big as Danel, he flicked him off like a bug, knocking him to the ground. "Do you realize how much she's worth? What the king would pay to have her back? I intend to collect a hefty reward for returning the king's virgin to him." He laughed uproariously.

His arm snaked around her neck, holding her fast against his chest. His other arm pointed a sword straight at Danel.

"She's married now!"

"I'm sure that doesn't matter for what he has in mind." He turned and backed down the hall.

Her sandals scraped the tile floor as he dragged her. His body stench assaulted her nose, and she clawed at his arms with her nails.

Danel scrambled to his feet, but he was now too far behind to do much good. She watched the emotion play on his face, deciding what to do. Stay and fight? Go get help?

He spun and raced back out the door.

Her abductor turned around, marched faster. She kicked and squirmed, making it as difficult as possible, but couldn't slow him down much. Soon he reached his destination. With no guards at the door, he kicked it open and barged in.

This must be the king's chambers. An enormous high-ceilinged sitting room, full of stone gods on pedestals and cushions on the floor. Tapestries on the walls. Four of the king's personal guards flanking a double cedar door to the right drew their swords and lunged at the warrior.

He halted. "No! I bring the king a gift! I will present to him the escaped consort of last year." He removed his arm and shoved her forward.

She hit the floor, landing hard. Pain radiated from her knees and hands through the rest of her body. She sucked in several deep breaths until a pair of sandals appeared in her vision.

"Stand up!"

She slowly rose and stood. Silent. Looking straight ahead.

If he killed her, he killed her. Even if he kept her here, this would not be her home.

Yahweh is my dwelling place.

The bodyguards studied the warrior. After several moments they must have deemed him trustworthy, and one knocked on the door, then entered the royal bedchamber.

Time dragged on. The king was old. It must take some time for him to waken and dress.

Finally the door creaked open and the king appeared. He neared Arisha. A smile appeared.

Blood pounded in her ears. Her mouth was dry. *Yahweh, help me.*

"Ah, yes. I remember you." His voice made her skin crawl. "I remember the day I picked you out. Your beautiful eyes, your skin. And I remember when I came to claim you, you had disappeared. I was forced to settle for someone less beautiful than you." He ran a wrinkled finger down her cheek, onto her neck.

"They told me you must have died out there alone. They said no one could have survived the desert."

Obviously they were wrong. And I had help. But I will never tell you that.

"How did you survive? Make it to the Israelite camp?"

She remained silent.

"You need to answer me!" The king roared. "How did—"

The chamber doors burst open, and Danel's grandson—Mika? Is that what he called him?—ran in.

The soldier stopped several strides from her. "I knew she was here." He cast a quick glance at the other soldier. "Excellent job, Magon."

"Thank you, Mika."

He bowed to his monarch. "I am Mika. I am the leader of the newest company in your army. I am the one who realized who she was, and had her brought to you."

"Mika. You are Danel's grandson?"

"I am."

"I knew your father. Tell me—do you worship Yahweh as your father does?"

Mika thrust his chest out. "I worship the gods of my father. I had her brought to you to prove that our gods are and always will be more powerful. She thought she could escape her fate, but Asherah has brought her back."

"And Asherah will reward you well. As will I." The king grabbed her arm and dragged her into his bedroom.

❧

*H*EART RACING, PALMS SWEATING, DANEL slammed into the doors, shoving them open and stumbling into the courtyard. He surveyed the frantic scene before him, searching for Zadok, Joshua, Caleb. Anyone.

Although the battle seemed to be winding down—the Israelites had brought more than twice as many men as Arad had soldiers—

pockets of combat still remained. He found Joshua and Caleb standing on a stack of boxes dragged from the market, studying the scene, looking for weaknesses, sending extra men to help where needed. He raced to them.

"I was taking Arisha to a safe place." He spit out his words between labored breaths. "I was overpowered by one of Mika's men and now he has taken her to the king. You must go help her."

"Where? Come show us!" Joshua jumped down and headed for the palace.

Gasping for air, he pointed behind him. "Back the way we came. The big hallway to the left. You'll find it. I won't be much help anyway." *Haven't been so far.*

Danel trudged to the wall. He rested his hands on his knees and closed his eyes, tried to swallow the lump in his throat. The one thing he thought he could do to help, and he had completely failed.

Did he even send help in time to save her?

Doubtful.

Yahweh, please don't let my incompetence cost Arisha her life. Or anything else.

His breath and heart beat finally under control, if not his shame, Danel looked up. Into the angry eyes of his grandson.

～

THE BATTLE NOW WINDING DOWN, ZADOK sprinted through the halls, looking for Arisha and Danel. Where would Danel have put her? A room? A storage closet? The palace complex was filled with so many places to hide a girl. He might never find her.

He'd just have to wait, and trust the old man—and Yahweh—to keep her safe until the battle was over. He turned on his heel to return to the courtyard and nearly ran into Caleb. "Wh-What are you doing in here?"

Caleb mouth twisted. "Later. Follow us."

Zadok didn't want to think about why they might be here. The pieces started falling into place in his mind. The possibilities were all too ugly. He followed them just a few steps before they all took a left turn and bolted down a wide tiled hallway. The ornate doors at the end stood open.

Four bodyguards lined the entrance to yet another set of doors.

Zadok halted as if he'd slammed into a stone wall.

His stomach threatened to come up to his throat.

His wife was in the king's bedchamber, and four armed guards stood in the way.

~

*A*RISHA BACKED AWAY FROM THE gray-haired sovereign, searching for anything she could use as a weapon if needed. The man was quite old and not too steady on his feet. Surely she could outrun him, if she could get out of the room. But those doors looked so heavy … and there were still the guards.

"Why do you fight it? Asherah has decreed that you return, and here you are. And at exactly the right time. Ordinarily I would wait for the full moon to celebrate the marriage of Baal and Anat with you, to ensure our city's fertility for the coming season, but since you are no longer a virgin anyway, I see no point, do you?"

How could he laugh and leer at the same time? His face was twisted into a gruesome shape.

She backed further away, bumping into the bed.

"Yes, that's it. Into bed with you. I'm sure you have never slept anywhere so luxurious, have you? Might make the night almost bearable, hmmm?"

That laugh again.

He slipped his robe off his bony shoulders and let it drop to the floor. His tunic followed. At least he kept his loincloth on. So far.

He climbed onto the bed. "Lie down."

She backed away on her elbows.

Her heart beat double-time and her stomach churned.

He came nearer. Still nearer. "Take off your clothes."

"Why don't you come closer first?" She smiled sweetly at him, and beckoned him with her finger.

He raised his brows, but he crawled closer.

She wiggled her finger, and he straddled her, his arms on either side of her. She lifted her chin as if to kiss him, and at the same time pulled her knee up hard into his groin.

The king fell to the side, his hands between his legs, rolling back and forth. She feared he would cry out, but he was in too much pain to utter a sound.

Arisha grabbed a pottery vase next to the bed. She slammed it hard into his skull. He stilled instantly. Pieces of the jar clinked as they tumbled onto the floor.

She held her hands over her mouth, watching his chest for movement. Was he dead? Had she killed the king? When she saw a shallow breath, she jumped off the bed and ran to the door. She yanked on the golden ring in the center, but either she was too short to gain enough leverage, or the door was just too heavy.

She lay her head against the wood. Now what? Just wait until he wakes up? In an even fouler mood? And do it all again? Or would the guards burst in first?

Either way, things did not look good.

But now was not the time to lose hope. She had made it this far. She would keep going. No matter what.

~

ANEL STOOD BACKED AGAINST A wall before Mika, his sword useless on the ground at his feet.

His eyes spewed hatred. "I just came from the king's chambers. That girl you helped escape—yes, I know it was you who helped her—has been returned to the king, where she belongs. Had you left things as they were, she would have simply participated in the marriage ceremony of Baal with the king and been returned to the temple. Now, who knows what he will do with her? So you see what your God has done for you? Nothing!"

Danel's heart sank. Not only had he lost Mika, long ago, now he had condemned Arisha to death. How had he gotten it all so wrong? "Mika, why are you so angry? Angry at Yahweh? Angry at me? All I have ever done is love you."

"Lies! You have kept me from my father's legacy, tried to keep me from fulfilling his dream for me, from becoming a great soldier like he was."

"True, your father was a great soldier. He would have been commander, I have no doubt, had he not been killed in battle. But do you know why he was killed?"

"He was fending off too many attackers at once. Everyone knows that."

"That is the story your mother told you. But it is only part of the truth. The truth is he disobeyed orders, and took his company into the enemy's camp before Arad's army was ready. The enemy overpowered them, and our army had to go in earlier than was planned. A great many lives were lost because he sought glory for himself."

Mika's eyes narrowed. "I don't believe you."

"If we survive this, you can ask anyone my age. They can help you separate truth from legend."

Mika brandished his short sword. He moved closer, placing it under Danel's chin. "*I* will survive. You, I'm not sure about."

Danel took shallow breaths with Mika's forearm against his chest. "The other truth is, you are far more like your father than I ever realized. He acted more like a soldier at home than a father, a husband. He often took out his frustrations on your mother. I finally lost count of the bruises she showed up with."

"You are lying again." Some of the bluster had gone from his voice, but he did not move the blade from Danel's throat.

"Let him go." Aqhat appeared over Mika's shoulder.

Danel would have breathed a sigh of relief if his chest could move.

"No." Mika did not take his gaze off Danel.

"Mika, don't make me do something I don't want to. I have loved you since you were born, but Danel has been my closest friend for more than twice that long."

"Mika, please."

"No," the younger man repeated.

Aqhat grabbed the arm holding the weapon and pulled Mika off Danel.

Mika swiped at Aqhat, but Aqhat backed away.

Danel watched the knife-play with increasing horror, still unable to breathe even though Mika no longer compressed his lungs.

Aqhat cut Mika's arm, barely. "Mika, stop now."

"No." Mika lunged for the commander, his sword slicing deep into Aqhat's leg. Crimson blood spewed onto his leg, his sandals, the street.

Still, Aqhat held back.

Mika once more dove for Aqhat, aiming for the man's heart. Aqhat blocked the move, knocking his arm skyward. Mika struck again and again. The two were locked in struggle for what felt like an eternity to Danel.

Aqhat finally aimed for Mika, his knife plunging into his chest.

Danel's grandson collapsed onto the stone. His chest stilled.

Danel slid down the wall, silent sobs racking his body.

Aqhat came to him, grabbed him under the arms, and half carried, half dragged him to a doorway around the corner where he could remain unseen. He set him on the ground, propped against the wall.

Danel pulled his knees to his chest and dropped his head onto his arms.

"I'm sorry ..."

Danel looked up to see Aqhat's tortured face, staring into nothing.

"I had no choice," he whispered, as he ripped a piece of his tunic and tied it around his wound.

Danel nodded. "I know. It's not your fault. He made his choices, long ago."

~

*A*RMED GUARDS OR NOT, ZADOK couldn't simply stand there and do nothing. There were four Canaanites, three Israelites. Not quite even, but ...

He unsheathed his sword.

A huge soldier came toward him, growling. Apparently deciding he was the weakest, another joined him. *Let him come to you.* When the first came close enough, he moved his sword over his left shoulder as if to swing wide, left to right. Instead, he slipped the weapon to his left hand, and brought it down sharply on the leg of the soldier on the left, going for his thigh as far to the back as possible. He must have hit the right place, because the soldier dropped at Zadok's feet, unable to stand.

The other guard slashed at Zadok. Searing pain sliced through his right arm, and blood flowed down from his bicep and dripped off his elbow. He dropped his sword, and the guard kicked it away.

Anger, fear for Arisha, pain, all combined within him, and he fought back with his dagger, Kamose's dagger, in his left hand, aiming for the soldier's chest. The Canaanite returned the attack, but Zadok sidestepped and avoided further injury, while driving his blade into his opponent at the same time. The studded dagger was sharp enough to cut through the leather breastplate. Blood spurted from the wound. The enemy stumbled. Zadok stepped behind him, grabbed his head, and slit his throat.

Joshua and Caleb had dispatched their guards, and the three rushed at the door.

Arisha sat huddled in the corner, cradling a metal vase.

Another pottery vase, or pieces of it, lay scattered near the bed.

Along with a stunned monarch.

Zadok rushed to Arisha and pulled her into his arms.

Caleb and Joshua looked from Arisha, to the king, to the broken pottery, and back.

"What happened?" asked Caleb.

"I didn't want to be his consort." She shrugged.

Caleb stared, wide-eyed. Joshua started laughing.

Caleb went to the bed and examined the king. He caught Zadok's gaze and motioned with his sword to the king and then the door.

Zadok steered her from the room with his left arm. She didn't need to see Caleb finish the king.

In the sitting room, she stepped away from him and eyed his wounds. "You're dripping blood!"

He glanced down at his side. The blood had seeped through again. His arm still bled as well. "I'm sorry."

"You don't have to apologize. You came for me. Again."

"I told you. I will always come for you."

Though if it were in his power, she'd never leave his side again.

~

*D*ANEL SAT IN THE COURTYARD, his head numb, his heart feeling like it had been ripped from his chest.

The only home he had ever known, his precious Arad, had been destroyed. The king he had served since he was but a prince, killed.

Yes, they asked for it. They attacked Israel for no reason. Refused to acknowledge Yahweh. Continued to sacrifice and perform outrageously wicked acts of so-called worship to a stone idol.

And now the city was gone, without the loss of a single Israelite. Israel had promised to destroy the city if Yahweh gave them back their hostages. And they did.

Yet none of that hurt as much as losing Mika. He had lost Mika long ago. But to be threatened by him, to see the look in his eyes, to know Mika would kill him, gladly, to gain power and prestige ...

He wiped a tear away. Nothing could change any of it now.

He still had Yasha, and Duni and Izabel. Aqhat and his family were safe as well. The children were happily riding on the shoulders of some of the men in the town center. What remained of it.

Their light spirits and the children's giggling brought some relief to his tattered soul.

A bloodied Aqhat sat beside him. He didn't speak, but stared ahead.

"I'm all right, Aqhat. Truly, I do not blame you."

"I cannot tell you how much it hurt to do that. I would have given anything ..." His voice was strained.

"I know. I wish you didn't have to. But it is finally over. Forty years of waiting, and we both made it through, my friend. There were times, in these last weeks, when I wasn't sure."

Aqhat finally turned his head and caught Danel's gaze for the first time since that horrible moment. "Yes, it's over. Time to begin again."

~

ARISHA STOOD AMONG THE FALLEN in the center of Arad. Safe now, she began to absorb the extent of the destruction around them. In the king's chambers, concerned only with avoiding his revenge, she had been oblivious to all else. The new morning's sun shined a brutal light on the demolished city.

Not a Canaanite soul remained standing. Broken pottery and smashed fruit lined the streets. Doors hung haphazardly on houses. Outside the walls, cattle called to be milked—to farmers who would never come.

"Are you all right?" Zadok held her close. "Seeing all this?"

She nodded. "It's not my city anymore. It no longer frightens me. I'll go anywhere you want." She raised her face to him. "I love you."

The corners of his mouth tipped up in his heart-melting smile. "I know." He lowered his head and kissed her.

When he broke the kiss, she lay her head on his chest to hear his heart beat. The familiar feeling of peace and strength enveloped her. She loved it, but now she didn't need it. She had found her own peace and strength.

Joshua approached Zadok. "I'm sending you and about a quarter of the others—the youngest, probably—back to camp now. The rest I'll keep to gather weapons and armor, maybe some food. But you, go. Take your wife home. Tend to the sheep." He grinned. "We won't be too far behind."

Relief settled on Arisha like a warm blanket.

Home. The word had never sounded so good.

*Take a Sneak
Peek at...*

PRIZE OF WAR

CHAPTER ONE

...and the daughter of Caleb was Acsah.

— 1 CHRONICLES 2.49

"I'm a *prize*? What do you mean I'm a prize?" Acsah's throat burned as she fought to keep the tears from spilling. How had this day turned upside down so quickly? The sky closed in on her as she stood on the open roof of her home. She struggled to breathe, couldn't pull in enough air.

Her *abba* folded his arms across his broad chest and clenched his jaw. "You are my only daughter. I intend to see you are protected. And since you can't seem to make this decision yourself, I felt I had to step in."

"My *imma* never would have allowed this."

Pain clouded his eyes. "Your imma would have seen you married by now. Perhaps I have been too indulgent."

"How do you know ...? But what if ...?" Thoughts swirled, too many and too fast for her to complete one. "Abba, why?"

He uncrossed his arms. "Acsah, you know I love you dearly, more than life itself. I have talked to Yahweh about this. I have talked to Leah..."

Acsah's gaze shot to the woman standing next to him. Why would her aunt betray her like this? "You agree with him? How could you?"

Leah neared. "Because I love you like a daughter. This way, Yahweh Himself will choose your husband. And he will be brave, strong, a true warrior." She stretched out her hand, but Acsah backed away.

"I don't *want* a warrior! That's the last thing I want!" Her traitorous hot tears finally had their way, coursing down her cheeks. She raced from the roof, down the stairs, and through the house. Outside, she ran past the wide gates of Hebron and into the countryside beyond. Was there no way out of this deal her abba had made for her?

Breaking into a sweat, she passed Abba's golden wheat fields and sprinted up the rise leading to the enormous threshing floor beyond. Reaching the flat, packed ground at the apex of the hill, she stopped, chest heaving. She bent at the waist, her hands on her knees until she caught her breath, then collapsed on the hard ground.

What kind of old, scarred monster would she end up with? How ugly would he be? Would he be cruel? Demanding? She buried her head in her arms on her knees, sobbing until her tears were spent.

Drying her wet cheeks on her headcloth, she scanned the verdant hills of Hebron, resplendent with the fragrant flowers of early summer. The fertile land mocked the emptiness in her heart.

She surveyed the abundant grain waving in the seemingly endless fields. Being the daughter of Israel's mightiest warrior Caleb may have locked her into a marriage she did not want, but it also brought her innumerable advantages. She rose and adjusted her clothing. The time for despair had passed. There was work to be done. People depended on her.

She strode back to her house and filled a small bag with grain. As she walked along the main road that fronted the outside circle of houses, she tucked the pouch into her sash. She crossed one of the many smaller streets leading from the ring road into the center of the city. Judith's house sat on the corner.

Acsah opened the courtyard gate and let herself in. "Judith? I've come to help with the bread."

Three older women sat in the common room of their modest home near a small oven. Each sat before a large, flat-topped, stationary stone called a quern, with a smaller handstone they moved back and forth over the grain to turn it into flour. "We were beginning to think we wouldn't see you today," said Judith.

"I'm so sorry. Just a talk with my abba. Nothing to worry about." She joined their circle, sitting before an empty quern.

"How is Caleb? Such a good man." Naomi patted her arm.

Acsah ignored the comment. She removed a handful of wheat from the bowl in their midst and began crushing the kernels. As flour was produced, she added it to another container and then began again.

Their chatter drowned out the scratching, crunching sounds of turning wheat berries to flour, and the flour into bread. Hours had gone by before the task was accomplished.

"I'll take the bowls back for you. You rest for now. If you'll pass me that, Miriam?"

Acsah balanced the bowl the widow handed her on top of the first one, leaving the stack of flat, round loaves that would feed the women for the rest of the day. She carried them to the storage room at the back of the house and set them on the table. Before she left, she emptied the contents of the small bag of grain she'd brought into the widows' larger jar to replenish what they had just ground, and returned with a small bowl of dates and raisins.

"Time for me to go, savtot. I'll be back tomorrow." They weren't truly her grandmothers, but since she had none by blood, and they had no relatives nearby, they all enjoyed the special relationship Acsah nurtured among them.

On the way home, she thought more about Abba's pronouncement. She simply had to persuade him to change his mind. As soon as the idea formed, she knew it would never happen. She'd never known him to change course. He made decisions slowly, deliberately, after examining all the facts. After much counsel and prayer. Then he did everything possible to see his decision was carried out.

The epitome of a warrior. A commander.

She had no more chance of avoiding this marriage than the walls of Jericho had against Joshua seven years ago.

~

*O*thniel's head was so full of competing thoughts he barely noticed the lush green fields he walked through. The road from Hebron to Bethlehem was usually calming and enjoyable, but so far he'd missed most of it.

Caleb's report after his scouting mission to the nearby city of Kiriath-Sepher echoed—especially that one unbelievable statement: "I offer my daughter Acsah as a bride."

Uncle Caleb was wealthy. He had land and silver. He had influence. He could offer anything, make anyone's life easier, better. He could set a man up for life. Why in the world would he offer his only daughter?

Not that Othni objected. To the contrary. He would do almost anything to make her his. His heart beat faster at the idea. He thought back to their life on the other side of the Jordan River, back to when they'd been children. Acsah had been not only his cousin, but also his best friend. Days of chasing rabbits and building fortresses blended into picking berries and sitting under trees, dreaming of what life would be like in Canaan.

Then they crossed the River. Her tenth summer, his fifteenth. After that, things got complicated.

He hadn't seen her in four years. What did she look like now? Surely she'd grown even more beautiful. She was a woman now— more than of age. Why hadn't she married yet?

Why hadn't he?

Because every woman he'd thought about marrying, he'd compared to her. And none of them measured up. None had her flashing eyes. Her pink cheeks. Her wavy, dark brown hair, which was so dark it was almost black...

That would all be over as soon as he conquered Kiriath-Sepher.

But first, he needed to talk to Salmah. Salmah had been with Caleb nearly every day of the wars until they came home. He hadn't run like Othni had. He'd had no need to.

Would Caleb even talk to Othni now?

Winning Acsah's hand was the only thing in this world that would make him risk disappointing Caleb again.

～

*A*csah paced in the courtyard in front of their home, the sweet fragrance of pomegranate blossoms drifting on the air. Bright red flowers, the shape of ram's-horn trumpets, dotted the trees. The colors and scents, which normally invigorated her, crowded her space.

Maybe she could talk to Aunt Leah first, enlist her help in persuading Abba to change his mind. Acsah moved to the side of the house where Leah and Uncle Jonah's rooms were attached. She peeked through the door into their central room, but Leah wasn't there.

After rehearsing a number of things she might say to attempt to change Abba's mind, Acsah finally settled on two or three. She had to try, though it was probably useless. She spun on her heel and returned to the wide, open room that occupied the right two-thirds of the lower floor of their home. The stone pillars that held up the roof loomed larger than usual this morning.

She leaned over the low stone barrier to her left and rested her head on Donkey's nose, rubbing his neck for a long moment. "You don't have to worry about getting married, do you?" She scooped out some grain from the feedbag in the corner and held it out to him. His lips tickled her palm as he nuzzled her hand. "Not that you could have any babies if you did." Too bad her life couldn't be so simple.

Acsah headed for the stone stairs in front of the storage room that ran across the back of the house. Reaching the top, she inhaled a deep breath. If only she could suck in courage as easily as air. Maybe she could duck into one of the two sleeping rooms that took up the back part of the roof.

No, she might as well face him now.

Abba and Aunt Leah sat on a round leather mat, and Acsah lowered herself to the floor next to him. "Abba, may I talk with you about what you said this morning?"

"Yes, *motek*." He grinned. "But I won't change my mind." He could call her *my sweet*, but underneath his smile, his will was as hard and sharp as the bronze in his sword.

She glanced at Leah, then back to her father. "Why must I marry a soldier? Can't I marry someone else? Maybe one of the others?"

"You've already turned down five men." He frowned at her and held up a hand, fingers spread wide. "Five."

She squirmed. "I know, but ..."

Aunt Leah touched her arm. "Tell me what was wrong with them. Why did you always say no?"

Acsah shrugged. "I don't know. Baruch was too old. Aviel wanted to move to Lachish. So far away—I'd never see you. Gershom ... Gershom ... he ..." She sighed deeply. "But Abba, I can't marry *anyone*."

"Why ever not?" He widened his dark eyes, his bushy brows disappearing under his crop of gray hair.

"Because ... because ..." She chewed on her bottom lip.

"Why?" His voice was firm, his eyes narrowed.

This was not how the conversation was supposed to go. She folded her hands in front of her, squeezed them together until her fingers ached. "Because then you will be alone. And no one should be alone." She pulled her knees to her chest and dropped her head onto her arms.

Her father's strong hand rested on her head. He waited, smoothing her hair until she stilled. "Acsah?" His gentle voice soothed her raging nerves.

She raised her face to his, drew in a shuddering breath.

"Why are you afraid to leave? What do you think will happen?"

"I- I don't know. I just know I can't."

He reached for her and took one of her hands between his rough ones. "But motek, you must. It is the way things have always been, the way Yahweh intended. Daughters grow up and leave to marry. I assure you, I will be fine."

He didn't understand. How could he? He hadn't been there that day. A thought occurred to her, and she tilted her head. "Why did you never marry again?"

He shrugged. "At the time, I only wanted to care for you. And there were wars to be fought, and then time went by, and here we are." He aimed his penetrating gaze at her. "Would you feel better if I were married? If I had someone here with me?"

It would.

But it didn't change the fact that she would never wed a warrior.

∾

*O*thni winced. Rahab had worked hard to prepare an abundance of delicious-looking food, and he couldn't remember having tasted any of it. Had he even spoken to her, or to Salmah, during the entire meal? He put on a smile and swallowed the last of his bread, then drained his drinking bowl.

Rahab reached to fill it again then set the pitcher on the mat spread in the courtyard of their Bethlehem home. She scooped a toddler off Salmah's lap, set him on the brushed dirt floor, and stood. "Come, Simeon. Let's let Abba talk to his friend."

Instead Simeon settled onto Othni's lap and tugged on his beard. "You are Abba's friend?"

"He is a very good friend."

"Then why have I only seen you a few times?"

Rahab gasped. "Simeon!"

Othni chuckled, dislodging the child's fat fingers. "I have been fighting in other places."

"My friends don't go far away." Simeon frowned.

"Your friends are little boys, not soldiers."

"Oh." The boy shrugged and clambered off Othni's lap.

"Simeon, we are going inside. Now." Rahab shook her head and picked him up.

"He doesn't live up to his name very well, does he? He who hears and obeys?" Othni laughed as Rahab carried the four-year-old inside.

"We keep hoping he'll grow into it. The *hearing* part he gets. It's the *obeying* part he still needs to work on." Salmah's hearty laugh rumbled deep in his chest. "Just wait—you'll see someday. Anyone you have your eye on?"

"That's why I'm here."

Salmah leaned forward, grinning. "What can I do? I have no daughters for you. Only one tiny, disobedient son."

"You know Caleb is planning to attack Kiriath-Sepher."

Salmah picked a ripe fig from the bowl and peeled it. "It's one of the only cities left."

"He wants help."

"No surprise. He was injured so badly, I'm amazed he wants to take part at all."

Othni winced at the mention of Caleb's injury, then shoved it from his mind. "Amazed?"

"I guess not. I'd be more shocked if he were willing to stay behind."

"He's looking for a commander. He's offered an ... incentive."

The older man raised a brow. "Silver?"

"No. He has offered Acsah as a bride to whomever conquers the city."

Salmah let out a low whistle.

"He did what?" Rahab's sharp voice came from the doorway. She'd been listening?

Othni spoke over his shoulder, repeating what he'd told her husband. "I'm not sure why he would do that."

Rahab returned and sat next to Salmah. She rested her chin on her hand and pursed her lips, but said nothing. Next to Salmah's husky build, her tall, slender frame was even more striking.

"Well?" Salmah eyed his wife.

"I know she has refused others."

"You've talked to her about that?" Othni knew Rahab and Acsah had been close when the Canaanite woman first came from Jericho years ago. Before she'd married Salmah, she'd lived with Caleb's family. But they'd stayed that close? Then again, he'd been up north, so how would he know?

"I see her often. She's found no one she wishes to marry, although I saw nothing wrong with any of the young men." She drew circles in the dirt. "I'm not really sure what she's looking for. I'm not surprised Caleb finally stepped in. She's nearing an age when most men would no longer consider her."

"She's not as old as you were when I married you." Salmah winked at his wife.

She grinned. "Yes, but you're smarter than most men." She turned to Othni. "You still find her desirable?"

He nodded. "And beautiful." Her face drifted though his mind. "Salmah, will you help me plan an attack on Kiriath-Sepher? You went with him the first time, so you must know everything I need to know, yes?"

Salmah nodded.

"I *must* take this city. Many heard Caleb's offer. Groups of men huddled up right away, starting on their plans. They have Caleb's ear." He didn't need to expound on Caleb's opinion of him. "I need all the help you can give me. I love her. I always have."

Salmah searched his face. "I'll help you. And I'll go with you."

Othni's gaze darted to Rahab. Her eyes closed for a moment, perhaps contemplating yet another battle for her husband. She opened them and smiled at Othni. "You will both be in my prayers, and in Yahweh's hands." She returned to her son.

Othni watched her leave. "Her faith is amazing. Especially considering she's a Canaanite."

"I think that's why it's so strong. She had to trust Him for her very life, before she even knew Him." Salmah played with the seed from the fig. "Here's what I learned about Kiriath-Sepher. For the Canaanites, it's a royal city. Bigger, and more important than Hebron was, at least to them. The walls are higher and thicker than Hebron's, and about as high as four or five men. They're made of enormous stones, perfectly shaped to fit together without mortar of any kind. There is an earthen revetment outside the walls, going up about two-thirds of the wall and not quite as wide. There are many towers, and there are gates on all four sides."

Othni blew out a long breath. "A direct attack would never work."

"I think the only way is by a protracted siege or by trickery."

"Like Joshua took Ai? Or Bethel?"

"Not Bethel." Salmah waved away the suggestion. "We'll certainly never find a traitor there."

He nodded. "True. Which leaves a siege or a ruse."

"Or someone, somehow, getting in and opening the gates."

Othni frowned. "If the giants built the walls and the gates, wouldn't the locks be much too high for one of us to open?"

"Also true. So that's probably not our best option."

Othni reached for a date. He ripped it in two and removed the stone, then put one half in his mouth. The fair-complexioned giants of Hebron invaded his memory. Twice as tall as Othniel, thighs as wide as his body. Joshua's armies had expelled them once, nearly six years ago after Israel first conquered Jericho. But as Joshua and his men moved on, the *Anakim* moved back in, and Caleb was forced to defeat them again in order to claim the city Moses had promised him.

"Let's see." Othni tore the other piece in half again. And again. "A siege will deplete our resources as much as theirs, maybe more. But if we attack and then fake a surrender, we can send in a good number of men, perhaps with gifts, hide more men—armed men in baskets. It's been done before."

Salmah shrugged. "It has. And if we hadn't been at war with every other city around here, and if they weren't giants, that might work. But I think it's far too risky here."

"What if we attack, then retreat and draw them out ..."

"That might work better. Or we could trap them between two forces."

He nodded. "We have to see how many of them there are. They can defend the city with very few as long as they're inside. Once we draw them out, we have the advantage."

Salmah grasped his shoulder. "You might make a good commander yet."

If Othni wanted to win Acsah, he would have to make certain Caleb finally could see that as well.

~

Othni had left Salmah's house as soon as the sun peeked over the eastern mountains in order to make the long walk back to Hebron before the evening meal. A hearty meal, a good night's sleep, and perhaps he'd have a decent chance to impress his uncle.

The next day, the would-be commanders gathered in Caleb's massive courtyard to present their plans one by one. Othni watched as man after man was sent away after failing to meet Caleb's expectations.

One young man—barely a man—flailed his arms like a baby bird trying to fly the first time. "But it worked before. We march around once a day for six days—"

Othni did his best to suppress a laugh. He glanced around and noticed several others hiding chuckles as well.

"We are not doing as we did at Jericho." Caleb's face reddened, his hands splayed at his sides. "Go." Eyes closed, he growled the word.

The young man slunk out through the courtyard.

An older, chubby man advanced. "If we gather men from all of Judah, we can attack them with full force. With Yahweh's help this will work. We can use battering rams—"

"Battering rams will never be successful," Caleb said, "against the stones in Kiriath-Sepher's walls."

The man looked baffled.

Caleb hadn't revealed much about Kiriath-Sepher in his speech to Hebron's men, but he undoubtedly would have told anyone who'd asked anything they wanted to know. That would be just like him, to see who would gather the information they needed before formulating a strategy.

The mighty warrior took a deep breath. "The stones in those walls are as wide as the height of two men. They are far too heavy to be dislodged by a battering ram."

"But we have Yahweh—"

"And we must also use common sense." Caleb pounded a fist into his palm. "Yahweh's power is not an excuse to be foolish. Next."

The portly man left, and a tall man Othni had seen talking to Caleb the day he made the announcement—obviously a favorite—sauntered over. Othni's chest burned. What made that man so special? He was tall, sure, but not that good-looking, at least not to Othni. Hair too straight. Nose too big. Laughed too loud.

Caleb's weathered face brightened. "Enosh. What is your plan? I'm sure you have thought it out well."

Enosh puffed out his chest. "I suggest a siege. It's the only reasonable option. We cut off their water supply. They get all their water from the two wells nearby—one north of the city and one south. Without water, they cannot survive."

"Won't they have supplies in the city? Water? Food?" Caleb arched a brow, accentuating the scar that ran from above his right eye to the corner of his lip.

"Cisterns full of water, I'm sure. But how long can that last?"

"Wait over there." Caleb pointed his chin toward the largest pomegranate tree in the courtyard.

Enosh's smirk as he passed fanned the fire in Othni's chest. Why was he so cocky? Did he know something the others didn't? He was the first Caleb had asked to wait, so maybe he did possess some secret information.

"Othniel."

Snapping to attention, Othni turned to the soft but firm voice. "Uncle."

"I'm surprised to see you here. A little young, aren't you?"

He fought a sigh. "I fought in Hebron, Gibeon—"

"That didn't work out so well, did it?"

Othni clenched his jaw. "I've fought for Benjamin the last four years, in Mizpah, Ramah, Beeroth, more. Did you speak to the commanders there?"

Caleb tilted his head. Was that a smile? Surely not. "What's your plan?"

Othni repeated everything he had discussed with Salmah.

After an almost imperceptible nod, Caleb gestured toward the tree. "All right, wait with Enosh."

Caleb dispatched the last two men quickly. His limp was slight as he joined the pair in his courtyard. "You two have the best plans. I shall need to consider them further."

Movement inside the house drew Othni's vision.

Acsah. His heart beat faster, and heat crawled up his neck. How beautiful she was—full lips, cheekbones set high against her dark eyes, a touch of pink on her cheeks. He hadn't seen her since ... when? Since before they left Gilgal to defend Gibeon.

She accepted a platter from a young girl, probably a servant, and stepped into the courtyard with bread and cheese and a pitcher of juice. Locks of her long hair slipped out from under her scarf, and she tossed her head to get it out of her face. She neared them and set the food on a pedestal.

Caleb beamed at her. "Thank you, motek."

"Would you like anything else, Abba?"

"No, thank you."

"Thank you, Acsah. How very thoughtful of you." Enosh touched her arm and grinned.

Othni tensed, his teeth grinding together.

Not that he had any more right to her than Enosh. In fact, Enosh probably deserved her more. He lived here in Hebron, likely saw her every day, knew her.

But he hadn't loved her his whole life, like Othni had. Spent the last four years trying to earn the right to ask Caleb's permission to marry her.

Acsah smiled weakly at Enosh, glanced briefly at Othni, and retreated. She didn't recognize him—at least she didn't appear to. He'd grown a cubit or two, added a good bit of muscle and a beard. He was no longer a boy.

"Anything else either of you'd like to say?"

Neither Enosh or Othni spoke.

"I'll have my decision tomorrow morning. We'll leave the next day." He turned toward his house and Enosh strutted from the courtyard, as if he had the command in hand already.

Othni snatched a piece of bread and trudged toward the street.

Caleb's voice stopped him on his way out. "Othniel, may I speak with you a moment?"

"Yes, Uncle." He ripped the food into pieces as he stared south toward Kiriath-Sepher.

In the morning Caleb would decide who would lead the attack on the Canaanite city—which in turn would decide who would marry Acsah.

For Caleb, an important decision, of course.

For Othni, nothing less than his entire future was at stake.

ACKNOWLEDGMENTS

My deepest thanks to:

The people who give my life meaning: my husband John, and my children, Emma, Mira, Dara, and Johnny. Thank you for putting up with hours on end of Mom in her office, or in her favorite chair in her bedroom, with the laptop and the kitty.

Kathy Donovan, of Checkmate Farms in Bluemont, Virginia, who spent the better part of a chilly day with me to teach me about the amazing, beautiful, fat-tailed sheep. Any misinformation in this novel is mine.

Prof. William M. Schniedewind, Kershaw Chair of Ancient Eastern Mediterranean Studies and Professor of Biblical Studies & Northwest Semitic Languages, UCLA, for his expertise. Again, any errors in this novel are mine.

My faithful beta readers—Lynn Rose, who read this more than once, Carrol Mercurio, Dr. Sue Pankratz, and Ceenu Jebaraj.

My fabulous critique partners and fellow authors Jennifer Slattery, Marji Laine and Tanya Eavenson.

Roseanna White Designs for bringing Zadok and Arisha to life on the gorgeous cover.

Jeannette Windle for editing the manuscript and pushing me to "pump it up."

And you, dear reader, for your time. I know it's valuable and I thank you for spending some of it with my characters.

Learn even more about these characters and their world, as well as the stories to come, at www.caroletowriss.com.

ALSO BY CAROLE TOWRISS

∽

BIBLICAL FICTION
'JOURNEY TO CANAAN' SERIES
Book 1 - By the Shadow of Sinai
Book 2 - By the Waters of Kadesh

Prize of War

∽

CONTEMPORARY ROMANCE
Just Until Christmas
The Other Brother
A Different Kind of Christmas

ABOUT THE AUTHOR

 An unapologetic Californian, Carole Towriss now lives just north of Washington, DC. She loves her husband, her four children, the beach, and tacos, though not always in that order. In addition to writing, she binge-watches British crime dramas and does the dishes for the fourth time in one day.

For more information and to sign up for my newsletter:

caroletowriss.com
carole@caroletowriss.com

Printed in Great Britain
by Amazon